IT TAKES
Monsters

It Takes
Monsters

A Novel of Suspense

MANDY McHUGH

SCARLET
NEW YORK

IT TAKES MONSTERS

Scarlet
An Imprint of Penzler Publishers
58 Warren Street
New York, N.Y. 10007

Copyright © 2023 by Mandy McHugh

First Scarlet Press edition

Interior design by Maria Fernandez

Library of Congress Control Number: 2023908386

ISBN: 978-1-61316-444-0
eBook ISBN: 978-1-61316-445-7

10 9 8 7 6 5 4 3 2 1

Printed in the United States of America
Distributed by W. W. Norton & Company

To all the girls who used to read
scary stories under the covers.

1

It was a beautiful Friday in October when Victoria Tate decided to murder her husband.

Standing over the sink with a mug of coffee, she watched the morning unravel on their quiet cul-de-sac. The idea had been floating around her mind for years, if she was being honest. Nestled and familiar like old curtains flapping in the breeze. Not that Warren suspected anything, of course. Why would he? She'd never given him a reason to doubt her loyalty. She was his second in command, his adoring wife.

He was the boss. The CEO.

And the title chafed her.

A little voice whispered that what she was planning was wrong. A sin. Victoria hadn't gone to church in a long time, but she was pretty sure that if God didn't want her to kill her husband, then he wouldn't have made him such a prick.

Once upon a time, she'd believed those three letters would be attached to her name. She was a force at Livingston Corporation. Thriving. From lassoing big-ticket clients to negotiating contracts that would make Mark Cuban cry, Victoria proved time and again that not only did she belong at the dinner table, but that she was hosting the entire goddamn meal.

It should have been a no-brainer.

Then, stupidly, she'd married Warren. It was what everyone had expected her to do, regardless of her accolades. She was a Livingston. Livingston women got married and had babies.

Victoria thought she could be different.

She could have the husband and the home in Kent Wood Manor and the successful career. She didn't have to choose. Her father had owned Livingston, after all. Nepotism aside, she was the best at what she did. She thought he would understand.

How wrong she had been.

Ten years down the road and Warren wanted to dump her like yesterday's garbage. He didn't want out of the marriage. That would be too simple. She almost wished divorce was on the table. Instead, he wanted her dignity, one of the defining characteristics that made Victoria Tate who she was.

We're running out of time. A few years is all I'm asking for, Vic, he'd said. *A family could be good for us. It could be good for you. The sabbatical forms will be on your desk in the morning. We can clean out your office together and figure out a solution—for your accounts, for—for a nursery. All of it. Trust me, Vic. This is what you want.*

He'd smiled like the matter had already been decided. She guessed in his mind it had been. Black and white was kind of his thing. Warren wanted a kid. Victoria was going to give him one.

End of story.

Having a child was not the issue. She had nothing against children or women who made it their life's goal to be the perfect mother. It was simply that Victoria had no clue if she wanted to be one of them. Wasn't she supposed to *know*? Wasn't every woman ingrained with some biological pull once they reached a certain age?

Victoria didn't feel a maternal tug, but she didn't have the luxury of pondering what that meant. Warren was taking away her choice.

Victoria couldn't wrap her head around his logic. Warren hadn't interacted with a kid since the children's hospital fundraiser dinner the previous year, and that had solely been for the photo op. He wasn't going to leave his job. He wouldn't sacrifice his early morning golf outings or late-night meetings for a screaming newborn. He most certainly wouldn't throw a burp cloth over his YSL button-down, let alone change a diaper.

That would fall to Victoria, and how was that fair? She loved her life the way it was. She loved her independence.

A child would change all of that. Acknowledging her misgivings didn't make her a bad person; it made her rational. Practical.

Warren, on the other hand . . .

How could he be so callous? Blindly assume that she'd drop her clients for a car seat? How could he take everything from her without even asking for *her* input? It wasn't like he'd have to endure the physical changes, the hormonal swings, the delivery. She wasn't some empty vessel waiting to be filled. They were supposed to be partners, in love and in labor—pun intended—but Warren's declaration that she was leaving Livingston and she was having his child had confirmed her long-held suspicions. He didn't see her as an equal.

He didn't see her at all.

She gripped the mug hard enough to feel the ceramic crack and then forced herself to relax. She didn't lose control of her emotions often, but this morning she was finding it difficult to maintain her composure. Anyone would, Victoria thought. It wasn't every day that a person's entire world shifted. The life she'd constructed teetered on the brink of an abyss. She and Warren skirted the edge in a dark dance for power.

Like hell was she going to be the one to fall in.

2

On a normal Friday, Victoria would finish her coffee, shower, and head to the office. Her meetings would wrap up, her accounts would be balanced, and she'd finalize her schedule for the upcoming week. Most often, her day would be punctuated by a scoop of chocolate chip cookie dough and whatever true crime documentary Netflix suggested for her while Warren indulged in whiskey.

Today, however, she wasn't going to work. Not when she'd have to sit in front of an HR rep and sign her life away. Warren would be mad, but she couldn't bring herself to care about that. She was mad too.

Setting her cup aside, Victoria tucked the front of her shirt into her jeans and slipped into her Sperrys. She grabbed her keys with a quick glance at the mirror over the foyer table. One low ponytail later and the Bored Housewife starter kit was complete. Cookie-cutter chic. Easily forgettable. Exactly the vibe she was going for.

She was ready.

The ordinary morning happenings of Kent Wood Manor were in full swing by the time she reversed out of the driveway. Neighbors collecting the local paper in their robes. Parents exchanging small talk at the bus stop. Would she be one of them? Victoria wondered. She would be, right? She would have to be. Coordinating outfits with the other mothers and Pinteresting bento-box lunch ideas.

Nope. Victoria squashed that train of thought before it derailed into a full-blown panic attack.

Despite the chill, Joe Waterman's landscaper—Tad? Ted?—was already mowing the lawn, nodding along to whatever music blasted through his ridiculously large headphones.

Rashad Banks in his navy-blue base sharkskin suit buffed a spot from his Mercedes M-Class. He winked as she passed, which drew a smile in return. He was handsome and he knew it. Had that whole BDE thing going for him, which was a popular topic of discussion in the neighborhood "book club."

Victoria used that term loosely. A group of horny middle-aged women drinking wine and drooling over smut while their kids were at school was a more accurate description.

Warren wanted her to be one of them. She shuddered.

The Sparrows, retired busybodies with too much time on their hands, rocked in Adirondack chairs and waved, big dopey smiles glued to their Florida-weathered faces like an ad for a prescription drug.

Near the end of the street, Betty Knottier, resplendent in neon leggings and matching sneakers, pumped her arms like a shadow boxer, lips pursed in exertion.

"Morning!" she called.

"You look ridiculous," Victoria said through ventriloquist teeth and gave a beauty queen-worthy wave.

Normal. Predictable. Just another glorious morning in Kent Wood Manor.

At the development entrance, Victoria turned left instead of her usual right, heading away from the city into the rural landscape that comprised the other half of Kent Wood County. Back roads and farmland opening before her, she found her favorite true crime podcast and tuned out, letting her thoughts wander to the details of crime scenes and forensic mistakes. Cornstalks whipped by while the hosts dissected facts about fibers, soil samples, and genetic material under fingernails.

Victoria examined her own manicure, a sensible length with a neutral color. Warren didn't like *flashy*. Flashy didn't win deals. *Or change diapers.*

A burn settled deep in her chest. She imagined her fingers digging into his neck, nails pink and pretty against his reddening flesh, collecting his genetic material in the struggle.

That wouldn't do. Victoria would be smarter. She wouldn't leave evidence.

She would wear gloves, she thought, parking in front of Miller's Hardware. Just in case.

3

The hardware store screamed of nostalgia and reeked of sawdust and gasoline. Vintage metal signs advertised soda and car services. The shelves were made of thick wooden planks, worn from years of use. It was cute. Quaint.

Best of all, it had no security cameras.

"Help you?" asked the man behind the cashier's desk. White hair stuck out from his stained baseball cap, but wiry muscles stretched beneath his gray thermal shirt.

Working man's muscles. Something Warren would never have. He'd slip a disc lifting a bag of potatoes.

Okay, that was a little bit bitchy, she thought, looking at her own arms. She guessed the same could be said of her. Pilates toned but not strong, by any means. It wasn't like she was lugging hay bales in the afternoon sun.

Honesty, like good and evil, like everything else, was arbitrary.

"Drop cloths?" Victoria asked. "And some leaf bags, if you still have them."

"Ayuh, we got 'em." He stuck out a gnarled thumb and hitched it to the right. "Two rows back for both. If you hit the nails, you've gone too far. Hard to miss, though."

She thanked him and moved quickly past the rows of tools and appliances. The plastic drop cloths were piled in wire baskets at the end of the aisle. She grabbed two rolls. Paused. Took two more. Three. Four. And a few rolls of painter's tape.

Items secured, she skirted the corner and found lawn bags stacked on an end cap. Perfect. She added two big boxes to her pile of Dexter-level spatter proofing and headed for the register.

The man stood at the counter wiping black grease from his hands with an equally blackened washcloth. "All set?" he asked, dropping the cloth into a bin at his feet.

She placed the last of the items on the small counter. "Yes, thank you."

"Find e'rything okay?"

"Yes, thank you," she repeated.

He tallied up the prices on scrap paper and entered them into the register. "We don't accept credit cards here, ma'am. Just so you know. Never did care much for those big companies. The fees'll suck you dry."

"That's fine." It was why she'd gone to Miller's in the first place. Hopefully that was the last of the small talk.

"Doing a little home improvement?" he asked with a chuckle as the bell above the door jingled.

She nodded. Something like that.

"Victoria?" a voice squawked behind her. "Oh my god, what a small world. I was just thinking about you."

Shit.

Betty Knottier, Neon Queen of the Speed Walkers. She was still wearing her blindingly bright athletic wear, but she'd exchanged her runners for a pair of day-glow Crocs.

"Betty," she said, "so good to see you!" They exchanged a quick hug and a cheek kiss. That woman was all about the cheek kisses. Victoria struggled not to swipe the ghost of spit from her face.

Betty's cloyingly sweet perfume hung heavy in the air between them. "What are you doing here?" she asked, all big-toothed and wide-eyed, shouldering her oversized purse with the grace of a donkey.

"Just picking up a few things."

The cashier clucked his tongue, inserting himself into the conversation. "Looks like it's gonna snow tonight," he said. "Early this year."

"Ugh, how do you find the time?" Betty mooned, ignoring him with a pointed eyebrow arch. "I need some of your motivation. If you could bottle it up for me that'd be great, because if I worked half as much as you did, I'd be a slob kabob by happy hour. And you're painting again? Didn't you just have the trim done? I remember seeing the utility vans outside your house for a few days."

Victoria didn't miss the disapproving frown. God forbid the unsightly work vans parked on the street. She'd probably been watching to make sure they left before the HOA cutoff, with a bag of low-calorie popcorn and a seltzer.

"We did, yeah, but they missed some sections," she said with a smile that she hoped looked more natural than it felt.

"Then they should come fix it." Betty scrunched up her nose in faux outrage. "Who did you use? I'm sure if you let them know you're dissatisfied with the work they'd come back."

"Call me a perfectionist," she said. "I don't want to rely on someone else to do the job right. Details are important."

"Yes. Yes, they are."

Victoria didn't appreciate the Mona Lisa smirk that accompanied Betty's agreement. "Well," she said, motioning toward the register.

"Hey, did you hear about the Mahoneys?" she asked, lowering her voice to a conspiratorial whisper. "Not the Sherman Ave. Mahoneys, the Edgewood Court Mahoneys. The ones with the yapping dog? They petitioned the board to install an above ground pool. Can you believe it? I mean, it's clearly against the rules, but they're arguing they should get an exemption for health reasons. Health reasons? He eats a sausage McMuffin every morning, and he wants to talk about health? I told Fiona, I said—"

Oh, for Christ's sake, Victoria thought. "I'm sure everything will be fine, Betty." Betty's energy furled inward in a mixture of confusion and rejection. "I'm sorry to cut this short, but I should get going if I want to get this done before the snow."

She really did not want to gossip in front of the cashier, who was eyeing them both with more than a fair share of judgment. Nothing drew attention faster than conflict.

She'd have to keep that in mind.

"Of course, don't let me keep you. We'll get a drink soon, all right?"

"Sure. I'll check my calendar and get back to you."

"You do that." Betty grasped Victoria's forearm and squeezed twice. "Send my best to Warren." With a flip of her dried-sweaty ponytail, she sauntered away.

Well, shit, she thought. *So much for keeping a low profile.*

4

L eaves whipped around the parking lot in crisp rusty arcs. The temperature seemed to have dropped ten degrees since she'd left the house, the wind raising goose bumps on her arms. October snow wasn't uncommon in Upstate New York, but that didn't mean she had to like it. Or the potential complications such a storm would bring to her plans.

The weather wasn't her only obstacle, however.

"Freaking Betty Knottier," Victoria mumbled, retrieving the car key. She popped the trunk and dropped everything inside unceremoniously before sliding into the driver's seat.

What were the odds of running into her obnoxious neighbor? Of all the places and times. She could've easily hit the Home Depot closer to the Manor. As much as Betty advocated the "shop local" mentality, she hadn't met a chain store she could say no to. Why Miller's?

Maybe she had a legitimate errand. Or maybe she was sticking her neon-colored bloodhound nose where it didn't belong. It wouldn't be the first time. Controlled chaos was Betty's specialty. It hadn't even been a year since her last drama unfolded, when she'd inserted herself into the nighttime activities of her next-door neighbors. George had been having an affair. Stacy had been in denial.

Betty had been curious.

She took to following George and eventually caught him leaving his girlfriend's house, sex hair be damned. The photo she posted to the Facebook HOA page spoke volumes. Victoria watched the mess from afar but concluded that the entire scandal said more about the kind of person Betty was than anything that happened between George and Stacy.

Victoria, however, had no desire to be the new featured drama on Nextdoor.

She started the next episode of *My Favorite Murder* and pulled out of the lot, tapping erratically on the wheel. Each mile tightened the notch of tension in her shoulders. Face flush and skin warm, she rolled down the windows and gulped mouthfuls of cool air until the drowning sensation passed.

Of course she was on edge, she told herself. It would be weird if she wasn't. People didn't off their spouses every day.

But she could do this. She *would* do this.

Not because she was born a Livingston and had some medieval birthright claim to the company (although there was some truth there). Not out of some ill-conceived notion that women belonged on top; as much as she believed in the feminist quest for equality, murdering Warren didn't fall under that umbrella.

It was the *injustice* of the situation: the fact that one man could sweep in with his dick-swinging energy and demand she bend a knee. An order to give up her body, her freedom, her choice. If Warren had broached the topic beforehand, maybe Victoria would've considered his point of view. As a courtesy. She wasn't unreasonable. She wasn't a monster. And even if she wasn't one hundred percent convinced that motherhood was right for her, she would have been willing to listen.

A few years.

She would be a relic by then, professionally speaking. As much as she hated to admit it, men could leave the game and be welcomed back with open arms. Two-martini lunches never went out of style.

Most women weren't given the same treatment, especially after a maternity leave, when the inherent assumption was that she would have to drop everything for a child. Had some places made progress? Sure. But Victoria was under no illusion that Livingston was one of them, not with her father setting the precedent for Warren. She could kick and claw her way back in, but it wouldn't be enough.

Victoria pressed the Bluetooth button on the wheel. Maybe her sister could offer deeper insight. "Call Teagan."

After four rings the recording began. "You've reached the voicemail of Dr. Teagan Livingston. I'm unable to take your call right now, but—"

"It's your personal phone, Teags, why are you introducing yourself like a quack on an infomercial? You colossal narcissist."

Knowing Teagan, she was probably watching the screen and waiting for the call to end. Then she'd wait a few extra minutes before texting a response: *Sorry, I was busy grafting someone's face back on because I'm a* doctor, *in case you forgot, doing* doctor things, *what's up?*

"A plastic surgeon, it's barely a doctor," Victoria said, smug in her dismissal.

Well-respected doctor or not, Teagan was decidedly insecure when it came to Victoria's opinion. She tried to hide it behind follower counts and celebrity name dropping, but it carried a note of desperation. Teagan craved her approval, and part of Victoria—one that she tried not to look at too closely—loved not giving it to her.

Did that make her petty? Perhaps. But for the first time in her life, Victoria couldn't find it in herself to care.

5

Victoria stacked the Miller's haul on the table. Insides jittery, chest tight, her hands were steady as she gripped the counter. She was making the right call. This was the only course of action.

Nerves were normal.

Her phone whistled, startling her out of the internal pep talk. The world didn't stop because she was facing the biggest moment of her life. Money was pushed, clients were irritated, and business kept moving. Sixteen new emails since she'd checked this morning, all from her VIP list. She may not be CEO, but Livingston couldn't function without her.

She shook her head and tapped the first message from Jeff Blevins, the ever-present thorn in her side. Account execs weren't supposed to keep tabs on each other's client lists, but Jeff had been trying to poach from her for the last three years—ever since Warren had picked him for a prestigious leadership summit where all the major players went to schmooze and pat themselves on the back.

Of course it hadn't been Victoria. They couldn't *possibly* risk having the team accuse him of nepotism. Her numbers drew enough speculation as it was. Jeff was the obvious choice.

And here he was, emailing her before business hours about one of her clients. *Heard this through the grapevine,* he wrote. *Thought you'd want to know.*

How altruistic.

Gratuzi and McCloud, her biggest account, had decided to jump ship. Three years she'd spent building a relationship, nurturing a meager one-off service fee into insane profit margins, and now? They were citing customer service issues as their reason to withdraw from their arrangement and go with Livingston's biggest competitor.

Customer service? Code for bullshit. Victoria could read the red between the lines.

It had absolutely *nothing* to do with the fact that Warren insisted he handle the last round of negotiations. Or how he'd inexplicably transferred them to a subpar service team where more than half the reps were in their first three months of employment and knew nothing about the systems.

Livingston had already lost two of its most lucrative accounts this month, and before Warren had dropped the surprise you've been-ousted baby bomb, she hadn't blamed them for leaving. Big fish always smelled trouble first.

They'd been able to hide the departures, at least temporarily, from the shareholders, mostly because Victoria knew how to smooth the rough edges of desperation.

There wasn't a chance in hell the façade would stay intact for another quarter. Also, it wasn't a good look that Jeff had found out about this before she did.

"Shit," she said, shooting off a few quick responses to frazzled account execs that she would circle back after the weekend with a fresh game plan.

She wouldn't have to make up for Warren's slack for much longer. Not if her plan worked.

As the last email sent, an alert for a calendar change popped up on the screen. *This can't be happening,* she thought, reviewing the notification. Everyone wanted to be wildly unpredictable today, it seemed. Wasn't like she had a murder to execute.

Victoria pulled up her call log and tapped Warren's name. No answer, which was odd. For all his ineptitude, Warren didn't miss her calls, especially when he was supposed to be free until his dinner meeting. She hung up and tried again. This time, the call went straight to voicemail.

Was Warren ignoring her?

Well, that wasn't going to fly. She swiped to her contacts and hit the main line.

"Livingston Corporation, how may I direct your call?" Warren's secretary, Judy, a comely woman with a small gap between her front two teeth and a penchant for ramen, crooned into the speaker.

"Hi, Judy, it's Victoria."

"Mrs. Tate, how are you?"

"I'm well, thanks," she said, diving straight to the point. "My calendar just updated and I was hoping you could confirm the change. What's going on with the Harvest Gala? The RSVP was for next weekend."

"It was supposed to be," she said.

"What happened?"

"Oh, it's awful," Judy said, frown evident in her voice. "Margaret's mother has taken a turn for the worse, I'm afraid. They were hoping for good news, but her last test results weren't great. So they bumped it to tonight in case Margaret needs to make arrangements."

Margaret Connors, *the* Kent Wood socialite. She and her ridiculous husband, Barnaby lived in a mega-mansion on a private cul-de-sac at the other, filthy richer, end of Kent Wood Manor. For anyone else, rescheduling an event of such magnitude with no notice would be impossible, but for Margaret Connors, the proud stay-at-home wife who ultimately controlled Barnaby's wallet, the city would move Christmas to June if it meant the cash flow continued.

"I didn't know her mother was still alive," Victoria said. "She's never come up in conversation."

"Well, she won't be for much longer," Judy said before immediately backtracking. "I apologize, Mrs. Tate, that was incredibly crass of me."

"No worries," she said. *Neither will Warren.*

Judy's voice lowered to a conspiratorial level. Victoria could almost see her twirling a strand of her copper waves as she divulged the news. "One of their housekeepers told me she has cancer. Stage four, in her pancreas. Terrible, right? Margaret is completely torn up. She wanted to fly her up from Long Island, but she's too weak to be moved, so they've hired the entire staff of a private practice to give her round-the-clock care. Margaret's taking the jet down first thing in the morning and plans to stay, but she refused to cancel the Gala. So it's tonight. All of that stays between us birds, of course. I'm not usually one to gossip."

Unless there was another person within earshot. "What time does the Gala start?" she asked.

"Seven o'clock at the Kent Wood Mansion."

"Does Warren know?"

Judy paused. "Mr. Tate has been in meetings for most of the morning, but I'll check with him before he leaves for lunch."

"He's leaving for lunch?" she asked dubiously. Warren ordered from Lorenzo's on Fridays. Every Friday, without fail. Grilled branzino with rice pilaf and two cannoli. His only cheat meal of the week.

"He had me make a reservation for two at the new Thai place downtown."

"Did he say with who?"

The keyboard clacked through the speaker. Another pause. "He didn't. He's on a conference call with Hobart's CFO, but I'm sure he wouldn't mind if I patched you in."

"That's all right, thanks for letting me know," Victoria said.

"Of course. Happy to help. I'm here until four if you need anything else."

The call ended, and Victoria stared blankly at the rolls of plastic and painter's tape. A reservation for two. Warren would never choose a Thai place. Vanilla was spicy to her husband.

So who was he dining with?

6

Victoria navigated the online appointment system for Atelier's Salon and scheduled a blowout for the last available slot of the day. The last thing she wanted to do was waste an hour in front of a mirror, but if she'd learned anything from her father over the years, it was to keep her business clean. Following surface-level expectations was necessary to maintain her air of innocence. If she showed up to the Gala unprimped and flat faced, Margaret would one hundred percent call her out, drawing attention where she didn't want it.

She scooped up the materials from Miller's and stuffed them in a bottom cabinet, out of sight in case Warren decided to come home early. Being observant wasn't a trait Victoria would ascribe to him often, but he had his moments.

Her stomach grumbled, which struck her as both funny and odd. How normal it was to feel hunger when she was coming to that fork in Robert Frost's proverbial woods. Granted, most people misinterpreted that poem, not realizing that the path never mattered; she was going to end up in the same place regardless of which direction she chose. In that, Victoria found comfort. A sense of rightness.

One way or another, they would've always wound up here.

With an apple in one hand and her phone in the other, she skimmed the messages in the Kent Wood Manor group chat. News of the Gala was spreading fast. Her neighbors rallied in excitement while fretting about the weather. Many complained about the burden of securing impromptu babysitters.

That's going to be me, she thought. *Warren* wants *that to be me.*

Scrounging for childcare at a moment's notice. Competing with the other mothers for who pays the most or who has the best snacks in the pantry for some teenager flicking through TikTok. Begging for an iota of responsibility while trying to figure out which dress hides her post-baby weight the best.

Okay, she didn't have time to stress about what Warren wanted anymore. She needed to focus and that wasn't going to happen with a thread full of neighbors arguing over curfews and parking fees. Wishing everyone luck with Gala prep, she padded across the darkening foyer up the stairs to their bedroom.

When Victoria had met Warren one star-crossed evening, he'd bought her a beer and delivered the cheesiest pick-up line she'd ever heard: *So aside from being sexy, what do you do for a living?*

It was still cringeworthy, but she also smiled at the memory. The ruffle of his dark hair, the curls at the nape of his neck, how shaggy yet tailored he seemed. The way his blue eyes gleamed under the bar lights.

She had loved him that night; she was sure of it. He was smart and witty and unbelievably charming. Victoria had been surprised at how hard she'd fallen but didn't fight the attraction.

Her father had adored him. Her mother had approved (which was high a praise for Clare Livingston).

She didn't realize how royally she'd screwed herself until it was too late.

Until her father had handed the company to Warren.

At first, Victoria had thought it was a test, some ill-conceived plot he'd cooked up to push her limits and prove her worthiness. A very Jeremy Livingston thing to do. So she'd risen to the occasion. Grew her client list. Banked crazy hours. Increased revenue. She'd hosted dinner parties and registered for a goddamn yoga class to sweeten the relationship with the CEO of the largest female-run financial institution in the Northeast, but the ah-ha moment never came. Warren stayed at her father's side, and Victoria was banished to the shadows.

The longer the denial, the more certain she'd become. Her father wasn't changing his mind. Not even Teagan had been able to find the logic.

That she and her sister had agreed on something spoke volumes.

Victoria hit the lights and sat on the tufted cream bench in the center of the closet. Her evening gowns were spaced evenly apart on velvet rods to protect them from wrinkles. Some fashion faux pas were acceptable, often debatable. White after Labor Day, denim on denim, pattern mixing. Those rules could be broken, but nothing said careless like wrinkles.

And maybe trace evidence.

Victoria would be guilty of neither.

Every Gala had a theme, and this year's was the Art of Nature. She doubted Margaret and Barnaby had spent any discernible time outdoors, but that wasn't important.

People came for the extravagance, not to see who could best understand the assignment.

Victoria's gown fit the bill for both, however. She'd chosen it months ago, scouring websites, department stores, and designer trunk shows until she had her *Say Yes to the Dress* gasp. The rich reddish-purple hue was technically called tyrian and would've been right at home on *Game of Thrones*.

Made of lightning and fit for a queen.

From the kitchen, the phone rang. Warren insisted on having a house phone for emergencies. Only punch-drunk telemarketers and automated survey bots called landlines anymore. Another archaic notion which proved that Warren was incapable of adapting to a progressive mode of thinking. Left up to him, Livingston would stay in the glory days of the nineties, all handshakes and hired escorts.

The answering machine activated, blasting Warren's voice into the silence.

"Hey Vic, it's me. Missed you at the office this morning, and you haven't answered any of my texts. Should've told me if you weren't coming in. I want to go over the contract before I send it to Lauren in HR. She'll have the final e-doc for you to sign once we get this taken care of, so check your email and get that back to me ASAP. Judy's got boxes coming for your office on Monday. I hope she got a hold of you about the Gala. Okay. Talk soon."

Contract. Boxes. Monday? Like hell she was signing that document.

She jumped when her cell vibrated in her pocket, Warren's name blinking onto the screen. She wondered if it was possible for someone to strain an eyeball rolling it too hard.

"Warren," Victoria said.

"Nice of you to pick up," he said, and she mouthed a silent curse at his snarky tone. "I just left a message at the house. Why aren't you at the office? Where are you?"

"Home. I felt off this morning and cleared my schedule. About to head to the Plaza, though. Duty calls."

"Ah. I see."

He didn't see. "What's up, Warren?"

"I . . . nothing. You heard my message? About the e-doc?"

Heat rose up her chest. "I heard."

"Great. Glad we're on the same page." The relief in his voice was palpable. She was about to call bullshit when he pressed on. "Listen, I've got to cut this short. I'm about to conference with James. Had to cut some corners to make the Gala work. I just wanted to make sure you knew about the contract. We'll talk more tonight."

Lie, she thought. James ran an international financial organization based in Cape Town. If Warren knew anything about time zones, he would've known that it was almost ten P.M. there. What's more, Victoria happened to know that James was on a digital-free retreat.

"How was Lorenzo's?" she asked warily.

He hacked a cough. "Hm? Oh, good. Same as always. Fish was a little dry."

God, Warren was a terrible liar. He was hiding something, and while she couldn't deny that she wanted to know what that something was, she didn't press her luck. There was no need. Warren would either tell her the truth or he'd die with his secret.

"There's always next week," she said. "All right, well, I have to get going."

"Sure. Right. Listen, don't wait for me tonight, Vic. I'll just meet you at the Mansion."

She stood and crossed the room, counting the footsteps from the bench to the bed. Continuing down the hall and stairs, she paused at the closet and hooked her arm through her coat sleeve. "You're getting ready at the office?" She looped a scarf around her neck and opened the garage door. Christ, it was cold. She cinched the scarf tighter and jumped into the car.

"I have everything I need with me," he said. "Going home would be impractical."

Didn't that sound loaded. "Okay, I'll see you there."

"Bring up a bottle of red from the basement too. The vintage merlot. I think we'll both need a glass after tonight."

The engine thrummed. She switched to speaker and pulled down the visor, rubbing at the smudged mascara in the creases under her eyes. "Why?"

"I'll meet you at seven," he said, ignoring her question.

So he was going to continue to be cryptic. The call disconnected as she eased onto the street.

Warren's comments left a bitter taste in her mouth. There was no way he'd figured out what she was planning. Not a single person would suspect Victoria of being capable of homicide, least of all her husband. She'd set herself up well in that regard. Volunteer work and charity and never—not once—uttering a word of disapproval at Warren's promotion.

But if he wasn't suspicious of her, why was he lying?

7

Victoria pulled into Kent Wood Plaza and spent an hour at Nine West, wishing she'd made the drive to Neiman Marcus in Paramus. Kent Wood was seriously lacking when it came to designer selection, so she settled on a classic black stiletto heel with strappy details that would meet the bare minimum of the Connors' dress code. Wasn't like she was showing up in Crocs, though. That was Betty Knottier's job.

Shoes handled, Victoria braced against the wind and took the covered sidewalk to the salon, tucking her chin into her coat. The door sealed with a whistle, and she was devoured by the cacophony of hair dryers and conversation.

Kimber Charles appeared wearing a black sleeveless sheath dress and studded oxfords. She'd been the premiere stylist in Kent Wood since the early aughts, when she relocated from the city to start fresh after a messy divorce.

Her jet-black hair was straightened into a blunt bob that grazed her chin. Her foundation was contoured and flawless. Her large brown eyes were accentuated by smoky hues and lash extensions, and her full lips were nude but not washed out. Not many women could pull that off without a filter, but Kimber exuded a natural confidence.

Over the years, Victoria had grown to appreciate Kimber for more than her trendy aesthetics. She was sharp. Determined. Took shit from no one.

A woman after her own heart.

"Victoria, darling, so good to see you," she exclaimed, locking her fingers in the crooks of Victoria's elbows and pecking cheeks.

"Thank you so much for squeezing me in."

"Anything for my favorite client," she said, inspecting Victoria's roots and ends with a neutral expression. "You've been using that toner I recommended. Love to see it. I'll have you looking like Charlize Theron in no time."

Bombshell *Charlize or* Monster *Charlize?* she thought. *Big difference.*

Kimber guided her through the swell of the main room to a chair at the end of the aisle. "Classic blowout?" she asked, fluffing the layers around Victoria's shoulders. "It's gotten so long. I'll give you a trim while we wait for a sink to open up."

"Actually, no. I'm not sure," Victoria said. "Got any suggestions for something a little more . . . daring?"

Kimber smiled. "With your bone structure? I've got a few ideas, but why don't you take a minute and flip through this for some inspiration." She handed Victoria a copy of *Us Weekly* and patted her arm amicably. "I'll finish up with Mrs. Middleton. You know how grumpy she gets if her perm doesn't scream 'microwaved in the eighties.' Then I'm all yours, darlin'."

Victoria thanked her and absently flipped through the pages of celebrities. Warren preferred her hair the way it was. Victoria hadn't worn it any other way since she'd known him, just varying degrees of the same long layers.

Much like her mother had styled hers.

Victoria really didn't want to think about why she might be mirroring those generational beauty beliefs—not when her actions were the opposite of Clare Livingston's definition of *woman*. Beautiful. Soft spoken. Delicate. Most importantly, a woman was nothing without a man to hold her up.

A woman could be so many things, though. That's what her mother had never understood. Victoria was so much more than a pretty, spineless rag doll.

How had she forgotten that?

With an odor of hair product and vanilla, Kimber appeared at her side. She studied Victoria in the mirror, lashes casting spidery shadows beneath her eyes. "What do you think?" she asked, pressing her hip into the chair. "Did inspiration strike?"

In more ways than one, she thought.

"I know exactly what I want," Victoria said with a hint of a smile.

Warren's fate had already been decided.

It was time to cut the deadweight.

8

The garage door rattled shut, sealing her in darkness. Victoria avoided the rearview mirror, her sheared reflection still an oddity. She dug her fists into her thighs and concentrated on her breathing. Anger. Fear. Anticipation. It was difficult to determine which was leading the charge. The last time she'd felt this alive had been on the eve of her father's death. Unable to take control of Livingston, yes, but free from his restraints in a way that left her gasping.

She wanted to feel that way again: boundless and terrified of the open water yet eager for more.

Inside, Victoria dropped her coat and purse on the chair and kicked off her boots. She shivered at the unfamiliar sensation of the draft on her shoulders, but the resulting chill seemed more like a promise than a regret. Following her gut hadn't steered her wrong today.

Gathering the materials from the cabinet, she jogged upstairs and inspected the bedroom. The plastic wasn't going to cover everything. The ceilings were too high, and the tallest ladder was stored in the shed to which Warren had the only key. She had enough to cover the immediate areas, however. That would have to suffice.

The drop cloths were just a failsafe, after all. Her Type A personality refused to let her ignore the potential for disaster. As long as Warren followed her lead, as he did most other nights, there would be no need for murderproofing. The act would be tidy and contained. What she'd gleaned from her true crime podcasts was that too little planning led to mistakes, and too much planning led to overthinking the execution. Victoria figured that covering her ass in case tonight led to unexpected blood was somewhere in the middle of those two extremes.

Wrapping herself in a robe, she opened the first box of supplies and got down to business.

The next hour passed quickly. She lost herself in the whoosh and crinkle of materials. Sometimes she would hum a tune. That new Lizzo song was quite catchy. Feel-good and representative of the hope she felt blooming in her chest. Mostly, though, she used the time for reflection.

She thought about Warren, of course. Their beginning and their inevitable conclusion.

She thought about her mother, how frequently and fervently she emphasized the necessity of beauty.

She thought about her father: his sweeping demands for her to be the best, even if that meant exposing her worst tendencies. Excellence was never good enough. She had to strive for perfection, no matter the cost. Friendships. Lovers. Sanity. Victoria was under no illusion that, conventionally speaking, murdering her husband to sever their ties and preserve her free will was frowned upon.

That didn't stop the little voice in her head from whispering that all things considered, Jeremy Livingston would be proud of her decision.

Taking a life. Regaining a life. Balance.

Here, she lingered. What would Warren's final thoughts be? Would he recognize that his end was looming? Would he reach for her in the darkness?

Victoria imagined him floating away, the lids of his eyes fluttering in unconsciousness. Perhaps that was why she missed the arrival of her sister.

One minute she was taping down the corner of a particularly tricky section of drop cloth, the next her bedroom door flung wide open, slamming into the wall as Teagan charged forward. She waved a knife wildly, casting frantic glances around the room like she was expecting Michael Myers to pop out of the closet.

"Jesus Christ." The knife dropped to Teagan's side as she stared at Victoria. Seconds, minutes, she had no idea how long she stood there, fish-mouthed and silent, trying and failing to figure out what the hell was happening.

"Tor," Teagan said, dragging her name through molasses, "what did you do?"

Nothing—yet—she thought, suddenly infuriated by her little sister's accusatory tone. "You broke my door."

"The door," she repeated, as if she couldn't be hearing her right. "Sure. The *door* is the issue here." Teagan's gaze wandered. "What is this?"

Victoria made a noise of disapproval and stood, crossing her arms and giving Teagan the look. The I'm-older-and-you're-annoying look. She'd mastered it over the years and used it to her advantage whenever she could. Including right now.

"What are you doing here, Teagan?"

For all her father's emphasis on building a Livingston empire, Victoria and Teagan hadn't quite figured out how to be around each other. Sisters, yes. They shared a bloodline that she recognized and honored. But honing the essence of what made sisters more than siblings? That inexplicable tie that transformed a relationship to a bond? That had always been missing for them.

Teagan did not stop by for casual chats or girls' nights. Her abrupt appearance raised all of Victoria's alarms.

"Me?" Teagan squealed. "What even—what is this? What are you doing? And what the hell did you do to your *hair*?"

She snuffed the urge to mimic Teagan's dumbfounded expression. Instead, Victoria smirked and fidgeted with the blunt edges. The pixie cut had been a bold choice; Kimber had agreed. But with every inch that had fallen to the floor, Victoria had felt the years of suffocation sloughing off too.

"Yeah," she said, her expression softening. "I needed a change."

"This isn't just change, Tor; this is cleaning out the whole damn account." She gripped Victoria's chin, turning her head this way and that, inspecting the styled pieces. "You haven't had short hair since "

"Since," she interrupted, "I was ten and you decided to play Sweeney Todd?"

Teagan scoffed. "It was like an inch of hair, drama queen. Let it go."

Let it go, she thought, mentally kicking Teagan in the shin. Their mother had literally banished her to her bedroom for two days when she saw what Teagan had done. There had been an emergency trip to the salon, where the stylist agreed that *nothing could be done to save her*. Her face burned at the memory.

"I should've shaved your eyebrows off," Victoria said, wrenching out of her hold.

"Aw, come on, are you going to stay big mad about that forever?"

"Yes."

"It was hilarious."

"A riot," she deadpanned.

Teagan closed the gap between them. "Hey, in all seriousness: you can talk to me about anything. Chopping off your hair is a massive cry for help."

Victoria rolled her eyes. "I'm not crying out for help, Teagan, god. I'm trying something new. Not a crime."

"Technically."

Bitch, she thought, before a trickle of insecurity took hold. "It looks good, though, right? Kimber said it accentuates my long neck and cheekbones."

Because as much as Teagan sought her approval, Victoria wasn't immune to the need for acceptance. She waited patiently as Teagan's eyes raked across her face, her judgment calculating like an Instagram filter.

"Objectively, yes, it looks good," Teagan concluded. "But it's still weird."

"Wow, love you, too, Teags." She felt better, though. *Weird* left room for adjustment, and Teagan would get used to her new look, just like she'd get used to existing on her own.

Victoria tossed the roll of painter's tape on the bed before rolling up the excess plastic sheeting. As if this was the most normal thing for her to be doing on a Friday night before the Gala.

"Don't be a bitch, you know what I mean," Teagan chided. "I walked in expecting Rapunzel and found Tinkerbell."

"Why are you here?" Victoria asked curtly. "And why do you have my cleaver?"

Teagan turned the knife over in her hand like she was seeing it for the first time. "You didn't answer the door or your phone. I got scared. Thought maybe you had an intruder."

"You and your horror movies. You need to stop watching Shudder."

"Hey, I watch the news too," Teagan said.

"Like that's any better. And what did you think you were even going to do with that?" she asked.

"Um, stab?" Teagan shrugged, almost dropping the knife.

"Jesus, you're impossible." The absurdity of the situation rolled over her in subtle waves. Teagan was more likely to stab herself in the leg than actually land a blow against an attacker. Her sister was the stuff of fluff. Cotton candy and angel plushies. And here Victoria was mid-murder preparation. "I thought surgeons were supposed to be good with a blade. Maybe that's butchers."

"Well, I have handled my fair share of meat, so."

Victoria rolled her eyes again but chuckled. "Cute."

"Get it? I was talking about—"

"Yes, please, it's funnier if you have to explain the joke."

"All right, all right. Kill joy," Teagan said.

"Child."

The sisters settled into the lightened moment, a tentative truce in a room full of plastic.

9

"I'll fix your door if you're upset," Teagan said after a beat, "but I maintain that I was acting under duress. I was worried about you."

"You don't have to worry. I can take care of myself."

She sounded like Warren; objectively, Victoria knew that. Blustery and assured. Did every married couple start sounding like one another after a certain amount of time? Was it inevitable that you'd absorb the vocabulary and mannerisms of your spouse? How long would it be before she was able to detangle her personality from the person she'd become to appease her husband?

The thought was both tedious and slightly terrifying.

"Of course, you can," Teagan said. "You're invincible." She placed the knife on the dresser and flexed her biceps like a superhero.

She stood by her previous statement that her sister was a child. How someone who routinely made dick jokes and prided herself on her extensive pop-culture knowledge became a medical professional was a mystery Victoria would never solve. *Speaking of medical professional,* she thought. "I thought you were in *surgery.*" She flexed her fingers around the word. Air quotes may not be cool, but they were a surefire method to piss off one, Teagan Livingston.

"Nobody does air quotes anymore, Victoria," she said. Predictably. "Your age is showing."

"Are you here just to insult me?"

"That, plus I need to borrow a stupid dress for the stupid Gala. What I really need to know is why you've got more plastic than Dexter going on. Are you murdering someone in here tonight?"

"What?" she snapped. "Christ, Teagan, no. We're," she fumbled, reaching for the first explanation that came to mind. She hadn't prepared for an interruption at this stage. "Didn't I tell you? We're having the ceiling repainted."

Not her best lie.

Teagan looked up at the spotless ceiling and frowned. "Shouldn't the painters be doing the prep? That's what you're paying them for."

"It's better if I do it myself." Victoria shuffled to the closet, hoping her flippant dismissal was enough for Teagan to drop the matter.

"What company did you hire?" she asked instead.

"I'm certain I told you already," Victoria said, keeping her back turned. Why wouldn't Teagan ever do things the easy way? Claws out, it would have to be. "I wouldn't expect you to remember with your *super* busy, incredibly important schedule. Tell me, how are the boob jobs going?"

Teagan's amusement died in a blink, her expression turning dour and sullen. "Plastic surgery is not just boob—oh my god, you know what? Go to hell. If I had known you were going to be such a bitch, I wouldn't have come."

"Feel free to see yourself out then," she said.

She didn't. Getting rid of her sister was like brushing off glitter. Following Victoria into the closet, she inspected the organized shelves and thumbed at various blouses, pulling and tugging at the fabrics, occasionally twisting her face to broadcast her opinion of her sister's wardrobe.

"Something, something beggars and choosers," Teagan said with a huge sigh. "I still need to borrow a dress."

Victoria skimmed the hangers and landed on a sleeveless blue wrap. She held it up and eyed Teagan for approval.

"Not that one," Teagan said. "I'll look like a Smurf."

"What was that about beggars and choosers?" she asked, searching again. A bedazzled mini caught her attention. Sparkles and attention: so very Teagan. "This?"

"I'll try it," she said, starting to undress. "Will Warren care that I'm taking over the space?"

"No. I'm meeting him at the Gala."

"Finally kicked him out; good for you," Teagan joked, setting Victoria's teeth on edge. Her sister's humor was landing a little too close to the truth for her liking.

"I didn't kick him out," she said flatly. "His keeps his tux at the office, and I like having my own space to get ready. It's important to maintain boundaries, even in marriage." She selected three more gowns and flung them at Teagan.

"Ouch," Teagan said, rubbing the spot on her chest where a hanger hook had dug in.

"You wanted dresses," she laughed. A gentle smile lifted the tension in her eyes, and Teagan reciprocated. The air around them settled, electricity fizzling out to a calm thrum.

And then, they were just sisters. Just Victoria and Teagan.

Victoria suspected that Teagan liked these fleeting moments the best, when the things that came with age and experience—the things that wedged and separated, or went unsaid—when all of that was forgotten, and it was just the two of them.

Livingston sisters against the world.

Those days were distant memories, at least for Victoria. Perhaps they were never there to begin with, simply long-gone wishes she'd convinced herself were real. She understood that there were pieces of herself that she refused to share. Her relationship with Warren had muted those vulnerable parts of her too.

Teagan shivered out of the first dress with a scowl and a snide comment about taste. Victoria scoffed but remained silent.

She'd forgotten what it felt like to trust another person. Could she open up to Teagan? Spill the dangerous words and dark imaginings?

No. But the temptation was there: to connect. To believe.

To break.

10

Teagan stepped into the next dress and spun. "What do you think?"

The satin fabric clung to her hips and hung from her shoulders in gentle swoops. The color of plump lemons, unblemished and radiant. "You're stunning."

"Thank you, thank you. It's got a real *How to Lose a Guy in Ten Days* vibe to it, right? Eat your heart out Kate Hudson."

"Good to see you've held on to your modesty," Victoria said, hanging her robe on an empty hook. She stepped into her own gown as Teagan twirled in front of the mirror. Ever the center of attention.

Victoria's selection wasn't meant to hide in the shadows either. A spectacular trumpet-style dress with a corseted bodice and thigh-high split. Unlike Warren's outdated beliefs about motherhood, a good thigh split never went out of style.

Was she really comparing Warren to her evening wear?

Maybe her righteous indignation was tainted with a slight veil of pettiness after all, but Victoria had earned that grudge.

"Damn, Mrs. Tate. New do and showing a little leg? Won't the Puritans at the town hall cast their pitchforks and torches?"

"No one's burning tonight, sorry to disappoint," she said with an exaggerated aw-shucks snap.

Teagan grasped her shoulders and leveled a serious stare. "Tell the truth, what'd you do with my sister? Are you one of those body-snatching aliens?"

"No."

"Pod person?"

"Zip me, asshole," Victoria said.

"Hold on, hold on, the profanity, heavens to Betsy," she teased. "Hold your hair up for me. Oh, wait," she said, and cackled like a hyena.

"You're *hilarious*. You'll have a solid career in comedy when the lipos dry up."

"If there's one thing that never dies, it's the lipos. I had two today. The last one? Lipo—for *her*—as an anniversary gift—for him."

"You're kidding."

"Husband encouraged her. Happens more than you'd think. She passed the BDDQ with flying colors, though" Teagan said.

"You're screening your patients now?" Victoria asked, eyebrows lifted in surprise. From what Teagan would have her understand, cosmetic surgeons weren't required to run psych evals on their patients, but she did her best to establish realistic expectations.

"No. Her therapist sent me the body dysmorphic disorder questionnaire after our initial consult, but it wouldn't have mattered either way." She bunched the two panels of Victoria's dress together and zipped as she spoke. "She followed me on TikTok and practically begged me to film her for the channel. Got some great shots, but it never ceases to amaze me how far people will go to make their partners want them."

Victoria was quiet for a solid minute before she said anything. She'd never tried especially hard to impress Warren. Sure, she'd felt an attraction in the beginning, call it a spark or butterflies, that wasn't the point. Victoria was not the same as that woman. She wouldn't compromise her desires to make Warren happy.

Or was she lying to herself?

Hadn't the vanilla manicure and long blonde hair been for his benefit as much as hers? Hadn't she yielded to him for years? How was what she'd done any different than anniversary liposuction?

"Don't you ever get tired of playing to vanity?" she asked, crisply dismissing that train of thought.

"Everybody's vain, Tor. Some of us just don't care to hide it." Teagan flopped on the plastic-covered bed as Victoria moved to the vanity. "Here's a better question: How do you sleep on this thing? Like a giant bag of marshmallows."

"I don't sleep."

"You don't sleep." She waited a beat. Victoria waited it out. Knowing her sister, another diatribe was brewing. "I don't want to tell you how to live your life—"

There it was. "Then don't." She couldn't dull the sharp edge to her tone. She didn't want to. Teagan was venturing on a land mine of loaded questions, and Victoria was willing to detonate them all with the slightest bit of pressure.

"But you remember what happened the last time."

The last time.

The days before their father had passed flashed violently. The thin skin on the back of his hand tugging around the IV port. The bruising under his eyes. The raspy breath as he whispered to her.

Please.

"This is not the same thing," Victoria said with a note of finality. "Not even close."

"What do you mean 'you don't sleep?'"

"Forget I said anything."

"I just think that—"

"*Enough.*"

Teagan clapped her mouth shut. The mood stayed tense, though, picking at Victoria's fraying nerves when what she really needed to focus on was how the next few hours were going to unravel with Warren.

"Let's go downstairs," Victoria said. "Have a glass of wine with me."

Teagan clucked her tongue inside her cheek, yellow dress shimmering in the soft lighting. "You had me at wine."

11

I n the basement, they spun lazily on bucket seats at Warren's bar. Victoria rarely used it, relegated to the upstairs for the social gatherings he insisted she host, but tonight was special. She tried on Warren's space like an old sweater, and it felt good. Right.

She poured two glasses of Pinot while Teagan rambled on about her latest romantic escapade. Forever incapable of settling down. Jumping from one hookup to the next. Never staying still long enough to grow roots. She wasn't judging Teagan, though.

Or maybe she was, but as the older and wiser sister, Victoria was allowed to hold Teagan to a different standard.

Okay, that was also bullshit. She didn't care about Teagan's promiscuity. Even the word itself bothered her. The negative connotation that being single and exploring somehow made her a lesser person. This wasn't some Victorian era melodrama where a bare ankle was scandalous, and Victoria clearly wasn't hanging her hat in the matrimonial bliss column.

If she were being honest, it wasn't the sex that she took issue with. It was the freedom she envied. The unburdened ability to make her own choices. Where would Victoria be if she'd never married Warren? Would her father have given her control of the company? Would she have been overshadowed by another partner who adhered to the old-school values of the boys' club? Would she still be considering murder?

"Vicky-Icky, did you hear me? Hell-o?"

God, the nicknames. Victoria detested the nicknames Teagan had given her over the years. Rhyming, ridiculous, super embarrassing. Teagan knew this but made them up anyway. Her immature streak knew no bounds.

Teagan waved dramatically for her attention, her face contorted into dumb expectance like this wasn't the first or fifth time she'd said her name. Victoria sipped her wine and scrambled for any detail from the story Teagan was telling. Something about his hands? Or the plans? Fuck it, she hadn't been listening at all.

"Sorry. Spaced out there for a second."

"Do I need to remind you about how conversations work?" Teagan asked, letting her annoyance take over. "One person speaks. The other—"

"I said I was sorry, gees. What more do you want?"

"A blood oath would be aces," she said.

"I'll get right on that," Victoria deadpanned. "Go on, corrupt me with tales of your misguided sexual adventures. I swear I'm listening."

"No, dear sister, I think I'm done sharing for today. I'm always the one to spill the beans."

"There are just so many beans, it's hard to keep track," she said, gesturing with her glass.

"Beans are all the same. Beans are boring. Tell me something new with you. How are you? What's going on in the world of Victoria Eloise Reginald Tate?"

Victoria checked the time again and rubbed an invisible spot on the bar top. "You're incredibly persistent, you know that?"

Teagan preened. "Did you expect any less?"

"From you? Not a chance."

Her tone softened, and that was almost as bad as the obnoxious nicknames. "Really, though, how are you?"

"I'm good," Victoria offered. "Nothing new with me."

"Except the hair."

"Yes, except that."

"Which has nothing to do with the ceiling getting repainted."

"Not a thing." Ten minutes until the town car was scheduled to arrive.

"Or your marriage."

"Christ, Teags, sometimes a haircut is just a haircut."

"You know what your problem is?" Teagan asked. She brushed a wisp of long auburn hair off her shoulder and sat a little straighter.

"I didn't know I had a problem."

"You do," she said flatly. "And I'll tell you what it is. You're too serious. You don't know how to relax. *Ever.* You're always working. Or planning an event. Or networking. Or researching for a client. I'm tired just listing this stuff. You're stressed way the fuck out, and that is sucking all the fun from your face. What little fun there was to begin with."

"I'm fun," Victoria said halfheartedly.

"You watch TikToks of people cleaning their houses."

"Murder scenes, Teagan. I watch crime scene cleanups."

"That's not the flex you think it is. Why not take a vacation? Have a little romp in the sun with your handsome husband."

Because Warren is demanding I quit my job to have a child, and I would rather kill him.

If only she could speak those words aloud and end Teagan's prying.

Not that explaining her feelings had ever stopped her sister before.

If anything, it had burned whatever rickety bridge had connected them in the first place.

Their father had just been diagnosed with cancer. The doctors had given him a year to live. Victoria had wanted to streamline the process of her succession at that point, creating mock-ups of projections and a complete five-year plan.

He'd resisted.

Be patient, Teagan had said. *Dad will come around. No one could run the company better than you, but he's not ready to give up the reins yet. You know how he is. He thought he'd live forever, and now he's got less than a year. Let him come to you in his own way. He will. I promise.*

That promise had been as real as Teagan's ass. Victoria had taken her advice—because their father favored Teagan. Because she'd thought that preferential treatment might pay off for once. But he hadn't come around. Instead, he'd gone to Warren. The man who crowdsourced Facebook for his beard oil.

When the official announcement had come, Victoria had been blindsided, eating lunch with her traitorous husband at a café across from the office. Her phone had buzzed, Teagan's name rolling down the screen. There was a second of dread that this was the text she'd been waiting for. The *Dad's dead* message.

Have you seen the PR? Daddy named his successor. It's Warren.

She'd read the message three times. Warren. Warren. *Warren?*

She'd met her husband's gaze before the press release finished loading, finding the truth in his dopey mouth-tucked frown. He'd looked like he was about to ask her if she needed a lollipop. A shitty consolation prize.

"How could you?" Victoria had asked.

"Vic—"

"I'm your wife. Your partner. You watched me pour hours into proposals and pitches and didn't say a goddamn word? Every day—for weeks, Warren, weeks—you just lied to my face."

Warren had caressed her cheek, some performative healing gesture that had only fueled her anger. "I wanted to tell you."

"Wanted to tell me—"

"I tried to fight for you."

"Not very hard," she'd said. They had both known it was true.

Warren didn't bother contesting her point. He'd dropped the soft-blow, sugarcoated spiel he had clearly rehearsed and leveled with her. "Vic. Come on. It's Jeremy fucking Livingston. The Reaper."

He'd spoken about her father like he was an idol. She had wanted to break every one of his fingers as they twined with hers.

"I know who he is," she'd said. "He's my father."

"But you also work for the man. You know the industry better than anyone else. You have to understand that you don't say no to Jeremy Livingston."

"Jesus Christ, Warren. You can't be serious."

"It's been killing me keeping this from you, you have no idea—" She'd scoffed at that, but he hadn't noticed. He never noticed. "—but now it's all out in the open. And look, nothing has to change between us, not at home or at work. Okay? Trust me."

Trust. Like he knew anything about what that meant. "Everything will change. You'll be CEO."

"And you'll be my right-hand woman." He'd taken said hand in his and winked, fucking *winked,* like they were partners in crime. Both in on the secret.

Gathering the pieces of her ego, Victoria had cleared the emotion from her throat and withdrawn from his grasp before he could feel her trembling. "Of course, darling," she'd said. She couldn't lose control. She had to get a handle on the situation and figure out a way for her father to renege on whatever deal he'd made with Warren. "I'll be your number two. Congratulations. I'm so happy for you."

The words had curdled on her tongue even as he'd rewarded her with his most charming smile, all teeth and tongue and blink-wink that was more endearing than successful. The blue of his eyes twinkling in victory.

That had been the first time she'd underestimated him, and she vowed to make it the last.

12

Victoria observed Teagan as she moved behind the bar, nursing the flare of jealousy. "Do you remember what Dad used to call you?" she asked.

"What?" Teagan squinted at the label of an amber-colored jug. "Can I drink this?"

"It's basically paint thinner, but knock yourself out. Do you remember or not?"

She unscrewed the cap and winced at the smell. "Never mind." The bottle went back on the shelf, and Teagan met her gaze. "*Reine,*" she said smugly, pronouncing the word with a shaky French accent. *Ren.* "He always said I was the queen of his heart."

"Right." Victoria raised her glass. Air cheersed. Drank. "*Queen.*"

If you looked up "Daddy's girl" in the dictionary, Teagan's picture would've been a full-page spread. Their relationship had been idyllic, especially compared to the train wreck Victoria was forced to navigate. For a long time she chalked it up to being the oldest. Having to set an example. That explanation only went so far, though. Victoria fought for a second of Jeremy Livingston's warmth, but Teagan lived in the sun.

"Don't be jealous, Tor," she said.

"Do you remember what he called me?"

Teagan thought for a minute, head cocked to the side. "Is this a trick question? Wasn't it . . . wasn't it just Victoria? Maybe your whole name when he was super pissed."

"You were Reine. I was Rainmaker."

"Yeah, I wouldn't take that too seriously. Doubt he knew what that meant." She shuffled her hands like she was dealing out money. "Dad didn't care about keeping up with social trends. He still called it The Facebook when he died."

Leave it to Teagan to completely miss the freaking point and belittle her emotions at the same time, she thought.

"When I was a kid, I thought he blamed me for the rain," Victoria said.

"Right, you were so weird about the weather." She opened another bottle of liquor, shrugged, and took a sip, lips smacking on the end with a shudder. "You stole the disposable camera I got for my eighth birthday and used the entire roll of film to take pictures of that one bad storm."

"I was trying to get a picture of lightning. Turns out, that's really fucking hard to do."

"You still owe me a camera," Teagan said.

"Bill me."

"Might as well. You can afford it."

She stuck out her tongue, enjoying the banter and the back and forth. Victoria was . . . surprisingly, not having a bad time.

"So that's why he called you Rainmaker? Because you liked storms?" Teagan asked, reclaiming her stool. The skirts of their gowns swished lazily back and forth. Victoria leaned back against the bar, rolling her head across her shoulders. The bristly hair against her skin gave her chills, but she didn't miss the weight.

"I mean, I really thought he held me responsible for the weather. That I was this . . . force behind the storms—that I controlled them somehow. He'd find me when the alerts went off and say, 'Cranky today, Victoria? Try not to destroy it all.'"

"Dad could be a jerk sometimes," she said.

That's the understatement of the century, Victoria thought, sipping her Pinot. "In the summer, I'd watch the really bad ones from the balcony off the study, just . . . closing my eyes and willing the clouds to come for us."

For lightning to strike.

It seemed right to tell Teagan this story, Victoria thought, to give her a chance to show that she understood where she was coming from before tonight. It was as close as she could come without flat out confessing.

Maybe she didn't have to do this alone.

"Can't actually walk on clouds, you know," Teagan said, interrupting her thoughts. "They're just vapor."

Teagan, for the love of—"The point is that Dad made me believe I was *wrong*. That there was something about me that wasn't normal."

Teagan was unusually quiet, staring into her glass. She dragged her thumb along the rim, hypnotically slow and contemplative. Finally, she spoke. "That's a bit dramatic, don't you think?"

"Dramatic." Teagan didn't understand. She would never understand. Victoria had her answer. "You didn't know Dad like I did. You saw what he wanted you to see."

"I knew how he treated you."

"And yet you still played right into his ego."

"And you didn't?"

"I did it because I thought I was taking over the company—not to shove his affection in your face. Not even close to the same thing."

"Potato, tomato. Keep telling yourself you weren't the favorite."

Victoria pinched her face into her best "Sure, Jan" expression. "Please. Mom thought I was a failure for continuing to work at Livingston after I married Warren. And Dad . . ." *Chose Warren. Over me.* "They were never going to love me. We both know that. Not like they loved you."

"Tor . . ." Teagan frowned. "All of that shit is in the past now. We're wildly successful women living the dream. Who gives a shit about whether or not our parents tucked us in enough when we were kids? What's this really about?"

The morality of killing my husband. "You wanted me to talk about something personal. Is this not what you pictured?"

Teagan set her glass down. "I thought we could at least try."

"Would it change anything?"

"Do you want it to?"

"You wouldn't even be here if you didn't need a damn dress," Victoria said. "Can we stop pretending our relationship is anything more than a biological obligation?"

"Wow." Teagan brushed her hands and moved to stand. "Okay, I can't do this. There's no winning with you."

Perhaps, Victoria thought, she'd taken it too far. Been too honest. But she was tired of filtering. "No, there's not. He hated me, and I'll never know why. There may not even *be* a why—but I carry that with me every day. Knowing that my own father pretended to care about my future just so that he could keep me at a safe distance. And I'm still paying."

"What does that mean?"

From outside a horn bleated, cutting the tension like a hot butter knife.

"Driver's here," Victoria muttered, blinking away a sheen of unexpected wetness.

"Tor—"

"Ready?"

Teagan's mouth opened, closed, opened again. She exhaled a frustrated sigh and turned for the stairs.

Victoria waited until she heard the front door click shut before releasing a shaky breath. Teagan had, at least, gotten one thing right: The past was done and buried. She didn't believe in superstitions or fate. She also didn't believe her life was mapped out by some omniscient being. There was something—a heaven, a hell, a never-ending cosmic void—but those were intangible. Abstract. And as such, they weren't worth the time it would take her to finish a prayer.

Free will was everything, and Victoria chose to put her faith in that.

Adjusting her dress, she headed upstairs and marched out the door. Not as a queen—that title was taken—but before the night was through, Victoria was going to be a king.

13

There was alcohol in the town car, much to Teagan's delight. Tiny bottles in hand, the mood lightened, and they settled into small talk. Celebrities and current events and Betty Knottier's weird obsession with neon colors. Teagan decidedly did not bring up Warren again, and that was just fine with Victoria.

She had planning to work out.

They took a handful of decent selfies despite Victoria protesting the angles and the act itself. Selfies made her feel simultaneously too old and incredibly immature. Teagan bragged about the hits on her latest video, and Victoria didn't make any snide comments about her being a fake doctor.

A mile or so from the Gala, the conversation died out. They watched the passing landscape while a random playlist of nineties throwbacks danced between them. As a Britney song started, Teagan turned the volume down.

"So, at Livingston. You're like a badass female version of Ray Donovan."

"Kind of," Victoria said. "I'm not the person you call when you've killed someone and don't know what to do with the dead body. I'm the person you call when you've tried to kill someone and *failed*, and now that person is running around your property messing with your plan."

"Ah. A hitman."

She snorted. "That's how Dad liked to think of himself, I'm sure. Really, my job isn't that glamorous or exciting, but I love it."

I love it, she thought, panic stretching across her chest. *And he wants to take it.*

She couldn't let him.

"You okay?" Teagan asked, concern dotting her brow as much as the Botox would allow.

"I'm fine. Tired."

The car slowed, then stopped. The driver peered into the rearview, two thick, gray eyebrows hovering above a pair of wire-rimmed glasses.

"Pardon, madams," he said. "We'll be arriving at the Kent Wood Mansion's security checkpoint momentarily. You'll need to have your IDs ready."

"Aye, aye, sir," Teagan said with a salute. She rooted in her clutch and whispered in Victoria's ear, "Why'd he have to say *madams*? I'm calling the police."

"Be nice," Victoria said.

"When am I not?"

They reached the checkpoint and two men dressed in black suits approached. Brown-blond hair cut military style and gelled to perfection. Square jawlines. The taller guard had a cluster of freckles on his forehead, and the shorter guard had a dimpled scar on his nose.

Each had a tablet and an earpiece, and Victoria was sixty percent sure they were armed. The Connors were sticklers for security.

"Good evening. Names and IDs," the taller guard said.

With a practiced grace, Teagan hiked her dress up half an inch and squeezed her arms together, highlighting her cleavage. Subtlety had never been her forte. "Dr. Teagan Livingston and Mrs. Victoria Tate," Teagan said, emphasizing *doctor* and adding a layer of sultriness to her voice. "What's your name, handsome? Anyone told you that you look just like Jensen Ackles?"

"Keep it in your pants, Teags," Victoria whispered.

"What did I do?" she mouthed innocently.

The shorter guard smiled and scrolled through the list of names on the screen. "Dr. Livingston, solo. Mrs. Tate, I see you're supposed to be accompanied by Mr. Warren Tate?"

"Yes, we're arriving separately."

"Understood, ma'am." The taller guard returned her license and added a notation next to Warren's name.

"Could I see your license, doctor?" the shorter guard asked.

"My pleasure." Teagan slid two fingers into her bra—*when the hell had she put her license in her bra?* Victoria wondered—and withdrew the ID, passing it out the window with a wink.

He checked it over and smiled, all white teeth and cupid's bow. "The Connors have asked that we review the rules before you enter. First, pictures are allowed but cannot be livestreamed or posted to any social media platform without joint approval from Barnaby and Margaret Connors. In the event that you do upload unapproved content, the Connors are within their right to pursue legal action."

"No leaks. Got it," Teagan said.

The guard checked his tablet, but he'd obviously run through this script many times. "It is an open bar, but a donation to the charity of the Connors' choosing is recommended and *highly* encouraged. And, finally, please refrain from any and all illegal substances while on the premises."

"Damn, there goes my night," Teagan snarked. "Was planning on binging some edibles until I hallucinated a tiger."

"Why a tiger?" Victoria asked.

"They are majestic," the guard offered.

"I'd touch your tiger," Teagan announced.

"Teagan!" Victoria smacked her knee.

"Do you have any questions?" he asked, suppressing a grin.

"No, I think we got it. And here." Teagan slid a business card into the guard's palm. "My personal number's on the back. Use it."

He smiled and slipped the card into his pocket. "Well, all right. You have a good night, doctor." Then to Victoria, "Enjoy your evening, ma'am."

The windows rolled up, and the car moved forward.

"Aghhh, he ma'am-ed you," Teagan said with a cackle. "That's worse than madam. You should make an appointment with me next week. Mini facelift, maybe an eyelift to tighten the musculature and skin around your eyes? Do wonders for those budding crow's-feet and marionette lines. You'll feel like a whole new person."

"I like my face the way it is."

"Resting and full of bitch?"

"Better than frozen and mass produced."

Teagan cursed under her breath. "I don't know what your issue is with cosmetic surgery. Everybody does it. You're not better than me because you haven't had any work done, and I really wish you'd stop with the condescending bullshit."

Pot. Kettle. "I don't have an issue; it's just not my thing, and I wish *you'd* stop pushing your procedures at me. I don't want a nip or a tuck or a facelift."

She held her hands up in defense. "All right, Christ, you don't have to scream at me."

Maybe I do, she thought.

The Backstreet Boys cranked through the speakers, and, oh, how they wanted it that way when Victoria just wanted the night to be over so she could go home and murder her husband in peace.

"He was delicious, wasn't he? God, I love when their faces are symmetrical."

"Do you have an off switch?" Victoria asked.

"Nope."

"That'd be too easy."

"There's no shame in taking what you want. I thought you of all people would get that."

The car stopped and Victoria stared up at the Kent Wood Mansion, anticipation coursing through her veins. The driver opened Teagan's door first. She burst out, gave him a high five, and twirled to the sidewalk.

"Hurry up, I'm freezing my tits off over here."

"Wouldn't want anything to happen to those," Victoria said, emerging from the car. Handing the driver a twenty, she inhaled the crisp night air and linked elbows with her sister. The first downy flakes began to fall like frozen kisses, and Victoria counted each one like a silent prayer that everything would work out in her favor.

14

B uilt in the 1880s, the Kent Wood Mansion was ten thousand square feet of opulence and grandeur: majestic columns, a ballroom with an ornate stained-glass ceiling, and a large gallery showcasing local history.

An emerald-green carpet lined the wide marble steps for the evening. To an outsider, the arrival was probably a spectacle, but to those who walked the carpet, pausing for photographers like Hollywood's A-list, the entrance was delicious. It left them with big heads and lucrative fingers. They were important. They were untouchable.

They were fucking gods.

"Greetings!" An attendant squealed. She stood near a series of sequined-lined tables at the top of the stairs, waving her arms like she was conducting an orchestra. Her dress was pink, flapper style, and with every exaggerated movement the lazy fringe jittered.

Victoria recognized the attendant as one of the Harrisons from the smaller developments off the oldest section of Kent Wood Manor, but it was impossible to know which Harrison it was for sure. There were at least half a dozen, all boasting the same svelte physiques and avian features.

"Is she for real?" Teagan whispered.

"Be good," Victoria warned. You could never guarantee what was going to come out of Teagan's mouth. Filters only existed in the digital world for her.

"Welcome to the Harvest! Please, choose a mask and keep the line moving!" Flapper Harrison waved over a table full of masks divided into two categories labeled *Saints* and *Sinners*.

The Saints were ethereal and angelic, Venetian half-masks designed with whipped swirls and Swarovski crystals. Rustic maroons, mustards, and golds with metallic sheens and silky ribbons that descended to teardrop handles.

The Sinners were an eclectic combination of beautiful and horrifying. Porcelain dolls with cherry pouts and innocent, rounded features mangled by jagged leather scars. Feathered and bedazzled hybrids. Ghouls dotted with opal and amethyst.

"Are you a sinner or a saint?" Flapper Harrison asked.

"Perhaps somewhere in the middle?" A second attendant asked, stepping to the table. Same thin frame, same straight black hair. Another Harrison, except this one wore a sequined evening gown with a deep cut to her navel. Their masks were identical, though: two ostriches, beaks dripping with red crystals.

"What'll it be?" Flapper Harrison squawked.

"I'll take this one," Teagan said, scooping up a white crystalline blob. She lifted it carefully over her head and fastened the clip. "What do you think?"

"You're . . . an owl?" Victoria asked.

"Not just any owl," Flapper Harrison said. "A snowy owl—full of magic and mystery."

"Ooh, did you hear that, Tor? Magic and mystery," Teagan said, catching a few snowflakes in her hand. Then, under her breath, "What butt kissers."

"*Teagan.*"

"And for you, madam?" the other Harrison gestured at Victoria. She ignored her sister's snort at the address and focused on the question. "Which face will you wear for the evening?"

She examined the massive selection, nodding as Teagan pointed out her favorites. Third from the last, she found the one, slipping it on and testing the weight of it on her face.

More guests filtered around them, excitedly chirping over the masks.

"A cheetah? Could you be any more predictable, Tori-Borey?" Teagan teased. "Come on, go with the murder baby. Or the vampire dolphin."

"Teags."

"It's a lynx, actually," said Flapper Harrison. "A true beauty. The luster of the crystals mimics the reflective sheen of the lynx." She rounded the table to help Victoria adjust the strap. "There. A perfect fit."

"Gatsby's right," Teagan said. "It suits you."

Victoria thanked them for the compliments and ushered Teagan away from the table. Normally she wouldn't have minded the attention, but the added scrutiny only served to remind her that, for tonight, she wanted to blend in.

"The Harrisons are so freaking weird," Teagan said once they'd cleared out. "I know they're your neighbors, but come on. The Connors can't be paying them that much. Like, give it a rest, Janice, you're not a bootlegger's mistress. I'll see you at

Pilates tomorrow." She scrolled on her phone while she talked, the mask's feathers ruffled by her breath.

"They probably wouldn't have been invited otherwise," Victoria said. "They don't exactly run in the same circles. And I wouldn't want to get on Margaret's bad side."

"Yeah, well, that makes two of us," Teagan muttered, tearing herself from the screen. "Alright, Tor. Thanks for the dress. And the ride. And the, you know, sister talk. You're a peach. But I have some mingling to do. See you later?"

"Knock yourself out," Victoria said, eager to find Warren.

"Try to enjoy yourself, Tori-Borey," she said. "I know I will." She blew a kiss and sauntered through the doors with an exaggerated shake of her hips.

Victoria waited another minute as the snow swirled around her, politely waving to the people who passed. A knot tightened in her chest—of dread or excitement, she wasn't sure.

Here we go.

15

The cocktail hour waitstaff wore low-cut black tuxedo jackets and black-sequined masks. Banquet tables were arranged sporadically, each one overflowing with expensive food or beverages. The space was packed, bodies writhing to the sultry music beating through the speakers. Victoria squeezed through a group of men sporting pearl-snouted wolf masks devouring petite cuts of filet. One of the wolves growled and pinched her thigh as she passed.

"Succulent," he said and let out a howl.

Victoria was too stunned to respond, and the man was quickly swept up into the arms of another wolf. They shared a bite, faces mashed together, before the steak was gone and their lips continued working.

She probably knew all these people, but the Gala was different. Board members and city-planning committees. The Kent Wood elite. Tonight, though, everyone wore a mask. Who they were in the real world ceased to exist.

Fitting, she thought. She, too, was going to suspend her everyday composure in favor for a darker side.

Wriggling up to an open spot near the end of the bar, Victoria breathed a sigh of relief. The surface was smooth and warm, a safe mahogany embrace after the sensory overload of the feasting floor.

"Can I help you?"

One of the bartenders, tall and modelesque in a blood-red Grecian tunic, cocked her head to the side. The red feathers of her mask fluttered with the movement.

A cardinal.

"Shot of vodka, please," Victoria said.

The cardinal flipped a shot glass and poured. She smiled at a tall man in a sapphire hockey mask at the opposite end of the bar before handing it over. "Bottoms up."

The liquor went down in a flash of warmth. "One more," Victoria said.

The cardinal poured again. "You know, not too long ago, we wouldn't have even been allowed in this place."

"Is that right?"

"In its prime, the Kent Wood Mansion had only three rules: cash only, no locals, and no women allowed."

This felt like a script Margaret Connors had forced her employees to memorize. This woman was probably one of many actors Victoria would encounter tonight, charged with historical facts or ghost stories or whatever else Margaret thought would make the venue more interesting.

"Shitty rules," Victoria said, sipping her shot. "All I see are inebriated locals with credit cards."

"Solid observation," the cardinal littered, starting to move away. "There's a bunch of us back here, but I'm Temperance, and I've got the best pour, so if you need anything else, flag me down."

A bartender named Temperance. Ha.

"I'm good," Victoria said, swiveling to people watch. The air was thick with alcohol and heat. No sign of Warren yet, though, and the room continued to fill up. Chances of finding him in here were slim. Finishing her shot, she left a twenty for Temperance—she was guilty of many things but being cheap wasn't one of them—and followed the flow of be-masked guests through a set of double doors.

This room was smaller and smelled of lavender and eucalyptus. A woman wearing the stark white mask of a poltergeist and a matching fitted romper greeted everyone with earthy bags of essential oils wrapped in twine and Reiki crystals.

Victoria didn't find that relaxing. It was like stepping into *Silent Hill.* She half expected a giant axe-wielding man with a pyramid head to emerge from the shadows.

"Welcome to the Lounge," the ghostly woman crooned, holding a bundle out to Victoria. "Please enjoy these favors, compliments of the Connors with the hopes you find peace and light."

What a bunch of—"Thank you," she said with her customer-service smile.

"My pleasure," the ghost said. "Enjoy the private viewings. Please let me know if you have any questions."

"Private viewings?" she asked.

The ghost's cultured voice dropped to a conversational tone, smiling as she doled out another bag. "Peep shows, honey. Through the curtain."

"Oh." Victoria flushed under the lynx disguise, eyeing the heavy red curtain draped over the door across the room. "Thanks."

Hard pass.

She had no desire to see what kind of Baz Luhrmann-fever-dream-induced beautiful people Margaret had hired to entertain the masses.

A strict Catholic upbringing was partly to blame. Prayers before bed. Church most Sundays. Bible study one night a week until she graduated high school. These things contributed to Victoria's belief that her body was something to hide. To be ashamed of.

Her mother hadn't helped. Clare was repulsed by Victoria's body and took every opportunity to make it known. She ran her hands over the gown's corset, remembering the scratchy polyester of her prom dress as Clare pinched the bit of skin under her arm.

Your back fat is showing, she'd uttered in disgust. *I told you this would happen. Where is your discipline? How many helpings of sweet potato did you have at dinner last night? You should have picked a dress for your body type, Victoria, honestly. Teagan has no trouble fitting into this silhouette, but you should know better. Something with more structure to suck this in.* Another pinch, harder and unforgiving.

She had pitted the sisters against each other, using the insecurities of one to break down the other. For Teagan, Clare only bought padded bras, pointing out Victoria's growing cleavage with a deceptively neutral face. She ridiculed Teagan's nose and lips, either too wide or too thin, and praised Victoria for her full pout and sharp features.

Victoria repeatedly refused lipo, but at sixteen, Clare took Teagan for her first round of lip fillers and a nose job.

There was no going back.

Clare's primary criticism of Victoria was her weight. Curvier meant fatter, and fat was just about the worst thing you could be in Clare Livingston's book. She suffered twice-daily weigh-ins. Mandatory food journals. Clare measured her waist and thighs once a week with a fucking yellow tape measure she kept in her pocket like a dressmaker. An endless barrage of fad diets had ensued. Dairy-free. Meat-free. Raw foods. Carb counting. Calorie counting. Then, water pills. Personal trainers. Once, an ab belt. Every day for a month, Victoria slathered this foam monstrosity with a lubricant and fastened it to her waist. It had aluminum panels that were supposed to shock her muscles into shape, but if she didn't use enough of the lubricant, it just burned her skin, leaving a wide red welt in its wake.

When one "solution" failed, Clare moved on to the next attempt to shrink her daughter to the appropriate size. Because for Clare, body-fat percentage was inextricably linked to a person's character, but more importantly, to marriage. Fat didn't get husbands, and the end goal for every woman was a diamond ring.

Victoria didn't want diamonds, but she had learned the value of control, and she wanted that: agency over her company, her body, her life.

And all things considered, a husband was a small price to pay.

16

Victoria dumped the favor in the nearest potted shrub and mingled down the wide hall to where a line had formed in front of another room. She still hadn't found Warren, and no one she'd spoken to had seen him either. Plenty of small talk to go around, though.

Conversations tapered to a whisper. Margaret and Barnaby Connors were perched on two wingback chairs meticulously detailed with thorns and golden garlands.

The honorary king and queen.

Victoria's stomach twisted in resentment. Of course, they wanted everyone to be jealous. The Gala wasn't for the guests; it was an excuse for the Connors to flaunt their money without having to hide behind false modesty.

And she had no patience for that bullshit. Not tonight.

Victoria decided to make a quick exit down the hall to her right, only to be stopped by a man dressed as a jester, clad in a garish mixture of red and green that was frankly offensive to the eyes. His ivory mask curled into a wide toothless smile.

"Good tidings, fair maiden," he said in a high-pitched elfin voice.

"Hello. Excuse me," she said, stepping to the right.

He matched her stride, blocking her path again. "Does the evening find you well?" he asked, the shrill, cartoonish voice grating her nerves.

Pivoting left, right, an awkward mismatched dance, she attempted to get around him. The jester matched her strides like a guard playing defense. She debated pushing him out of the way but didn't want to make a scene.

"I need to get by, please," she said.

"I'm afraid you'll have to earn permission from the majesties first. Care to hear a joke?"

She opened her mouth to tell him to drop the act—nobody cared if he kept up the persona and could he just *move out of the way*—but the line of masked guests had curled around them.

Encouraging the crowd to cheer, he broke into a jig, slapping his feet underneath him and spinning in circles. He finished with a flourish, wild applause ricocheting off the walls.

Victoria took the opportunity for what it was and tried to sneak past, realizing all too late that the hand now clasped around her arm belonged to the jester.

"What do you call a person who doesn't masturbate?" he asked from behind his frozen grin.

"What?" someone replied.

"A liar." The jester bowed, rooting on the cheers. Victoria's heart rate ticked up another notch. The jester held tight to her arm, his gloved hand warm and dry. Two beady eyes watched from the holes in his mask, locked on her face in merriment. He waited for the laughter to die down. "Another, another. What's the difference between your penis and a bonus check?"

Victoria glanced over his shoulder into the room at Margaret and Barnaby. They were chatting with someone wearing a horse's head, mane swishing down her back, but Margaret's eyes flicked to Victoria.

"Someone's always willing to *blow* your bonus!" The jester mimed the lude act, much to the delight of the audience.

Christ, the bar was low.

The jester's warm grip tightened. "Give me your hand," he said in that creepy elfin voice.

"No, thank you."

"For a joke, I promise." He took it gently, caressing her skin in arcs, each one slowly working higher as he released a throaty moan.

Disturbing. "Stop it," Victoria muttered.

"This is my lady's hand," he proclaimed loudly. "And it's the most beautiful hand in all the land." Still rubbing, he got on his knees, freakish mask cocked to the side. Without warning, he grabbed Victoria's hips and buried his mask against her lap while she struggled to push out of his hold.

A daisy with yellow crystals yanked him off her. "Hey, asshole, you can't touch her like that."

"All in good fun, my lady," he said, slowly standing. "All in good fun. Just a little—"

Victoria smashed her clutch into the jester's head. The blow landed on the side of his jaw, dislodging his mask with a padded cracking sound.

He rocked back in surprise. "Fuck, lady, I was just doing my job." Without the formality he sounded like a kid. The cloud of anger receded slightly. "It was a stupid joke."

Her thoughts tangled. Had she overreacted? *He grabbed me.* Was I making a big deal out of nothing? *He stuck his face in my crotch.*

"Next time," she said, "think twice before touching someone without consent."

"Crazy bitch."

"Is there an issue, Fool?" Barnaby bellowed.

The fallen jester snapped to attention. "No," he said, a squeak catching in his throat. "Everything's just fine."

"Wonderful," Margaret pursed, allowing the pause to last long enough for the crowd to shift under her gaze. "We wouldn't want any trouble at the Gala, would we?"

A statement. A threat.

"Absolutely not," the jester agreed.

"Did you forget something, Fool?" she asked.

Victoria imagined the boy's face scowling beneath the mask's smile. He turned back to Margaret and cleared his throat. "Absolutely not. Your *highness*."

"Didn't think so." She seemed exceedingly pleased with his response. "Please send in the next guest."

He motioned Victoria forward unceremoniously, muttering something under his breath as she passed. "What did you say?" she asked.

He refused to answer. She tried to piece his words together as she crossed the room, turning the syllables and sounds until they fit. She could've been wrong, but it sounded a lot like, *You'll regret this.*

Like a comic-book villain promising revenge. It was almost adorable. Almost.

17

The Harvest King and Queen drank in Victoria's approach. Margaret, poised and beaming, pouted her ruby, overlined lips. Balayaged hair swept half-up in delicate waves, she tilted her head slightly to the side as if she were posing for an unseen photographer.

"Barnaby. Margaret," Victoria said, once more composed and the picture of grace.

"We ask that you address us properly while in the throne room," Margaret said, matte-black stiletto nails clutching the armrest. "And a bow wouldn't hurt either. We are Gala royalty."

Was she serious? Her mask was crystal-encrusted and flared out at the edges into perfect circles. It gave her the disconcerting appearance of an oracle, like a thousand eyes holding Victoria in judgment.

Yes, Margaret was well and truly serious. Because Margaret was an asshole.

Victoria curtsied like Clare had taught her so many years ago. Knees bent outward, not straight ahead, right foot swept behind, head bowed. "Your majesties," she said bitterly.

Margaret waited for her to rise, soaking up the adulation. She preened, running her tongue along her teeth. They were

Hollywood white, straight as a needle, and bared in amusement. "Better," she said. "Now. With whom do we have the pleasure of speaking?"

Like she didn't know. "Victoria Tate."

"Victoria?" Margaret's jaw dropped. She slapped Barnaby's shoulder and repeated her name. "Victoria fucking Tate."

Jeremy fucking Livingston, Warren's voice echoed.

"I heard, dear," Barnaby muttered.

"Darling, come closer!" Margaret stood and reached out both arms in welcome. Her heels were sky high, but she didn't totter. Rumors persisted that she did yoga in Jimmy Choos, but these would've scared Gaga. "Your dress! Your hair! My god, what on earth possessed you to do it?"

She floundered under the microscope. "Ah, I . . . don't know. I just . . . wanted to make an entrance. The Gala demands a showstopper, after all."

"Well, it certainly does," Margaret said, booping the end of Victoria's nose. "Nail on the head. Doesn't she look lovely, King Barnaby?"

"You hit our Fool," he said, gulping from a bejeweled chalice and wiping his lips. "That wasn't very nice."

Margaret dismissed him with a flagrant eye roll. "Ignore him, he's got his jockstrap in a twist because I wouldn't let him wear the pompadour. Can you imagine?"

"It would've been so cool, Margaret." He perked up a bit, gesticulating with the chalice. "Like, okay, picture this. Louis XIV with dayglow orange hair. Awesome, right? Wouldn't George Washington have been twenty times hotter with a key-lime wig? See, she agrees, Margaret. Playing it safe sucks."

In platinum-rimmed sunglasses, an ermine cloak, and a sparkly red suit, he could have been the headliner for the Elton John revival tour.

Playing it safe did suck. "Absolutely," Victoria agreed, not specifying which of his statements she was agreeing with when she just wanted an end to the whole exchange.

In the candlelight, Margaret's silver dress was holographic, a chainmail-esque fabric fitted at her waist. The asymmetrical hem showed off her toned legs and precarious heels. Wealth wasn't the only thing they were flaunting tonight.

"You're not *alone*, are you?" As if showing up sans spouse was Page Six scandalous.

"Oh, no, I'm not, I—"

"Where is Warren?"

"His meeting ran late, so—"

"Yes, I've heard he's been having a lot of . . . *meetings* lately." She emphasized *meetings* but didn't explain. Everyone in Kent Wood Manor was a gossip to some degree; it was almost an unspoken requirement to take up residence there, but Victoria didn't like the suggestion that her life was the subject of twittering busybodies.

If people were discussing Warren's work habits, what else had they noticed?

"I'm sure he'll be along any minute," she assured. "I came with Teagan."

"Oh, Teagan's here," she said, tone ambiguous.

This was not going well. Victoria decided to switch topics, get a little personal and make Margaret uncomfortable. "I was so sorry to hear about your mother," she frowned. "I hope she pulls through. Clare's death nearly wrecked me. Ovarian cancer. She was gone within a month of being diagnosed."

Margaret went ashen and took her place beside Barnaby. "How terrible," she said.

"If there's anything we can do—"

Her face hardened. "I'm sure there's nothing but thank you. I appreciate your kind words."

Barnaby chugged the rest of his goblet and belched, waving a hand in front of his mouth. "Oh, that's *awful*." He threw the cup. It hit the jester's back and bounced off, landing with a metallic clunk.

"Barnaby," Margaret scolded.

Barnaby snapped his fingers. "Fool." Snap, snap. "I need *more*. More whiskey. More food. Call a waiter and fetch me my drink."

The jester turned slowly. He stooped to pick up the cup. Victoria watched the steady rise and fall of his chest, the desire to tell Barnaby to go fuck himself radiating from every tense muscle in his stance.

"Did you hear me?" Barnaby slurred. "Get me another drink." The jester lurched forward and Barnaby released an embarrassing noise of surprise. "Stop!" he commanded. "What do you think you're doing?" His frightened words melted together.

The jester stopped in front of the throne and dropped the chalice into Barnaby's lap.

"Get it yourself," he said and marched out.

Margaret seethed. She whispered something to Barnaby. As she motioned for the next person in line, movements jerky with exasperation and anger, Victoria seized the opportunity to leave.

"Oh, uh, Victoria?" Margaret called, voice full of molasses.

She hesitated in the doorway. "Yes?"

Margaret stood, posed for the hidden photographer again, then strutted toward Victoria like the trek was her own personal catwalk. Which it probably was. For people like Margaret Connors, there was always a runway. "Enjoy what remains of your time," she said.

She smirked, knowing and foreboding, the light catching on the circles of her mask. She patted Victoria's arm, and with that, she turned and sauntered back to Barnaby.

18

Being away from the Connors brought a flood of relief. As if accepting her own decision to act tonight wasn't bad enough, getting on Margaret's shit list had fried what few nerves remained unaffected. Victoria walked quickly, skirting a room where various card games were well underway. Cigar smoke and the smell of weed lingered in the air as she passed, the chatter punctuated by sporadic shouts of celebration. She gave a cursory search for Warren, but cards had never been his forte, so she didn't linger long.

The hallway ended in an exit to the courtyard. Victoria squeezed her arms tighter to her body, rubbing away goose bumps. Cool air leaked from the door seams, wind whistling against the glass. Outside, the snow was falling harder, coating the topiaries and treetops with cotton-candy softness. The wide paths were serene, unblemished by footsteps.

It would be so easy to duck out there, she thought. To be swallowed by the silence and the cold.

The eagerness with which she yearned to slip away was jarring. When on task, Victoria was laser-focused and undeterred. Warren was simply another task to check off her list, she justified. Why was she hiding in a dark dead end when she had a job to do?

Figuratively, she thought. Deep diving into the whys and hows of her reasoning could be saved for another, less eventful, day.

She headed back the way she came, pretending to admire the oil paintings of battle scenes and horse races. Without the bustle of the receiving line and poker games, the corridor was shockingly empty. If she'd been the type of person to believe in such things, Victoria might've chalked it up to the universe telling her she was exactly where she was supposed to be. No distractions, no speed bumps. Guilt might come later, that was true, but it was still an abstract. A problem for Future Victoria to flesh out.

Whatever the fallout from Warren's death, she would handle it.

She stopped in front of a door emblazoned by golden letters. *H.G. Harvest Gala.*

Curious, she pushed it open and was startled by the optics of a cave. LED projectors transformed the walls into crimson abysses. Virtual stalactites dripped red into rippling puddles. A different set of projectors transformed the floor into a bottomless pit. The image shuddered, and chunks of rock tumbled into the void with a loud crash. The speakers in the corner of the ceiling echoed with the static of the volume.

She almost missed the two masked figures seated at a table in the middle of the room.

Mannequins, she thought, until the one on the left twitched. She managed to hold onto the shriek that rose in her throat, but just barely.

"Little strange to be sitting here alone in the dark, guys," Victoria chided.

Neither responded.

They were dressed in flowing black robes that hid the bodies underneath. The person to her right wore a black hood that covered everything except their eyes and mouth. An executioner. His black leather gloves creaked as he silently motioned her forward.

"Who are you?" she asked, hoping her words didn't sound as mushy as they felt in her mouth. The Connors loved their party games, but much like the rest of the evening, she couldn't pinpoint what exactly about this experience was supposed to be fun.

"Sit," the executioner bellowed in the mechanical, deep tone of Darth Vader.

A voice modifier was a nice touch, she thought. Really added to the creep factor.

Victoria puffed a nervous laugh, but she pulled out the chair despite everything in her lizard brain telling her to *run*. She was looking for Warren, not indulging in Margaret's party tricks. "Is this the part where you ask me about my favorite scary movie?"

Unfazed, the executioner ignored her quip. "Name."

"Uh—um, Victoria," she whispered, hating the hitch in her words. She swallowed her nerves and recalibrated. She refused to become unhinged by a Halloween costume. "Victoria Tate."

"Not *your* name," he said slowly. "Your target's."

Victoria forced herself to stay neutral. Her gaze flitted from the executioner to his partner, who sat quietly, unmoving. Somehow the intensity of his silence scared her more.

"I'm sorry, what is this?" she asked.

Vader laughed, a robotic jerking sound that curled into a single word. "Vengeance."

"I don't understand."

"We've made arrangements to . . . let's say, contract our services, but to do that, we need a name."

"What service do you provide?" she asked.

"Vengeance. Revenge."

"Is this a joke? You're a hitman?"

He tapped the spot on the mask where his nose would be and pointed. *Nailed it.*

And wasn't that just a little too ironic. Why would the Connors hire a hitman for the Gala? Wait. *Would* the Connors hire a hitman for the Gala?

The guest list was small, intimate considering the depth of the Connors' social circle. It wouldn't be a matter of security. And Victoria did have some doubts about their ethics. Warren had worked with them on numerous projects over the years, and because of that Victoria knew they had at least three offshore accounts registered to shell corporations.

Making the leap from money laundering to criminal networking wasn't hard to imagine. So, yes, Victoria admitted, she believed the Connors would know who to hire for a dirty job and how to do it off the radar.

But could it be that simple?

Why would they assume she'd want revenge?

Warren.

Had someone figured out he'd planned to oust her from the company altogether? The HR rep she was supposed to sit with today. Maybe Warren had sent the contract without her approval.

She turned the idea over. It was possible. Warren was an impatient man, especially when a deal was already finalized in his head. But Victoria doubted he'd send a highly sensitive, unofficial, unsigned contract to HR without having everything buttoned up first. Eager, yes, but never sloppy.

This had to be about something else.

Maybe this was the Connors' own vengeance. Last month, Warren had severed ties with a mutual connection after an international search came back with troubling results (a lien on a foreign property, if she wasn't mistaken. Warren, as usual, hadn't wanted to get into details, and she hadn't been able to dig into the files). Liens meant debt, and that amount of debt was a risk not worth taking. She wasn't sure if the Connors knew about the debt beforehand, but they certainly knew about their client's assets, and they weren't happy. They threatened legal action if Warren didn't reconsider.

Victoria assumed he would do just that. Send them a fruit basket with a kiss-ass apology to keep the status quo. But Warren had refused to budge. He terminated the account with no further explanation. The end result being that the Connors pissed off a lot of important people while losing a small fortune on the investment.

Did they want Warren dead too? Money was a serious motivation for just about anything.

That idea was almost enticing enough to make her confess to the executioner. Yes, she did have a cross to bear. Yes, she wanted someone gone. They could join forces, the brunt of the crime could be taken off her hands.

But she couldn't take the chance. Trust was not given freely.

"I don't have any grudges," she said.

The executioner tilted his head to the side. "You sure about that?"

"Even if I did, I would never have someone killed. That's insane. I'm not a murderer."

Yet.

"Technically no, you're not, and you wouldn't be," Vader said.

"Right, because I'd be relying on you to exact this hypothetical revenge. That's so much better."

"Isn't it?" he asked.

Victoria cleared her throat. For the first time since she'd dreamed up her plan, she didn't know how to answer.

19

Victoria contemplated the question, her eyes darting back and forth between the two figures. Like the executioner, the other man was dressed in a black robe and leather gloves. His mask, however, was a plague doctor. The surface had a metallic sheen that shimmered in the undulating lights. Two holographic holes covered the eyes. A long beak, crusted with black crystals and sharpened to a point.

The mask tilted to the left. She saw herself reflected in the orbits and shivered.

"Who are you?" she asked.

"Who I am is not important," the plague doctor said. The projectors dripped again. Strange shadows cascaded down the plague doctor's body. "What matters is the name you give to me."

She paused at the voice. A buzz of recognition ran through her.

The projectors thrummed, ticked, and the red walls transformed. It was like watching an endoscopy, the camera zooming in on the wall of an internal organ. The image throbbed: *lub-dub, lub-dub, lub-dub.*

A heart.

"You have a name," he said.

The *lub-dubs* quickened, as did the images. They veered left and right, the muscle contracting in tandem with the sounds.

They wanted Victoria to be afraid.

If she was being honest, they'd succeeded. The theatrics were only a small part of it. Flashing lights and loud noises. It wasn't like she was in any real danger. She could leave anytime.

Her fear ran deeper. It was the threat of being caught. That strangers could see what she was planning—who she was planning to be—like a warped scarlet letter.

"Name," the plague doctor demanded. "Give me the name."

In that moment, one thing clicked. That voice.

She *knew* that voice.

Pushing out from the table, Victoria stood and crossed her arms. "Okay. Fine. I'll give you a name."

"Good. Speak," Vader said.

Victoria cocked an eyebrow and waited a beat, letting them know who was really in control. The air was charged, tension thrumming in time with the grotesque images on the walls.

"My husband," she said. "Warren Tate."

As if on cue, the room went dark. The pounding from the speakers stopped. She could still hear the harsh rasp of breathing through their masks, though. Something about the noise, like dead wasp wings, kickstarted that spark of fear. She backed slowly away from the table.

What if I was wrong? she thought.

From the vacuum, the plague doctor spoke, erasing her lingering doubts. His tone was hushed, a husk of his previous volume, but she knew she'd played her cards right.

"Who is man that is not angry?" he said.

"You tell me, because I'm pretty damn angry," Victoria seethed. "Turn the lights on."

A chair squeaked, and Victoria was nearly knocked off her feet as one of the figures bounced into her, fleeing out the door. She squinted at the sudden sliver of light and hurried toward the door. A beep to her left, however, paused her mid-step. The lights grew brighter, revealing the plague doctor alone at his table.

The mask hung limply from his neck, pointed end precariously tilted toward his chest. His real face focused on Victoria, drawn and serious and unimaginably tired.

"Vic," was all he said.

Victoria raised her chin in response, fire bursting through her veins. "Hello, Warren," she said.

20

Swaying, Warren rose from the chair. The tang of his sweat hit her as he approached. It dotted his brow and ran down his neck, dripping beneath the stiff collar of his dress shirt that peeked out from beneath the robe. His eyes, glossy and red-rimmed, trembled as they tried to focus.

Victoria swallowed her disgust. *This* was the man in charge of an empire?

"You want me dead, Vic?" he asked.

"Who was that?" she deflected. "The executioner, who was that?"

"No one." Warren placed a hand on the wall to steady himself. The lights were full-bright now, and Warren looked ill.

"Warren "

"You didn't answer my question."

"Because it's a bullshit question you shouldn't have to ask in the first place."

He balked, whether at her casual cursing or her firm denial. "You admitted it."

"Admitted what?"

"You want me dead."

"Warren, are you high?"

"No, I'm not high. I'm—don't change the subject, Vic. You said my name. And not in the fun, sexy way. You said you wanted me dead."

"I did not."

"You did."

"Warren."

"Vic."

And so it went. The volley of marriage.

"You're drunk."

"So? Victoria, I know what I heard."

Do you, though? she thought at him, squeezing her lips into a skeptical line. "I was kidding. We've been married for how long, Warren? You *really* thought I wouldn't recognize your voice?"

Warren's body slumped, confusion written into every feature from forehead to slouched shoulders. "But I had a mask on."

You sure did, you beautiful idiot. "Last time I checked, masks didn't disguise voices. Especially when the person speaking is my husband."

He sighed. "Okay. You got me."

She got him.

She yanked off her mask and let it drop to the floor. "What is all this, Warren?"

"I . . ." He fumbled. His spine went rigid. "Nothing. Nothing, nothing. I was trying to play a trick on you but you're obviously too much of a genius to fall for it." A flask appeared from a secret fold in the robes. He drank hungrily and coughed at the burn.

This was the messiest he'd been in a long time. Victoria had been counting on him being three sheets to the wind tonight, but there was a big difference between drunk Warren and the belligerent asshole she was currently dealing with. He'd tipped the scales against her, and now she'd have to adjust her expectations. "Jesus, what is your problem?" she asked.

"I'm almost out of booze, and that is sad." He took another hearty gulp and shook the flask as if to prove his point. "Forget it, Vic. Let's go back to the party."

"I think we should call the driver," she said.

"Not yet," Warren crooned, giving her the lazy, charming smile that she'd become so familiar with since that first night they met at the bar. He reached for her hips, swiveling them gently. "Not yet." A kiss to her forehead. Her skin itched with his touch. "I'm going to hit the head quick and then we'll ramble on in. The fun's just getting started."

With that, he threw her a double-eyed wink and rolled out the door, sliding the plague-doctor mask into place as he left.

Victoria wasn't sure their definitions of *fun* were the same. Hers was clearly the better choice, however. Only one of them was making it out of this night alive.

See? she thought, following his trail. *Fun.*

21

Warren emerged from the bathroom and turned the corner on his way to the ballroom, his steps long and hulking and very Warren, when everything else about his demeanor was screaming OFF. Victoria didn't know why he was acting so weird, but frankly she was at her wits' end. They'd make an appearance at the dinner where she'd act loved-up and domestic, and then she was getting them the hell out.

Questions stacked one on top of the other in her head. Why and how had he pulled off that stunt? Were the Connors in on it? Who was the executioner?

Crickets from Warren.

She clacked a pace behind him, toes pinching in her shoes as she tried to maintain an air of normalcy—which Warren was doing his damnedest to implode. They passed another couple, elbows linked and smiles painted beneath matching cupid masks. *Irritating.* It reminded her that there were still people who thought men and women became one unit, one flesh, in marriage. A skin-fused abomination incapable of independence.

Victoria would not be Warren's skinsuit.

She grabbed his elbow as they neared the ballroom entrance. "Warren, stop."

He twisted, face slack with confusion. The pointed beak of his mask came dangerously close to poking her in the eye. "What is it, Vic? Dinner's about to start."

"I thought we'd walk in together," she said, molding her features into what she hoped was affection. "I won't pretend to know what happened back there, but we can put whatever it was behind us, can't we? I missed you today."

"Oh, Vic," he said, softening at her endearment. "Of course. I'm sorry, I'm just—I've been in my own head. This probably didn't help." He shakes the flask. "But I have the contract with me in the car. Do you—"

"I don't want to talk about work tonight," she said quickly, recovering with a charming smile of her own. No one could say that Victoria wasn't willing to use every tool in her box. "Tomorrow. We'll deal with it tomorrow."

"You're right," he said, thumbing gently over her cheek. "Let's try to have a good time."

Putty. Sir Warren to the rescue, only this time Victoria wasn't the damsel waiting to be saved. She guessed that meant she was the villain. Oddly enough, she didn't mind being the dragon in this story.

Someone had to be.

She eased an arm around his waist and pulled him close. The robes smelled musty with a hint of something floral. "Shall we?"

The ballroom was elegant, crisp lines and muted neutral accents. A string quartet played Vivaldi on a small platform near the windows, which were steamed from the heat of bodies.

Beyond the glass, there was a glimpse into the wintery garden outside. Apocalyptic. Like they were the only people left in the world, and this was their last night on earth.

For someone, it would be.

Warren and Victoria entered together, immediately swept up in the swell. Women from the neighborhood group chat and their interchangeable husbands exchanged air kisses. It was difficult to understand Warren with his mask on, so eventually he looped it around the back of his neck. The beak protruded like a fisherman's hook. He nodded in all the right places, asked questions, and dipped into his impressive repertoire of dirty jokes.

Everything Victoria had hoped for, but she couldn't relax the anxiety gnawing in her gut. She was waiting for him to blow up. They should've talked more about Livingston before the dinner, she realized. If he mentioned the contract to anyone, she wouldn't be able to go through with her plan. It would be too suspicious. Victoria was banking on Warren's overly cautious nature to keep his mouth shut.

So if she directed the conversation to topics that Warren didn't give two shits about to keep him bored and disinterested, that was pure coincidence.

A flourish of horns interrupted Naomi Cho's complaining about the manufacturer's warranty on the Audi she'd purchased. Warren sighed a *thank god that's over* under his breath. Victoria couldn't help but chuckle.

A different jester appeared in the center of the room. Same disturbing mask, but his outfit was purple and gold. The gossip wheel spun through the ranks about the original's moment with Barnaby.

He told Barnaby to go fuck himself. Hand to god, I was there. I heard Barnaby told him to get on his knees. The man is crazy. He threatened him with a knife.

Adult telephone at its finest.

"Hear ye, hear ye!" the jester bellowed through his mask. "Theydies and gentlethems, and all the ups and downs, ins and outs, tops and *bottoms*." Laughter erupted. He clicked his heels and produced a scroll from behind his back. It crinkled against his chest and unraveled in a whoosh. "Before we're seated for supper, the Connors would like to thank you for joining us tonight. They are—" He stopped, tilting his head at a woman to his right. A woman in a gold dress. "Well, well, what have we here?"

Teagan.

The owl feathers fluttered flirtatiously, if that was even possible. She sauntered up to the jester and curtsied, which garnered loud applause, because of course it did, it was Teagan and her perfect cleavage. She rose and grabbed the scroll.

Oh no.

"The Connors would love to remind you that you will never be as rich as they are," Teagan said. "But who cares about money? Money isn't everything. Or is it? Maybe money is everything, and these two assholes are just way ahead of us."

Damn it, Teagan.

"What is your sister doing?" Warren muttered.

"What she does best," Victoria said. "Never had a spotlight she didn't steal."

The jester grabbed her by the waist with a triumphant grunt. Teagan dropped the scroll as he lifted her into the air like Johnny and Baby; and wasn't that just the kicker.

"Hey," Warren said, elbowing her gruffly in the side. "You've gotta stop her."

"Teagan is a grown woman capable of making her own outlandishly bad decisions."

"She's embarrassing us," he hissed.

"What would you like me to do, Warren?" Victoria asked, her patience thin. She struggled to keep her voice low and measured. "Grab her hair and drag her out caveman-style?"

"Someone should."

Someone being Victoria. "I'm not her keeper, Warren. If she wants to make a fool out of herself, that's her business. I'm not getting involved."

Victoria cringed as Teagan wrapped her legs around the jester, the epitome of grace and effortless agility. The bells of his ridiculous hat rang wildly. She let her head roll back in laughter. The room was captivated, all eyes glued to her.

Warren pushed away. "I'm going to the bar."

"Warren. *Warren*," she called, but he was already gone.

Teagan finally tired of gyrating on the clown and climbed down amidst a thunder of applause. As the crowd parted, the jester cupped his hand to his mouth.

"Alack! *A-lay*," he gestured to Teagan. "The belle of the ball, a true beauty!"

"True beauty my ass. That woman has always been a whore," someone behind Victoria muttered.

"Gemma, you can't just call people whores."

"You can if it's true. She slept with half the baseball team in high school."

Two heavyset goldfish stood behind her with cheery-cherry pouts. Victoria recognized them as the wives of a few of Kent Wood's lower-level politicians, one of whom still taught English at the high school to maintain her humble upbringings. What a role model.

They caught her watching and backed into the crowd, whispering like children. Some people grew up but never matured, she thought.

"The hour has come!" the jester bellowed. "The Harvest Feast is upon us! But what is a feast without a host? Behold! Our royal highnesses, King Barnaby and Queen Margaret!" With that, he commenced shoving people out of the way, inserting cattle calls as he plowed through. "Make way! Make way!"

Smoke filled the air, the smell sweet and peppery. Lorde's "Royals" blasted through the speakers, the strings adding their own twist to the track. When the smoke cleared, there stood the Connors.

Barnaby's Elton John robe sparkled in a strobe light that dropped from the ceiling. Margaret was doling out pageant waves like her life depended on it. Elbow, elbow, wrist, wrist. Mouthing *hellos* and *thank yous* to her adoring subjects.

"Thank you, thank you, all." She pronounced *all* like *awl* and let the word extend. Julia Child's protégé.

"Thank you for coming," Barnaby added.

"We truly appreciate you celebrating with us tonight," Margaret continued, crossing one leg in front of the other in her skyrise heels. "Planning this event is tedious and time-consuming, but Kent Wood needs someone to step up to the plate. And year after year, I gracefully accept the challenge."

Oh, you self-important bitch, get on with it.

"You may be seated, peasants!" Barnaby interjected, hands on hips and chest puffed.

And with that, Victoria decided she'd had enough of the Gala. It was time to get the real show on the road.

22

Warren had found a spot at the bar in the corner and was nursing a tumbler of whiskey with a bowl of peanuts. He was talking with his hands, something he only did when he was drunk or nervous. The cardinal bartender Temperance smiled warmly as Victoria approached, but Warren didn't notice, too deep in his story about an unfortunate fishing-boat incident with a shark and his frat brother. She'd heard it a hundred times, but it was a crowd-pleaser.

She tapped his shoulder and watched his smile slip. He caught himself quickly, plastering a too-bright grin back in place, but she didn't miss it. Warren was disappointed to see her. If anyone had a right to be upset, it certainly wasn't him. What could he possibly be upset about? Too many people clamoring to agree with him?

"I'm still not feeling great, Warren," she said. "I think I need to head home."

"Okay."

Okay? "Are you ready to go?"

Warren finished his glass and motioned to the bartender. "Leave the bottle," he said, and slapped a hundred-dollar bill on the counter.

"That's not necessary," Victoria said.

He added a second bill. "Leave it."

"Sorry," Temperance mouthed with a shrug. She claimed the money and left the Jameson before turning away.

Warren removed the cap and drank directly from the spout. Some whiskey escaped his mouth, dribbling down his chin and the front of his silky black robes. He didn't bother to wipe.

"I'm going to stay a while," he said. Another swig.

Wonderful. "You're sure?"

"Yup." He snapped the end of the word and stretched his eyes wide in annoyance.

Victoria clenched her hand into a fist. Her nails dug into her palm and she silently counted to three. This wasn't going the way she'd imagined at all. Warren was supposed to happily come with her. She didn't make a habit of using sex as a negotiation tool, but she was dangerously close to putting that offer on the table.

"I guess I'll go then."

"Bye."

Warren was being downright rude. He had no right to be irritated with her—to act like *she* was the problem—but they were in public. She wouldn't let him get under her skin. "All right. I'll see you at home."

She kissed his cheek, careful to avoid the razor beak as he swiveled in his seat. *Dick.*

Warren's blue eyes dipped to the bar top as he twirled the bottle between his thumbs. "I don't think so."

Victoria jerked to a halt. "I'm sorry?"

"I won't be coming home tonight," he repeated. "Not tonight."

"Why wouldn't you come home?"

"Because I don't want to." Petulant.

"Why?" she asked.

He refused to meet her gaze.

"Warren."

"No."

The bar was emptying, but she wasn't stupid enough to think the people around them weren't listening to the drama unfold. She lowered her voice. "Why wouldn't you come home?"

He scoffed and took another pull from the bottle. Head hung low, his voice cracked. "Because you're killing me, Vic. You're killing me, and I can't take it anymore."

"Warren. Maybe have some water." *And shut your mouth.*

"Sure thing, boss," he said.

The cardinal picked *that* perfect moment to pop up, and Victoria suppressed the urge to smash her face with the nearest bottle. They shouldn't have been talking about this at the bar. At the Gala. With the Manor's crème de la crème within earshot.

The bartender smiled, but Victoria saw the force behind it. How much had she heard?

"What can I get for you, beautiful lynx?" she asked.

"That's Victoria, my wife," Warren added.

Astute. "Yes, we've met. Unfortunately, I'm not feeling well and I'm on my way out. Will you make sure Warren gets cut off within reason?" Victoria asked sweetly. "No more bottles."

"I don't need a damn babysitter, Vic."

She caressed his cheek before tilting his chin to meet her eyes, keeping her tone melodic and light. Warren wasn't used to her taking charge, not in any meaningful way. Steamrolling over her opinions or appropriating her ideas as his own, that was Warren's wheelhouse.

He was in for a rude awakening.

"You will stop when this woman tells you to stop. You'll thank her, leave a tip, and call for your car. Then you *will* come straight home. To me. Do I make myself clear?"

"Let go."

He jerked out of her grip. The sudden movement shifted the plague-doctor mask, causing the nose to swing forward. The beak sliced into her hand. She stared unbelievingly at the blood blooming.

No. Shit. *No.*

Warren stumbled off the stool, mumbling apologies, reaching out.

God, even when he wasn't trying he still ruined everything. Victoria corked her frustration. People would remember this moment. Warren, drunk and combative. Victoria, cut at the hand of her husband.

Shit.

She reached for a napkin, pressing it to her wound with a hiss. The pain wasn't too bad, but the napkin quickly soaked through. The bartender handed her another.

More guests crowded around them, drawn by the commotion. Victoria was enveloped by a dizzying barrage of inquiries.

"Are you okay?"

"She's bleeding."

"What happened?"

"I think he clipped her with the mask."

"It was an accident," Victoria interrupted, raising her voice to be heard. Rumors were birthed by the loudest mouth in the bunch. She needed to shut down as much misinformation as possible. Quickly. "An accident. He didn't mean it. I'm fine."

Warren's sweaty hand landed on her shoulder. His long fingers dug into her flesh, trying to pull her close, pawing at the wound like a bear. "I'm so sorry, Vic. I didn't—I wasn't thinking. This damn mask. I didn't even want to wear it."

"It's fine, Warren. Don't worry about it."

"I didn't mean to."

"Well, of course you didn't," she laughed. Silly husband.

He stared at the blood seeping through, pallor waxen. "Of course I didn't."

Victoria cast a wide smile to everyone to show that she was fine—just great, peachy fucking keen—and cleared her throat. "I'm going to the restroom to clean this up, and then I'll be heading home. You stay. Enjoy dinner. Give my best to the Connors. I'll see you later, Warren." To everyone else, "Excuse me."

She pattered toward the exit, refusing to turn when he shouted goodbye. She heard him say something in her wake that sounded like, "Did she get a haircut? Did her hair look shorter to you?" She didn't look to see who he was talking to.

Observant.

Ignoring the puzzled stares of the few guests she passed, Victoria marched toward the exit, stopping in the entryway to peel away the napkin and examine the cut. Not deep enough to warrant stitches, she didn't think, but an ugly gash, nonetheless. She balled up the napkin and tossed it into a small trash can next to a decorative vase.

"Shit," she whispered, trying to straighten her thoughts into a cohesive order.

"Oh my god, Victoria, are you okay?"

Son of a bitch, she thought, snapping her head up at the sound of Betty Knottier's voice. Flamingo-ed to the nines, she hitched up her hot pink, hideous taffeta skirt and scurried to Victoria.

"Betty. Yes, I'm good, just a little mishap with Warren's mask, nothing to worry about."

"I think I have some bandages in my purse, hold on." She yanked open the flaps of a lip-shaped handbag and rooted around until she found what she was looking for. "Ah-ha!" She ripped the paper, grabbed Victoria's wrist, and slapped a neon-green bandage over the wound before Victoria had time to protest. "There you go, girlfriend. Good as new."

Victoria squinted at the bright color. Why couldn't she have neutral bandages like an adult? "Thank you," she said with a tight smile.

"Don't mention it. Going back to the Gala?"

"I—uh, no. Heading out, actually."

"Ugh, jealous. I've got a sleep mask prepped at home. Can't wait to get out of these shapers. Don't tell WellShape I said that, though," Betty cupped her mouth conspiratorially.

Yes, because Victoria cared so much about Betty's Instagram partnerships. "Your secret's safe with me," she said.

Two young women pushed the doors open behind them, their energy high and infectious as they made their way toward the ballroom. They laughed together, poring over their phones in shimmery backless evening gowns.

Victoria remembered what it felt like to be in her twenties. Eager. Ambitious. Hungry. She was still those things, had always been those things, even with a soft-hearted Big Man blocking her way, but now she would be unstoppable. She would finally have her place in the world.

"Thanks again for the help, Betty, but I really have to go."

"Of course, don't let me stop you," she said, hand over her heart. "Are you waiting for Warren, or—"

"He's staying for dinner. I think the wine is giving me a migraine," Victoria said.

"Oh, you poor thing." She squeezed Victoria's forearm and puckered her magenta lips into a frown. "Sulfites. Sulfates? Whatever. Nasty business. Don't you worry, I'll take good care of him for you. Get on home before the snow gets any worse. Driving with a migraine must be awful."

Not nearly as bad as this conversation, Victoria thought. "Have a good evening, Betty."

"You, too, Victoria. Feel better." With a quizzical look, she was off, leaving Victoria with her murderous thoughts to guide her home.

23

Victoria bounded up the sidewalk, the train of her dress soaked and heavy. Her footsteps crunching in the snow, she raced inside pinching her toes together as the icy chill thawed. Roughly two inches had fallen since the start of the Gala and it was *cold*, an abrupt contrast to the sunny and seventy-five degrees it had been the previous week.

Maybe she'd put the house on the market once Warren was taken care of, she thought. Move some place she wouldn't need a plow. No bugs either. She'd never been good with nature. Warren had taken her camping the summer they'd started dating. It had been a hundred degrees, the bathrooms had been infested with spiders, and a sudden storm had flooded their tent. After slipping in the mud and landing flat on her ass, Victoria had tapped. The backyard was as outdoorsy as she got—hence why her plan didn't involve a remote cabin and a deep-woods burial.

The suburbs were a perfect spot for a murder if you knew what you were doing.

She unzipped her dress on the stairs, running through a mental checklist of what was left to do. Plastic crinkled beneath her as she padded to the master bathroom, all brushed chrome and granite surfaces the color of sand. This had been Warren's favorite room to design, which had been surprising to Victoria. More than once he'd gushed over the self-closing toilet seat to party guests. The pride he took in the showerheads rivaled his most lauded accomplishments at Livingston.

And then there was the upgraded soaker tub. His crown jewel. Where he soaked his achy muscles after a long run and simmered off the stress of the day with bath salts and essential oils.

One more thing Warren would never sacrifice for a child, she thought.

This was where, if everything went as it should, Warren would die. It was poetic really, and the plan was simple.

Victoria would make him his favorite drink: whiskey sour—with a dash of sleeping pills. Not enough to be suspicious on a tox screen—which, according to her true crime podcasts, they would undoubtedly run—but enough to guarantee that he wouldn't wake up while she worked.

She would coax him into the tub before he passed out, persuading him with extra bubbles and his favorite lavender oil; because for all his cocksure Big Man behaviors, Warren enjoyed a good soak. Proper lotioning. The occasional manicure. Plus, he was a sucker for romantic gestures—the showmanship of them, anyway: flowers delivered to the office, a very public engagement at a crowded restaurant downtown. Beautiful, empty. No surprise there. He preferred an audience, and while Victoria would be the only one to witness his final breath, she hoped his ghost would take solace in the exposure that was sure to follow.

So: nightcap, sleeping pills, cozy soak. The final step was the hardest—the part she was most nervous about. Once he was knocked out, Victoria would use her father's old hunting knife to make two neat incisions, submerging his wrists in the water.

A razor was perhaps the expected choice, but in Victoria's mind it had to be the knife. Her father hadn't taken her on a single hunting trip, but that hadn't stopped his reverence from bleeding into his lessons. Livingstons were not prey.

They would find the knife in Warren's hand. There would be a note, short and melancholy. She'd read it as if it were the first time, conscious of the police watching her as she took in the words, the paper probably shielded from her fingerprints by a plastic bag.

She'd say she'd had no idea that her husband was in the throes of depression, unable to cope with the insurmountable pressures of his job. The guilt he'd felt on a daily basis. His lifelong feelings of inadequacy and overcompensation.

Hanging her dress to take to the dry cleaners, Victoria slipped into a pair of black jeans and a black long-sleeve shirt. She'd received dozens of compliments on her appearance that evening, but none of the kind words compared to the excited chill she got seeing herself in the plain cotton fabric: capable, determined, dangerous.

Crouching to the bottom shelf of her dresser, Victoria pulled out a mahogany box and placed it on the bed. She lifted the brass latch and opened the lid. Surrounded by burgundy velvet lining was the hunting knife, the handle scratched and worn against the pristine blade. Her father had denied her the company but at least he'd left her the knife he used to stab her in the back.

One final dig. Even in death Jeremy Livingston was a callous bastard. Now she would use it to destroy them both. The justice of it all filled her chest with warmth. Everyone loved symbolism.

People would be shocked but not that surprised, not when they really considered it.

His pliable personality. His drinking. It made sense. That was the beauty of it. Her fingers ghosted the edge of the blade as she ran through what she'd say to Warren when he came home.

You look tired. Let's get you in the bath.

How about you take a nice, relaxing bath and I'll get you another drink?

Half an hour of rehearsing passed. Forty minutes.

Victoria wasn't worried. Warren would be home soon. All she had to do was wait.

24

It was almost two and Warren still wasn't home. As usual, his half-cocked choices were seriously screwing up her plans.

Bringing up his text thread, she tapped out quickly, It's late. Where are you?

Five minutes passed. No response.

She dialed his number, let it ring until the voicemail picked up.

Either he was ignoring her, or he'd meant it when he said he wasn't coming home. Where would he go instead? The office? It was too late to text Judy. She could do a drive-by, but there was a chance he'd arrive home while she was gone and she couldn't have him seeing the bedroom the way it was.

"Shit," Victoria hissed, stepping out onto the porch. Pumpkins sat woefully next to the posts, covered in snow. Flakes descended in large clumps, heavy and wet in the streetlight's glow. The street had been plowed, one of the benefits of allocating HOA funds to a private contractor. Most of the houses were dark, with only the old-timey black lampposts to mark their existence. Content in their sleepy bubbles while Victoria's life was on the brink of destruction.

Okay, enough with the pity party, she thought. She needed options.

Options.

First: Eliminate the obvious. She decided to call the Kent Wood Mansion security. A worried wife would do that. Someone would be able to tell her if he was throwing them back at the bar or if he'd left.

She googled the number and dialed, wrapping her arms around herself for warmth. Like Warren's line, the phone rang continuously. The Connors probably had their own security bypassing the main line.

Shit.

Teagan's car was still parked out front. An unblemished layer of white coated the exterior.

Are you still at the party? she texted. Have you seen Warren?

No dots. The receipt stayed on SENT.

Call it off, a voice said solidly in the forefront of her mind. *Before it's too late.*

She cursed, staring unseeingly into the night as time continued to work against her. Getting the drop cloths up and hidden was going to be a hassle, but what other choice did she have? Warren wasn't playing by her rules.

She had to call it off. For now.

Shivering, Victoria ran inside, taking the stairs two at a time to the bedroom. She locked the door behind her, a brief barrier should Warren decide to grace her with his inebriated presence, and pried up the painter's tape. She rolled the first sheet up, then a second and third, building the world's worst snowman. Why had she laid so much goddamn plastic? she wondered, frustrated by her earlier decisions about precautionary measures. But if Warren had made it out of the tub after having his wrists sliced, she would've had a whole different set of problems.

Next time she'd skip the drop cloths altogether and crush an extra sleeping pill.

Her phone vibrated. Stopping mid-roll to scoop it up, Victoria squinted at the screen in confusion. How could she be getting a message from her own number?

I hope you're happy.

"What the hell," she muttered, clicking the info icon in the corner. No other information was available. "Why, yes, stranger, I am very happy, but I'm rather preoccupied at the moment, so if you'll excuse me." She tossed the phone on the dresser and went back to peeling.

She ignored the chips in her nails and the scuffs the tape left behind. She ignored the buzzing behind her eyes and the urge to scratch out of her skin.

She was going to fix her Warren problem. It was going to take longer than she wanted, but this wasn't defeat. Postponing was the smart thing to do. She believed that, too, wrapped herself in confidence, until the doorbell rang.

25

V ictoria held her breath.

Had she imagined it? No one would just show up at this hour, especially not with the snow and the Gala. Warren wouldn't ring the bell.

Another ring interrupted her thoughts, followed by several loud knocks.

She rushed to the window. Someone was out there. A car, possibly a dark sedan, had parked in front of Teagan's. It was still running, snowflakes swirling in the headlights on the otherwise silent street.

I hope you're happy. You know what didn't make her happy? she thought. Strangers at the front door in the middle of the night. The anonymous text popped into her mind, the message eerie in this moment, as Victoria lost her hold on the illusion of safety.

More heavy knocks made her jump.

Definitely not a neighbor. Kent Wood Manor residents were polite to a fault, no matter the hour. A shadow moved down the sidewalk, slowly taking on the shape of a person. Could that be—no.

Yes.

Police. Worse than random strangers.

Her thoughts collided. Why were they here? Warren wasn't dead yet. How could they know?

Victoria left the mess on the floor. She snapped the box holding the hunting knife shut and shoved it in the bottom drawer of her dresser. Her clothes were an issue. The all-black ensemble. *I look like a cat burglar,* she thought. Snatching Warren's robe from the hook in the bathroom, Victoria tied it snugly around her torso, adapting the drowsy lethargy of one who has been rudely awakened from a deep sleep.

Good enough.

She crept down the stairs. Figures moved outside the foyer windows.

Run.

She took a deep breath and opened the door. "Hello," she said, eyes flitting from one person to the next, voice scratchy with pretend sleep. "Is everything all right?"

"Victoria Tate?" the woman in front asked. Unlike the uniformed officers behind her, she wore a peacoat over dark jeans and a T shirt.

She cleared her throat. "Yes, that's me. Is there a problem?"

"Mrs. Tate, my name is Detective Briana Meyers."

"I hope you don't mind if I ask to see your identification," Victoria said.

"Not at all." The woman tugged at her pocket. She presented Victoria with a badge. "I'm with Kent Wood Homicide."

Homicide?

Victoria's stomach sank. *They know, they know, they know,* her subconscious insisted. How could they? There was nothing to know. She hadn't done anything. *Someone tipped them off.*

They were here to arrest her.

This could be fake. The gold star looked a little too much like a child's prop, but she didn't have a clue what an actual badge was supposed to look like.

"What's this about?" she asked.

The peacoated woman frowned and stuffed her hands deeper inside her pockets. "Might be better to discuss inside."

Absolutely not. She couldn't let them inside. "Please," she said, betraying her own common sense and ushering them through the door. She pulled the robe closed under her chin. "Can I offer you all something to drink? Tea? Water? Coffee? It's awfully cold out tonight."

"Coffee would be great," the dark-haired woman said. "Thank you."

Polite. Would a cop be cordial if they were going to arrest her? And wouldn't they compel her out onto the porch? She couldn't be taken into custody in her own house, if the podcasts were to be believed. What if this wasn't about Warren?

"Mrs. Tate—"

"Victoria, please," she said, pulling a trio of mugs down from the top shelf and busying herself with the coffee maker. The officers sat at the table and watched her glide from cupboard to cupboard. She poured the first cup and handed it to Briana Meyers. "Cream?" she asked.

She shook her head and blew on the steaming liquid. "Black's fine. Same for them." She motioned to the others and sipped. "Thank you."

On autopilot, Victoria prepared the rest of the mugs and set out a plate of day-old pastries that Betty Knottier had forced into her hands after the neighborhood-watch meeting.

"So, what can I do for you, *Detective* Meyers?"

No reaction when she emphasized the title. Either Briana Meyers was a good actor or . . . well, Victoria didn't like the alternative. The longer she observed them, however, the more convinced she became that they were not here to arrest her.

That should've taken the edge off, but if anything Victoria grew more agitated with every passing minute.

Wrapping her fingers around the mug, Briana Meyers leveled her with a serious expression. "Mrs. Tate, I'm afraid we have some bad news. You may want to sit down."

To hell with that. "I've never been one to sugarcoat or beat around the bush, Detective Meyers. You might as well come out with it. Or should we wait for my husband? He should be home any minute."

Meyers grimaced, sending up alarm bells in Victoria's mind. What the hell was going on?

"We've just come from the Kent Wood Mansion," she said. "Were you in attendance at the Gala this evening?"

"Yes, I was there." Victoria's tongue was too big for her mouth. "I wasn't feeling well, so I left early. I'm sorry, what's going on? Did something happen at the Gala?"

"There's been an incident."

"An incident," she said, more of a statement than a question.

"Mrs. Tate, we're here because of your husband. Warren Tate, is that correct?" She pulled a tiny notepad from her pocket and flipped through the pages. The gesture was something out of a movie.

Victoria's pulse thrummed. "Yes, Warren's my husband." The sentence tasted stale on her lips. Moldy.

Briana Meyers frowned. It made her look old in the dim kitchen light, the soft wrinkles around the corners of her mouth stretching into sadness. "Mrs. Tate, I'm sorry, but your husband is dead."

"I—" *I can explain.* She actually started to say it, a gut reaction. *I didn't do it.* But she cut off the thought, processing what the detective had said. "I'm sorry?"

"Your husband's body was discovered a short while ago. I'm very sorry."

Body? Discovered? "H-how?" Victoria muttered.

"We can't go into details yet, but from everything we've been able to gather so far, we're pursuing this as a possible homicide."

In all the ways she had envisioned this moment, Victoria had never seen it happen quite like this. In her imaginings, she was guilty and playing innocent, hiding her bloodstained hands. It was suicide, not homicide. Yet this detective was telling her that Warren was dead. Murdered.

And she hadn't been the one to do it.

26

B riana Meyers was being too evasive. With her dingy
notepad and dark bags under her eyes, she flat-out refused
to tell Victoria what had happened to Warren. He was dead,
she knew that, and they were *fairly certain* it was murder; she
knew that too. But how?

Victoria excused herself and ducked into the half bathroom,
leaning against the sink with shaking hands. The robe was suddenly too hot. Too itchy. She pulled at the collar and splashed
water on her neck. In the kitchen, the officers' walkie-talkies
crackled. They had a brief exchange about whatever had come
in while she hid on the toilet.

Get a grip, she ordered her zombied reflection. *Get a fucking
grip.*

Taking out her phone, she quickly googled Briana Meyers. She
found half a dozen articles about charity events and local accolades. Nothing unusual. No scandals or blemishes on her record,
at least not on the surface. But she also hadn't been promoted in
years, and she wasn't making the rounds on the Connors' roster,
which suggested one of two things: one, she was an actual do-
gooder type, or two . . .

Well, two was that Briana Meyers was like Victoria.

She really hoped it was the former.

"Mrs. Tate?" A tap on the door. "Are you all right?"

Victoria startled but managed to not knock over the bowl of potpourri. "Fine," she said, tucking her phone into her pocket and pretending to wash her hands. She opened the door to the inquisitive face of Briana Meyers and skirted any further small talk by walking directly to the kitchen table. She plopped into the seat with the tired limbs of someone who hasn't slept in days. That wasn't far from the truth. When was the last time she'd gotten a solid night's sleep?

Meyers joined her. She tucked her hands in her lap, watching Victoria trace the rim of her mug with her thumb. "I have a few questions," she said. "When you're ready."

"I'm ready," Victoria said. "I—it helps me to have something to focus on."

"I understand," she said. The notepad from earlier made a reappearance. "If you need a break, let me know."

"Thank you, but I'm okay," Victoria said, sitting a little straighter. She wasn't okay, not even in the same ballpark, but she would concentrate on Meyers's questions. "What do you need to know?"

Meyers sat for another beat, trading glances with the officers, seeming to wait for Victoria to change her mind. When that didn't happen, she gave a nod of acknowledgment and dove in. "Had your husband seemed distracted lately?" she started.

"Yes, but that was normal with the end of the quarter approaching."

Straightforward answers from Victoria, she'd decided. Short and simple. No overexplaining. Less chance of getting caught in a lie, especially when she didn't know what she was up against yet.

"Was he a gambler?"

Victoria shook her head. "Warren's not the betting type. Had a terrible poker face and never took much interest in cards. We go to the racetrack in Saratoga a few times every summer, but he rarely puts money down. It's mostly because it's expected of us."

"Any history of recreational drug use?"

"Not that I'm aware of. He drank," she sniffled, "sometimes too much."

"Mm," came the reply. "Anything unusual about his behavior recently? Mood swings or . . ."

Meyers let her fill in the blanks, and Victoria stumbled a bit. Her initial reaction was to play up Warren's mood swings, his anger and fits of depression—none of which was true, but it was the narrative she'd been practicing. It fit well with her plan, but she hadn't *actually* murdered Warren, so convincing the detective that her husband was suicidal might be counterproductive.

She landed on, "I don't know, I guess he has been a little short-tempered. But he's been under a lot of stress, so, nothing stands out."

"What kind of stress?"

"Work," she said. "Everything ramps up this time of year. I've barely left the office as it is, and Warren is even more of a perfectionist than I am. He holds himself to such high standards because they expect so much out of him. The clients. Not to mention the demands that come with being the boss. It's a lot to always have to be on, to have all the answers and be the go-to person."

It was easy to explain it that way. Warren's job was difficult because Warren made it difficult. Meyers didn't need to know she was talking about herself.

Meyers nodded, making notes without comment and moving on to the next question. The peacoat was unbuttoned now, revealing a plain blue boatneck top with a small stain in the middle. A little circle of red. Victoria stared at the dot. Spaghetti sauce?

"Did Warren have enemies?" Meyers asked. "Anyone with a grudge?"

Salad dressing? Meyers didn't look like the type to order a cobb over a sandwich. "*No*," she declared. "Everybody loves—*loved*—Warren."

Well, except for me, she thought, choking on the change in tense. Victoria had a pretty big grudge, but love was complicated, right? Right.

"Is that so?"

"Sorry?" Victoria scowled. "I'm not sure what you're implying."

"Nothing." Meyers waved her off, but Victoria saw it for the ploy it was. She had to be careful. "Just covering bases. How would you describe your marriage? Were you happy?"

Whiplashed, Victoria sputtered. Who was ever really happy? she wanted to ask. In fact, she was beginning to think that happiness was a myth perpetuated by Hallmark, because as far as her rays of sunshine were concerned, happiness was much closer to a hole in the ground than it was to a white picket fence.

"We loved each other very much," she said instead.

"I have to ask," Meyers said, leaning closer. "Had Warren . . . Had you ever suspected that your husband might be having an affair?"

That irked Victoria. Warren was many things, but a cheater wasn't one of them. He didn't have it in him. Using his wife as a rung on the corporate ladder was one thing; she'd even wondered if maybe it hadn't been a coincidence that he'd hit on her that night at the bar. Maybe he'd known who her father was the whole time. But disrespecting the vows he made in front of God—and *Jeremy fucking Livingston*? He would've lit himself on fire first.

She said as much, folding her hands together and arching her best business brow at the detective. Meyers, face full of pity—and screw her for that, Victoria thought—flipped the notepad shut and stood to leave.

"We'll need you to come down to the station to file a statement," she said. "Can I call anyone for you?"

"I'm fine," she said. "I can handle it. Thank you, Detective." She pushed in her chair and walked Meyers and the two officers to the door.

On the porch snow swirled around them, slower now than a few hours ago. The worst of the storm was passing.

As soon as the cavalry pulled away from the curb, Victoria trudged upstairs. She didn't want to think. She didn't want to have to worry about what everything meant. Not yet.

Instead, she decided to finish deconstructing the murder room she wouldn't need because her would-be victim was already chilling at the morgue. Alanis wouldn't be singing about that irony any time soon. Throwing herself into the task, she was lost to the crinkling plastic and the *zwip* of painter's tape.

Once the supplies were handled, she undressed slowly and climbed into the shower. The water was hot, and the pressure was good, but she couldn't get past the singular thought that Warren would not be coming home again. It should've been grounds for some morbid celebration. Not a party—her husband was dead; that wouldn't be a good look—but a smile or fist pump or *something*.

Nothing.

She waited for the dip of guilt, but that didn't come either. Maybe that wasn't indicative of anything, though. Victoria hadn't killed Warren, so she didn't need to feel guilty. The absence of her moral compass didn't mean she was broken so much as it meant she was absolved.

Okay, she wouldn't go that far.

So many times she'd pictured this moment, expecting the thrill of independence. The reality of her situation, however, was not that straightforward. With Warren, in death as in life, it rarely was.

Victoria was in limbo, an odd space between reclaiming her life and burying the past. And that, she thought, simply wouldn't work for her.

27

The roads were slippery and deserted. Victoria embraced the silence that came with the late hour and the first snow, letting her thoughts drift aimlessly in the ten-minute drive to the station. This was the opposite of life flashing before her eyes, no montage of happy memories. It was half a stale bagel at her desk, the afternoon sun heating her office as Warren mansplained the reproductive process. It was the dry, wrinkled skin of her father's hand as she pleaded with his unconscious to change his mind.

It was the gruesome image of Warren's final moments her mind conjured. Gunshot wounds and muggings. Chipped teeth and road rash.

At the end of it all was the same deceased husband and her spiraling emotions.

Two hours after Detective Meyers first rang her bell, Victoria sat at a dull metal table in the central office of Kent Wood PD, a box of tissues to her left, a manila folder to her right. Meyers stood in the corner of the small room with one leg bent behind her and the stained shirt taut over her stomach.

Victoria answered her questions readily: what time she'd left the Gala, why she hadn't waited for Warren, if anyone could verify her location at the time of death. She didn't ask for a lawyer, and no one suggested that she needed one, a sign, she hoped, that things were moving in the right direction.

The current matter at hand was the body.

She had to see his body. To know it was real.

Meyers hadn't wanted to divulge the gory details—and gory they were—but Victoria had worn her down. It didn't take much. She assumed that the holdout was more of a test, a way for Meyers to feel out the spouse's reaction. For the time being, it appeared that Victoria's place on the suspect list was standard procedure. Many people had seen her leave the Gala early. Her alibi was tighter than the corset she'd worn on her wedding day.

Victoria appreciated Meyers's approach: quick and technical. There was no pity or shying away from the truth. Warren was dead, and it had been brutal.

Shortly after midnight, a couple attending the Gala stumbled across his body in the garden of the Kent Wood Mansion. Their identities were being withheld for the time being, but she figured it was only a matter of time before they were revealed. Nothing stayed secret in Kent Wood Manor for long.

The official cause of death was still unknown, pending the results of an autopsy, but he had been stabbed multiple times in the abdomen, chest, and neck.

Stabbed, she thought. Stabbed.

Many victims of stabbing reported that it didn't hurt at all. At least not at first, according to the various podcasts she'd listened to. Pain came after the victims realized what had happened.

Did Warren make that same discovery? Had he died in pain?

Had she wanted him to?

Victoria had been angry, yes. Determined to end his life. But she hadn't wanted him to suffer.

"Oh my god," Victoria muttered, visualizing the scene. Warren, sprawled on one of those fancy marble-slab garden benches she'd observed that night. The snow stained red.

"Mrs. Tate?" Meyers interrupted.

"Sorry," she said. "I was just . . ."

"I know." Her tone was understanding yet firm. "I have to ask about your hand. How did you get injured?"

"Oh. This." She plucked at the neon bandage, completely forgotten in the chaos of the night. "The Connors made everyone wear masks. Party theme, you know? Warren's had an incredibly sharp beak. He took it off before dinner, and it slipped and cut my hand. Looks worse than it is." She thought again of his plague doctor getup. The nose-scythe. "Was he wearing the mask when they found him?"

"I can't answer that, unfortunately," Meyers said.

She didn't sound contrite to Victoria. "I was just thinking it was very sharp."

"Apparently." Her eyes widened with another nod to Victoria's injury. "Were there witnesses to this incident? Someone to corroborate your story?"

Story?

Victoria wasn't an English major, by any means. Sometimes a word was just a word. But with Briana Meyers, that word was significant. It suggested a degree of doubt.

"The bar was quite crowded. I'm not sure who the other guests were, but the bartender—Temperance, she told me her name was—she saw it happen. And Betty Knottier was the one who gave me the bandage outside in the lobby. She's a neighbor from the Manor."

Meyers recorded these details in her trusty notepad. "We'll speak to both of them. We're trying to obtain a list of employees from the Connors, but I'm not expecting anything before late this morning. My guys will make the rounds of the development after shift change."

The air in the station was thick and stale, the heat working double time against the early chill. Victoria's lips stuck together. She focused on a thread of skin, working it between her teeth. "I can't believe this is happening. Everybody loves Warren."

Loved.

Meyers sat back in her chair. The thin cotton fabric of her shirt was crinkled and worn as thin as Victoria's patience. "Mrs. Tate, I have to caution you again about what you're asking here. Some people find closure, but others . . . the experience can be traumatic. Do you have anyone you can talk to?"

"Thank you for your concern, Detective Meyers," she said curtly. "I will be fine. I need this."

"You might not," she countered. "The lacerations will be mostly covered, but there was additional mutilation."

Victoria froze. "What do you mean, 'mutilation'?"

Meyers looked to the corner of the room before settling back on Victoria. She seemed to have come to a decision in that moment, breathing deeply before clearing her throat and replying. "His eyes were removed."

"His—what?" Meyers didn't explain further, leaving Victoria to process. "His eyes? Who would—why?"

A sharp pain needled through her temple. She folded into her lap, head in hands, rubbing the pain away. Meyers's proximity made her skin feel too tight, and she resisted the urge to pummel the detective into the nearest wall just to have some space to breathe.

"Mrs. Tate," Meyers said softly, "if you're really doing this, I need you to prepare for the shock of it. He won't look like you remember him."

"Somebody stabbed my husband multiple times, left him to bleed to death, and cut out his eyes, and you're worried about my feelings?"

Whatever she did, Victoria would not trust Briana Meyers.

"And your well-being," she said, a deep frown carving her face. "Due to the particularly violent nature of this crime, and . . . other factors which I'm not at liberty to discuss just yet, the case has been expedited."

"I'm not sure I understand what you're telling me," Victoria said. She'd changed into jeans and a simple sweater before leaving the house and was regretting that choice. The cotton was stiff and itchy on her neck. Sweat made the material cling uncomfortably to her underarms.

"We're throwing all our manpower behind it, the entire force. Things like this tend to start a panic."

In Kent Wood? *Panic* wasn't a strong enough word. Hysteria was more like it. The last murder in the community had caused a circus of nightmares. A man had been found shot in the shed in his backyard. His killer turned out to be a jilted lover, the babysitter or the nanny or some other clichéd connection, but that hadn't stopped the energy with which Kent Wood Manor put into demonstrating their fear. It had happened a few years ago, but at the time, Dan Delaney's murder had been more unavoidable than a shadow. Everyone was scared. They still talked about it.

And Dan Delaney hadn't been the CEO of a major corporation.

This was exactly the type of scrutiny that Victoria had wanted to avoid. Now, however, she was in the thick of it. She had no doubt that the rumor mill was already turning, which meant their lives, Warren's and hers, would be front-page fodder in a matter of hours.

"I understand," she said.

"And I promise you," Meyers said, full of solemnity, "we will find the person who did this."

Intimidation or consolation, Victoria didn't care to decipher.

It was interesting to note, however, that Meyers apparently had a bit of a hero complex. Capturing the bad guy. Sending him to jail. Those promises were empty, not hers to make.

Because Victoria had a new mission. If she couldn't kill Warren herself, she thought, she was damn sure going to find the person who did.

28

The morgue was in the basement of the hospital off a corridor adjacent to the kitchen. They didn't bring Victoria into the actual room, but instead showed her to a white closet-sized space with a small table and single chair. On a closed-circuit screen, a woman with curly white-blonde hair and a white coat pulled back a stiff white sheet with detached precision.

Victoria had to wonder about the unintended symbolism. Everyone associated white with weddings, but in many cultures white was the color of death. Here she was, wrapped up in the void, snow on the ground and a pale form on a cold, metal table.

Warren.

Victoria whimpered, a noise she would deny until her own dying day, and—oh, she was going to puke. Grabbing the wall, she steadied herself and waited for the sensation to pass. Sweat stuck to her forehead. Her muscles trembled as she wiped her lips.

Meyers set a trash can down at her feet and signaled to the woman. The TV went black, but Victoria could still see the outline of Warren's shape behind her eyelids. Focusing on her breathing, she inhaled deeply and released her breaths in shaky huffs. After a few rounds, the worst of the dizziness had passed, and Meyers escorted her out of the room.

She led her slowly to the cafeteria, guiding her wordlessly through the sterile dimly lit corridor. For the hour, it was relatively busy. Nurses and a spattering of visitors grabbed quick bites, hunched over their tables on phones or tablets.

Meyers stuck a Styrofoam cup into Victoria's hand. "It's shitty but sobering."

Victoria would've preferred a whiskey and ginger. A bottle or four of Cabernet. Sobering was seeing Warren on that large baking sheet. His skin—she'd never seen a color quite like that before, somewhere between gray and dishwater. The place where his eyes should've been haunted her already. They had done their best to cover the area without hiding the rest of his face, but that only served to remind her of what was missing.

Victoria sipped the black tar masquerading as coffee with her eyes closed, acutely aware of how much she relied on them. It was funny to her then: how once you started thinking about a certain part of your body, you couldn't stop. Like an unreachable itch. Or your tongue moving around in your mouth.

Every dust mote, every lash, every blink. The muscles holding them in place. The individual veins spidering across their bloodshot surfaces.

The black holes hidden behind Warren's sunken lids. Victoria wouldn't be shaking that image anytime soon. Whoever had attacked him had to be deranged, she thought. Maybe a legitimate psychopath.

No sane person could inflict that level of harm and walk away unscathed. Unbothered.

She understood that some might say she was hypocritical. Yes, fine, she'd wanted Warren dead, and yes, she'd expected to be okay after he was gone, not plagued by the act itself. Lady Macbeth's bloody hands were not her own.

This was all true, but the situations were not the same.

Killing Warren wasn't a long-unfulfilled homicidal urge. Victoria would have been acting out of necessity. She wouldn't have carved out his eyes and left him to die alone. She wasn't cruel. She was a rational person capable of feeling things.

"Are you ready?" Meyers asked, finishing a text and shoving her phone into her pocket.

Victoria nodded at Meyers and stood on wobbly legs. She tossed the cup in the garbage and followed the detective out of the hospital, neither one speaking about Warren Tate.

The fresh air was welcome, and she inhaled greedily, blinking against the first hazy rays of sunshine dawning on the horizon. The snow had stopped, leaving that icy serenity that comes in the first snow's wake.

As gruesome as it may have been, Warren had died on a beautiful day, after all.

29

The rest of the morning passed in a blur. Death, even when Victoria wasn't the cause, came with moving parts and a lot of paperwork. She signed various documents until her hand ached. She reviewed the itemized list of belongings found with Warren's body. Watch. Wallet. ID. One hundred and forty-two dollars in a platinum clip.

Teagan finally materialized, vomiting teary-eyed excuses for not getting there sooner. Meyers had watched this play out, thin-lipped and tired, as the sisters awkwardly embraced. Victoria, not used to Teagan's comfort, was probably at fault there, but she'd accepted the hug regardless.

They exchanged few words, covering the basics on too-hard chairs that squeaked on the linoleum. Teagan held Victoria's hand while she asked about funeral arrangements. Despite the black hoodie thrown over her Gala gown and her running mascara, she still somehow managing to look like a Hollywood starlet.

"When can my sister claim his body?"

What a weird question, Victoria thought. Weird question, weird idea: taking ownership of her dead husband's body.

"We're waiting on the completed autopsy results," Meyers replied, running a hand through her already-messy hair.

"Once the paperwork is settled and the certificate of death is issued, you'll be good to go—I mean, free to make arrangements." She fumbled with the phrase, cheeks flushing at the potential insensitivity. "In the meantime, if you think of anything, call me at that number." She handed Victoria and Teagan her card.

"Thank you, Detective," Victoria said, reaching for the door, Teagan's arm wrapped around her waist. Her head barely reached Victoria's shoulder, but she found that she appreciated the support. It was nice to have Teagan at her side for a change.

"Mrs. Tate," Meyers called.

Victoria paused, turning at the address.

Meyers stepped closer, smelling of cold sweat and bad coffee. The flyaways around her forehead were frizzy, but her gaze was level and fiery. "I just want to make sure you heard me earlier. Sometimes it takes a minute for the fog to lift, and this is important."

"Of course."

"We don't see a crime like this every day. Something this violent . . . more often than not, the attacker isn't a stranger but someone the victim knows. It's usually personal."

Victoria knew that. Murder Podcast 101. "Personal," she repeated anyway. The less Meyers knew about her macabre interests the better.

"You think Warren knew his attacker?" Teagan asked.

Meyers's eyes narrowed. "It's possible. We'll get a list from the Connors, but I'd be surprised if you didn't know ninety percent of the guests at the Gala, am I right?"

"Yes, but it's not like we knew who was wearing what. Everyone wore masks," Teagan said.

"Be that as it may, with the level of security measures the Connors took, and the strict protocols they had in place, it's unlikely someone was able to sneak in."

"But not impossible," Victoria said. "The guest list doesn't take into account the waiters or guards or janitorial staff, not to mention the Uber drivers or delivery people who might've had access to the Mansion."

Meyers startled. "Been thinking about this a bit?"

"Common sense." Victoria shrugged off Meyers's prying stare, holding her muscles steady while she was studied like a bug under a microscope.

Meyers retreated gradually, her gaze flitting between Victoria and Teagan. "Takes a lot of stamina to do what was done to the victim. Warren. Mr. Tate."

The detective didn't seem to be good with words, but that didn't mean she wasn't good at her job. "I'm too tired. What are you trying to say?" Victoria asked.

The door swung wide as Meyers stepped out of their way. "Be careful," she said. "And stay close to home."

30

Victoria was practicing her eulogy when her phone vibrated. She assumed it was Teagan. Since Warren's death, her sister seemed to have made it her personal business to smother Victoria as much as possible.

Teagan had been attentive. Overprotective. Victoria would've gone so far as to describe her behavior as clingy, which might have made sense for some siblings but was an alien concept for her. She was showing up with coffee before work. Texting throughout the day—just to chat, just to say hello, just to drive Victoria nuts with the use of *just*. A word of submission, of diminishing power, people *justed* when they were insecure. There was only so much of Teagan's out-of-character mother hen-ing that she could take.

Ignoring the messages only made it worse. Preemptively irritated, Victoria checked her phone and frowned. The text was from her own number. She'd almost forgotten about the anonymous text she'd received the night Warren died, but the memory came rushing back as she opened the thread.

> I cut out his eyes. What makes you think I won't cut yours out too?

Victoria read it until the letters swam together, dread flooding her gut and rising to her chest. This wasn't a sick prank, as much as she wanted to believe it was. Enemy was a strong word, and while Livingston had engaged in some heated competition over the years, she had always remained professional and courteous. If someone was holding a grudge strong enough to lead from the boardroom to a violent stabbing, it wasn't because of Victoria's business dealings.

Outside the office? Friendships centered mostly around group chats. Petty lines were inevitably crossed, but it was a stretch to think breaking an HOA rule would lead to homicide—and whatever this was. Her neighbors loved the Joe Goldbergs of the world and salacious gossip, but they weren't really the bloody-your-hands type.

More importantly, nobody was supposed to know about Warren's eyes. According to Detective Meyers, that detail was purposely left out of the news. Someone could have leaked the information, but this text wasn't an intrusive reporter looking for an edge on their next story.

The simplest explanation stood: This was Warren's killer.

Who is this? she wrote.

Dancing dots appeared, and then they were gone. Victoria waited, refreshing the feed. Nothing.

"Tor?" The front door creaked shut and Teagan's footsteps sounded on the stairs. She blew into the bedroom, makeup pristine and hair set in gentle old Hollywood waves.

A streak of jealousy ripped through Victoria. She missed her long hair. "You're early," she said.

"Have you looked outside?" Teagan asked, breathy and flushed. "There must be a dozen news crews."

Hands trembling, Victoria unzipped her makeup bag and rooted for the Dior tube, carefully applying a single coat of mascara to distract herself from the cocktail of emotions threatening to unleash. "I hadn't looked, but I'm not surprised." Two coats. If she couldn't have the hair, she thought, she could at least have the lashes. Not the spider legs Teagan glued to her face.

"It's going viral." A note of excitement slipped into Teagan's otherwise somber delivery. Funeral or not, the spotlight never lost its appeal. She was like a horny moth rubbing up against a light until its body melted.

And now Victoria was thinking about melted wings and horny things, and that was definitely not the direction she wanted to explore. "Lucky me."

"I'm sorry, I know you don't want to hear about this."

"You're right, I don't."

"It's just"—*There's that word again*, Victoria thought—"people are blowing up my comments sections, tagging me in Reddit forums. It's really something, how fast Warren's murder is spreading. Could you imagine if they did a Netflix doc?"

Zero chill. "Glad your head's in the right place," Victoria said, fussing with her makeup organizer.

She parted the curtains and peered down at the mass of people. Most of the snow had melted, but the temperature had dropped again. The crowd was bundled and ready for the long haul. Her neighbors might've been afraid, but no one in Kent Wood Manor could stay away from the excitement, however somber it may be.

Case in point: Betty Knottier.

She donned a simple black sheath dress with Chanel earrings the size of golf balls. They shook wildly back and forth as she talked to one of the reporters, one of the more popular anchors from a national tabloid. Betty was the picture of grief; she hadn't forgotten to bring her pouty lips and model poses to cry pretty for the cameras. Performative outrage 101.

"Ugh, she's such a douche," Teagan exclaimed, leaning over Victoria's shoulder to take in the view. "You get one C-list sponsor and suddenly you're a freaking Kardashian. It's like, calm your tits, Rebecca—because you know Betty is probably just a stage name that tested better with the cool kids at the country club. And speaking of tit-calming, my god, those implants. She paid someone money, actual American dollars, for that watermelon uniboob travesty."

"Not everyone can afford your expert skills, Dr. Livingston."

"I might have to interrupt her audition for *The Real Housewives of Kent Wood Manor* to offer my services."

"Teagan, I'm burying my husband today," she snapped, because this was a little too much all at once. The eulogy and the text and now making fun of Betty's poor delivery of a Sad Neighbor.

"You're not—"

"His headstone—you know what I mean; don't play dumb. For once in your life, could you just be quiet?" Teagan turned, argument already spilling from her tongue. Victoria forced her tone to be softer. "Please."

The fight left Teagan's body. She crossed her arms over her chest and nodded once. Silence followed, but it wasn't awkward. They were back on opposite sides of the fence, not pretending to be loving sisters. Victoria felt at ease in her presence for the first time since Warren's demise. It was grounding. Exactly what she needed to get through the next few hours.

Teagan heaved a sigh. "I'm going to wait downstairs. I'll let you know when the town car gets here." She didn't wait for Victoria to respond, and that, too, was a small miracle.

Victoria took a minute to inspect her reflection before gathering the things she'd need for the service. If she focused on tasks, tangibles to check off her to-do list, then she wouldn't think about Warren. Or the texts.

The problems faded into fuzzy particles as she lost herself to the rote words of her eulogy. Her phone buzzed as she stuck lipstick and a travel pack of tissues into her clutch.

"Tori, town car!" Teagan shouted from downstairs.

"Be right there," she said mindlessly, swiping to see the message. The screen illuminated with a grainy photo of a bedroom, almost like someone had screenshotted a video, but the subject was unmistakable

In the shot, Victoria's face was in clear view, fresh haircut and robe unmistakable. She was on her hands and knees laying out the drop cloths.

Another message popped up. I know your secret.

Her body flushed with heat. The longer she stared at the photo, the clearer it became that Victoria was in trouble. The time and date were clearly marked in the bottom corner. And although Warren's body had been found at the Mansion, Meyers had implied that it was possible that he might have been murdered somewhere else and then moved.

The time stamp was in the window of the suspected time of death. Alibi or not—body or not—this photo created doubt.

Someone had been watching. Victoria slowly let her gaze creep around the room. Could still be watching.

"Tori, let's go!" Teagan called impatiently.

"I'm coming!" Her hands shook as she tapped out the same message as before.

Who is this?

The dancing dots appeared immediately. Names are irrelevant. But if it makes you feel better, you can call me X.

"Tori, come on, what's taking so long?" Teagan's voice tunneled into focus as she appeared in the doorway.

Victoria stuffed her phone into her clutch with an emphatic snap. "Sorry. Nerves," she said, beelining for the exit. "I'm ready."

"Hey." Teagan touched her elbow and held her gaze with an intensity that rivaled Victoria's own.

Victoria was tempted to recoil from the gentleness, primed to explode. It reminded her of the night of the Gala. How close they'd been to truth. Or ruin. "We're going to be late."

"Just . . . wait, all right? Don't run away. Not this time."

"I've never run," Victoria said.

"Then stand still for long enough to trust me. I know we've had our differences, but you can talk to me about anything. I really am here for you."

Ha. This experience had shown Victoria that trust was a liar's most useful tool, a convenient screw. Not to mention she had to assume that the texter was still watching. X. Choosing her words carefully, Victoria said, "Thank you, Teagan. I appreciate that."

Ending the moment as quickly as possible, Victoria offered her a watery smile and linked their elbows. Satisfied, Teagan returned the affection, and together they met Detective Meyers on the porch. She gave a curt hello and reiterated condolences. Victoria would've handled herself much the same in the detective's shoes. She found the efficiency comforting.

Escorting them to the town car, Meyers shielded them from camera flashes. They clambered inside while she addressed the nearby officers, giving the signal to fall in line behind the procession.

The drive was quiet, and the service began without a hitch. Officers kept out of the way of the mourners, observing from a marked distance, searching for anyone suspicious.

Victoria knew from her true crime podcasts that it wasn't uncommon for killers to attend their victim's funerals. The thrill of getting caught was part of the experience. It was the same reason people who blew up buildings sent notes taunting the police. Scrapbooked their own sordid headlines.

They wanted everyone to know what they'd done.

X didn't seem to want notoriety, though. There'd been no grand gestures, no riddles or hotline calls to the police.

He'd only contacted Victoria.

31

Paperwork was both the bane of Victoria's existence and the balm of her day. Mindless, repetitive fill-in-the-blank assignments that were tedious, yes, but also left her feeling accomplished after a lengthy negotiation. Nothing was more satisfying than ticking tasks off a to-do list.

Unfortunately, that same sense of fulfillment did not carry over into her home life, where Warren had insisted that he be the one in charge of bills. They'd had discussions before they got married, fleshing out how they would share money, who would be responsible for which payments. A joint account had been the result, the practical (read: old-fashioned) choice, which now remained password protected by a dead husband. Since supernatural dollars weren't an acceptable form of currency, Victoria was now forced to go to battle with the utilities company and internet provider, as well as deal with a half dozen other things she hadn't worried about in over a decade.

She almost wished she were dealing with another text from X. Almost.

As Victoria was placed on hold for the third time in as many hours with the mortgage company, her mood soured. A podcast was rolling in the background, a repeat of *My Favorite Murder* set in an upstate New York town an hour north of Kent Wood, but she'd missed most of the summary arguing about verified identities and death certificates. She was about to pull the emergency tub of cookie dough from the freezer and eat her lunch by the spoonful.

The staticky drone voice of the customer service rep clicked back into her ear as the doorbell rang.

"Shit," she hissed under her breath, peeking through the window. Betty Knottier shifted in her highlighter-yellow trainers on the front porch, cradling a gift basket under one arm. "I'm going to have to call you back," she said, hanging up.

The movement drew Betty's attention. She peered through the glass with a cheery wave, and Victoria wanted to kick her in the teeth. Why was she so energetic? Why was she here?

Tugging the collar of her hunter-green shirt and rolling her eyes at the mirror above the foyer table (she had to get it out of her system somehow, she thought), Victoria opened the door.

"Hi, Betty."

"Hi!" she replied, the smile on her face stretching wide enough to hurt. Victoria half expected the skin at the corners of her mouth to crack and bleed. "I'm so glad you're okay. I knocked a few times and no one answered. I didn't see you leave this morning, so I was worried." Betty chuckled like she'd told the funniest joke in the world. "Was about to come barging in like the Kool-Aid Man. *Oh yeah!*" She thrust the basket forward. "This is for you. Figured you wouldn't need any more roses."

She motioned to the sad and wilting bouquets propped against the pillar on the porch. Most of the sympathy cards had folded into soft wads from exposure. Victoria had lost track of the number of well-wishers who'd stopped by unannounced with their casseroles and flowers. Even Jeff from the office had made an appearance after the service, big-toothed and slicked hair, slithering through the reception like the snake that he was, nodding condolences while slipping his business card into waiting hands.

Betty eyed the flowers, making no attempt to hide the crinkle of judgment on her face. The I-would-never-let-this-happen sneer that was exclusive to the suburban elite.

"Yeah, I should take care of those today," she said, mad at the blush creeping up her neck.

"No judgment on my part," Betty lied with a hand on her heart. If she'd had a gavel, she would've been laying down the sentence already. One year of community service for every offending bloom. No time served for grieving. Betty plucked at the items in the basket as Victoria kept it from tipping in her arms. "Speaking of care, I can't think of a better opportunity for a little self-pampering."

Victoria scanned the strategically arranged collection of running leggings, moisture-wicking socks, tanks, and sports bras. She thumbed the spa gift card with the enthusiasm of an enema patient before tempering her expression. Betty Knottier was insufferable, but the sooner she accepted the sponcon swag, the faster she could get rid of her.

"Thank you," Victoria said. "This is very kind of you, Betty, and I'm sure I'll make good use of these when I'm feeling up to it. Finding motivation to workout hasn't been top of my priorities lately. And actually, I'm kind of in the middle of something, so—"

"Actually, sweetie, if you have a minute, I was hoping we could talk."

Of course, Betty wasn't going to be dismissed that easily.

"Now's not really a good time," Victoria doubled down.

"It won't take long, I promise. Just a few minutes."

Oh, she really didn't want to let Betty in. They'd never been close, even before everything with Warren. She wasn't a bad person, in the most general sense of the word. A mother and doting wife with a penchant for MLM merch and an unhealthy obsession with social media. Where Teagan had found a niche to monopolize with her gratuitous plastic surgery videos, Betty hashtagged from one campaign to the next, touting skin care and smoothies and dog grooming accessories. She didn't own a dog.

So, no, she wasn't a bad person, but they had nothing in common.

Victoria opened the door wider and stepped back. "Come on in."

Betty entered, craning to look around the room without hiding her interest. "Did you get new sconces? I don't remember seeing them at the reception. Then again, we were all a little preoccupied that day."

They weren't new, but Victoria had moved them from the bedroom when she was searching for X's camera. One less place to hide a lens. The devil was in the details, but truth was in the bigger picture, and Betty seemed to be in the mood to paint.

"Warren's mother gave them to me," she said. "They were his favorite."

"Warren liked sconces?"

"He liked a lot of things." *Like fraying my sanity,* Victoria thought. "I did most of the decorating, but Warren had strong preferences. Wanted to own his spaces, you know?"

"What a comfort that must've been. Dave doesn't care what I do with the house as long as we abide by the rules. That and no roosters. His mother was very country chic in the nineties."

"Oh."

"Yes."

An awkward silence settled in. From the kitchen, the pod-caster revealed that the body had been discovered in various parts along the interstate. Duffle bags full of arms and legs. Betty's horror reminded Victoria that not everyone liked their noon breaks with blood spatter analyses. *Great.*

"Alexa, stop." Setting the basket down, Victoria wiped her hands on her jeans. Hopefully Betty wasn't as big of a gossip as Judy, but she doubted it, and she mentally prepared for the glares she'd get for listening to murder stories when her husband was barely cold in the ground. People still hated on Evelyn Charles around the corner for remarrying after her husband died of a heart attack—and it had been three years.

"Interesting listening choice," Betty quipped.

Yeah, there was no way Victoria wasn't going to catch heat for this. "Takes my mind off things."

"Does it?" *You're full of shit,* her tone read.

Victoria cleared her throat. "Coffee?"

"I'm good. Cutting back on caffeine."

"All right, so what can I do for you?"

"I wanted to see how you were holding up," Betty said, blunting her enthusiasm with an air of concern. "Woman to woman. We haven't had much chance to talk."

"Woman to woman."

"Precisely," she agreed, as if Victoria had answered her own unasked question. "Being lonely is hard, especially when you've shared a bed with someone every night for years. Shared a life together. I would know. Chelsea's a junior now and has her own extracurriculars. Friends. At the age when she wants nothing to do with her mother, that's for damn sure. Dave travels a lot. I know it's not exactly the same as what you're going through, but . . ." She shrugged, leaving the thought unfinished.

Lonely? Victoria hadn't had a chance to breathe since Warren's body had turned up. The few moments alone had been dominated by the stress of Livingston and X's games. She couldn't wait for this to be over so she could spend time by herself.

"I'm okay," Victoria said.

"I'm sure it helps to keep busy."

"It does."

"Warren must've left a lot on his plate."

That was a left turn from nowhere. "Sorry?"

"What with how—suddenly—he was taken from us. And with Livingston unmanned. I mean, I'm sure he told you everything anyway, but his clients must be completely adrift without him, especially the ones with unfinished deals."

Victoria's eyebrows knitted together. "It'll all work out."

"I didn't mean that in a negative way. I'm royally screwing this up, aren't I? Warren's accounts are none of my business. Forget I said anything. Let me try this again. I wanted to check on you, and I'm glad you're okay." She mirrored Victoria's tone. "I also need the minutes from the last HOA meeting. Do you happen to have the hard copy?"

The sudden shift from Warren's work to mundane HOA tidying was unnerving. "Yeah, I think they're upstairs; I'll go grab them. Just a sec."

"Great," Betty smiled. "Can I use your restroom while I wait?"

Victoria couldn't help herself. "Too many energy drinks?"

Betty's face sobered. "Hydration is important. Where is it again?"

"Second door on the left."

Betty thanked her and padded down the hall. The gentle snick of the door was soon replaced by the rush of water. Victoria waited a beat then jogged up the stairs. HOA minutes were typically recorded online; the people of Kent Wood Manor were staunch advocates of climate change reform and wouldn't dare waste paper. She'd only taken notes at the last meeting to keep from being bored to tears. Having a unified set of rules was one thing; the controversial finish of a decorative railing the Sparrows had installed was not the next great war the board was making it out to be.

She rifled through the stack of papers on her nightstand, tossing an errant receipt into the trash. Her phone buzzed with a notification as she searched through her purse. The memo pad was tucked into the side pocket, half-bent but legible. Stuffing it in the crook of her elbow, Victoria reached for her phone and froze when she saw a new message from X.

DON'T TRUST HER.

Maybe she shouldn't be putting stock into the texts of a supposed killer, but Victoria heeded X's warning. Red flags had been waving since Betty knocked, she realized with a calming sort of certainty. Instead of addressing the itching apprehension of *how did he know she was here*, Victoria embraced the validation.

Hustling downstairs, she found the kitchen empty and silent, shadows of tree branches dancing on the walls. She tiptoed through the foyer and peered down the hall. Listening. The bathroom door stood ajar. She inched forward and pushed it slightly to avoid the squeaky hinge, which proved to be entirely unnecessary.

With her back to Victoria, Betty emerged from Warren's office, pulling the door shut as quietly as Victoria was trying to do.

"Feeling better?"

Betty screeched. "Shit, you scared me. Yes, sorry. I—"

"What were you doing in Warren's office?" Victoria asked.

"I—got lost. Are those the minutes?"

"Yup," Victoria said, handing them over.

Betty snatched them and rushed toward the front door, her yellow sneakers flashing against the neutral accents of Victoria's home. A trapped animal scampering for escape. "Thank you for these. I know you're busy, so let me get out of your hair."

"Already? Sure I can't interest you in a cup of coffee?"

"I've got an appointment," Betty said. "Next time. We'll go to Lorenzo's and properly catch up. I'm sorry for your loss, Victoria. We're here if you need anything."

Betty whipped outside and Victoria trailed behind her, like the killer in a scary movie chasing the Final Girl.

Betty Knottier was absolutely not a Final Girl.

"Betty?" she called. It didn't escape her that a handful of neighbors were watching their interactions.

Betty's shoulders flung up to her ears, but she turned slowly. Waiting.

"Don't let me catch you near my home again."

A rebuttal didn't come, and Victoria was spared of making a bigger scene than she already had. Betty flushed deep red and scowled, speeding down the path without another word. Victoria's gaze burned into her back as she retreated, purposely ignoring the inquisitive stares.

Warren's office appeared undisturbed, tidy and warm. If anything was missing, she couldn't tell, but she wouldn't make assumptions.

She had put Betty in her place, but the question remained.

What had she been looking for?

32

A week after her husband's service, Victoria sat at his gigantic I'm-overcompensating-for-something mahogany desk preparing to sign the final documents that would confirm her appointment as interim CEO of Livingston Corporation.

The investigation was ongoing, but Livingston obviously couldn't function without a leader, so the board members had convened with a unanimous vote.

Victoria Tate, CEO.

She should've been ecstatic, even if there was a temporary asterisk attached; years of hard work were finally coming to fruition. This was everything she'd wanted.

And yet, as she signed the final line in a dress as black as the one she'd worn at Warren's memorial, passing the papers to the board rep wearing too much cologne and not enough deodorant, Victoria's thoughts turned once more to X.

There hadn't been any more texts since Betty's visit, but the silence was just as ominous. Victoria wasn't stupid enough to believe that that was the end of it. X was waiting. Deliberately holding out to make her sweat. To force her to make a mistake.

A clever tactic, one she'd employed numerous times herself.

She debated going to the police for all of two seconds before deciding that was a terrible idea. The spouse was always a suspect. While her alibi had helped, Detective Meyers was still asking too many questions. Broadcasting an incriminating photo of herself seemed like a guaranteed way to be put in an interrogation room—or a jail cell.

No police.

Victoria was wearing a slim-fit two-piece tangerine suit that Warren had never liked, tapered at the ankles and sexy as hell, if she said so herself. Perfect for day one as the head of Livingston.

With a handshake and a thanks, the board rep was dismissed and she was left alone in Warren's office.

Her office.

She hadn't expected the space to feel different. How many times had she stood in this same spot over the years? The bookshelves hadn't changed, the photos, the mounted accolades. But nothing was the same. This was hers now, and that meant something. A fundamental shift.

Behind the desk, three floor-to-ceiling windows overlooked the city center. The streets below were crowded and bustling. People going about their business, unaware they were being watched.

Was one of them X? she wondered.

Was he watching her now?

X would have to be dealt with, but that would have to wait until later. Victoria had bigger concerns, like undoing the many mistakes Warren had made in his tenure. She opened her laptop, eager to get to work. Victoria had ideas, and for the first time in her life no one was standing in her way.

A knock on the door interrupted her thoughts. Victoria turned to find Jeff. He'd opted for full business casual today, a trouser and button-down combo that was a little too clean-cut to be effortless.

"Victoria," he smiled. "Got a minute?"

"Less than. I'm due in the conference room."

Her first official client meeting was with the Connors, because of course it was. Barnaby wanted reassurances, Margaret wanted what Barnaby wanted (if only to keep his wallet greased and ready), and Victoria wanted the chance to observe them without their perfectly curated security detail. Home field advantage was a huge perk.

"I won't keep you," Jeff said, stuffing his hands in his pockets. "Just wanted to be the first to offer my congratulations to the new boss."

"Thank you, Jeff."

"No hard feelings on my end."

"Glad to hear it," she said. "You were a strong contender."

The candidate pool had been small, and Victoria hadn't been surprised to learn that the board had narrowed it down to the two of them. Climbing the corporate ladder was Jeff's real job, and Judy had informed her that he'd taken the news hard.

Punched the wall in Boardroom C, was actually how she put it, but Victoria wasn't going to split hairs. At least he'd wrapped his knuckles well. How he explained the injury to his clients was his problem.

"Crazy how quickly that vote came back. We all expected it to take longer, but I guess when you know you know. Don't worry. You'll do great until they find the permanent replacement."

That's *not transparent at all,* she thought.

"Excuse me." She pressed the com button on the desk phone, holding up a finger in pause and smiled at Judy's voice.

"Yes, Mrs. Tate?"

"Would you link me to the most recent docs Warren had for the Connors? They aren't showing up in my Drive."

"Of course. I'll get right on that."

"Thank you, I appreciate it."

"You know, Warren and I discussed how to handle the Connors moving forward." Jeff approached the desk, already reaching for her laptop. "Their new earnings structure and the updated investment portfolio—"

Victoria deftly shut the screen, stopping him in his tracks. "I've got it covered."

"I was just going to show you how we were doing the spreadsheet. Warren was particular when it came to the Connors."

"I'm sure he was, but this is my account now, and I'll proceed in my own way."

"But is that the best way? War always said your strategies were on the safe side, and you can't play nice when you're dealing with Barnaby's investors."

Why was it that the men in her circle had a bottomless supply of audacity? "Well, *War's* not here anymore. Is he? I am."

Jeff crossed his arms, expression unreadable. "For now. I have it on good authority that the board is considering its options. Warren's death was . . . tragic." He let the word hang.

Victoria rose, rounding her desk and holding his gaze. He was a few inches taller, but in that moment, she towered over him. "Jeff, as far as you're concerned, I am the authority."

"Right. Well. I've got a client waiting in B." Mood sufficiently tense, Jeff straightened, rolling his shoulders back and widening his stance. "Good luck, Vic."

She couldn't stop the shudder that ran through her body. Jeff didn't miss it either, if the predatory smile plastered on his smug face as he walked out of the office was any indication.

"Prick," she muttered, but she couldn't shake the unease left in the wake of their exchange.

33

Pushing Jeff out of her thoughts, Victoria settled into her work. She hadn't seen the Connors since the memorial reception. They'd showed up late with three gourmet food trucks in tow. *It's nothing, darling,* Margaret had swooned. *More than happy to help. Good food heals bad blood.* And when Victoria's face had contorted in response, Margaret had added, *The sashimi special was Warren's favorite.*

As if Victoria hadn't known that. As if Margaret had known Warren better because they'd shared a raw fish plate over tax records.

Concentrating on the charts on the screen, Victoria created a list of questions that needed answering, noting the areas where Warren was missing essential information.

The Connors arrived not ten minutes later, resplendent in matching designer suits that had her cringing in secondhand embarrassment. Toddlers wore matching outfits, much like Victoria and Teagan had been forced to for their many staged family portraits. Married couples? Barnaby was missing the Louboutins, opting instead for a pocket scarf with red piping, but the whole vibe read as, *My wife picked my clothes.*

Nevertheless, she wouldn't be swayed by their wardrobe choices. Appearances were deceiving, and underestimating the Connors was a surefire way to make a mistake.

Victoria didn't make mistakes.

"Hello, Margaret. Barnaby," she said, standing to meet them.

"Good to see you," Margaret said, clutching Victoria's elbows. "You look well, Victoria. How are you coping?"

"Fine. Appreciate you asking, though." She did wonder how long people were going to keep the kid gloves on whenever Warren was mentioned in conversation, but at least they weren't pointing fingers.

"We've been in contact with the detective. Briana Mayer?"

"Meyers." Maybe she'd spoken too soon.

"Yes," Margaret continued. "I have to admit, we weren't prepared for the level of attention that Warren's . . . passing has put upon us."

Sorry for the inconvenience, she almost replied. Not that she had anything to apologize for; she hadn't been the one to play Ghostface in the courtyard. And she really didn't like that her first inclination was to appease Margaret.

"If only he'd been able to choose where the killer attacked," Victoria said instead. "Location is everything."

Barnaby made a noise in the back of his throat and scratched his nose. Was that nerves or discomfort?

"Oh, Victoria, no. I didn't mean—I wasn't trying to "

Watching Margaret fumble over her words was a beautiful thing.

"They have several promising leads," she said, scrutinizing their expressions with her own razor-sharp condemnation.

"Really?" Barnaby asked, perking up. "What have you heard?"

"Only what Detective Meyers has told me."

"Has she mentioned the guest list? Have our names come up?"

Margaret elbowed him in the side, as subtle as a battering ram. "Perhaps we should focus on the business at hand?" she said, tone thick with shut-your-mouth-you-idiot energy. "We are sorry for your loss, don't get me wrong, but now is neither the time nor place to be discussing such a personal matter. We'd like to review your proposal, right Barnaby?"

Interesting, she thought. *Very interesting.*

One thing was certain: They weren't going to confess to anything in this environment. Not with Margaret in charge and the possibility of someone else overhearing.

Barnaby slowly nodded, the unspoken language between husband and wife finally translating. "Yes. The proposal. You *are* ready, correct?"

Victoria didn't miss the inflection. It was smart, turning the spotlight on her. Trying to catch her unprepared. This, however, was the kind of pressure in which she thrived. "Of course. Follow me."

Laptop in hand, she ushered Barnaby and Margaret down the hall toward the first conference room. She'd reserved the biggest—she was CEO; she could do that now without fighting over pecking order—and waited for them to take their seats while the projector screen rolled into place.

For the next little while, the world was lost to data and projections. First day with a title or not, Victoria was damn good at presenting her findings. What she hadn't anticipated was the updated information in the missing docs. She stalled while she read the numbers, asking benign questions about expenditures while she sorted through a plan of attack.

Warren had almost permanently screwed the Connors' account. Why wouldn't he have filed the incorporation articles with the state by the deadline? Such a simple—

"Mrs. Tate?"

"Hm?" Victoria acknowledged, not looking up from the document. She was used to Judy dropping in on meetings.

"I hate to interrupt."

The wariness in Judy's voice and Margaret's surprised gasp broke her concentration. She turned to the bright red of Judy's hair before noticing the woman standing behind her.

"Detective Meyers is here."

34

B riana Meyers was dressed in her usual uniform, as Victoria had begun to think of it: open peacoat, dark jeans, and an ill-fitting button-down. She wondered if those were department mandated or if Meyers refused to buy flattering clothes.

Either way, an unannounced visit from the lead detective working her husband's homicide was less than ideal.

"Detective Meyers, hello," she said, minimizing the browser.

"Mrs. Tate. Mr. and Mrs. Connors."

"Hello, Detective," Margaret said. "Good to see you again."

"To what do I owe this visit?"

Judy backed out of the doorway and scurried to her desk. No doubt to spread the word that Meyers had made another appearance. Wonderful.

"Can we speak privately for a moment, Mrs. Tate? Promise it won't take long."

Margaret and Barnaby exchanged a look between them while Victoria rose and followed Meyers into the hallway. They didn't speak on the way to her office, but she didn't miss how Meyers inspected the happenings around her as they passed.

Victoria shut the door and sat in the chair behind her desk. Meyers took the leather seat across from her, tiny notebook already in hand. Despite the confidence she was clearly trying to portray, she looked uncomfortable. Like she didn't belong in this environment with its designer suits and expensive accents.

"I wasn't aware you worked with the Connors," she said.

"Barnaby was one of Warren's first clients," Victoria said. "Since he's no longer able to handle their concerns, I've inherited the account."

"Fancy way to say your husband is no longer alive," Meyers said.

"Death is a rather taboo subject for the office. We can't all work in Homicide."

"I suppose not."

"I gather that's why you're here? Has something happened with Warren's case?"

Meyers let her gaze roam the office before landing on Victoria. "I've just come from an interview and I have a few follow-up questions that I wanted to ask you," she said.

This couldn't be done over the phone? Victoria thought. Meyers had follow-ups after many of her interviews, it seemed. She double-checked witness statements and details about the Gala that others reported. None of it seemed relevant, and most of it was handled at scheduled times.

"Must be some important questions if you had to come all the way downtown," she said.

"I find that it's better to have these conversations face-to-face. So much is lost in translation when you can't see the other person you're talking to. Besides, gives me a chance to grab a beef patty from the corner store off State Street. Best in the area."

"I'll take your word for it," Victoria said, because despite the disdain she harbored for her mother's rigorous and toxic dieting habits, she couldn't bring herself to buy street food from the same place people got scratch-offs.

"Anyway." Meyers shook off the awkward transition. "Like I said: I know you're busy. Doubt you want to keep the Connors waiting. Just a few questions that need clearing up, and then I'll be out of your hair."

"Of course." The few seconds allowed her to calm the nerves tingling through her body. Flexing her fingers into a loose grasp on the armrests, she let the detective take the lead, reminding herself that she had nothing to hide. She hadn't killed Warren. She was innocent.

Well, innocent was a stretch, but she wasn't guilty either. She also wasn't prepared for what Meyers said next.

"Tell me about your relationship with Scott Morton."

35

A trap.

    Victoria chewed the corner of her lip, waiting for further explanation. Meyers returned her stare, seemingly content to wait even longer. At a stalemate, Victoria conceded, hedging her bets to see where Meyers would take this. "I don't know a Scott Morton."

Meyers's expression rounded into skepticism. "Are you sure about that?"

"One hundred percent? No, that's impossible. I meet a lot of people through networking events, fundraisers, business inquiries," Victoria supplied. "But the name doesn't sound familiar, so if I have, in fact, had some interaction with this Scott Morton, I don't readily remember him."

"Mm."

Mm? What was that supposed to mean? "From your ambiguous response, I take it that I should. Or you were expecting a different answer from me."

"Have you been faithful in your marriage, Mrs. Tate?"

"Didn't you ask me this already?"

"I asked if Warren had been seeing someone else."

She may not have wanted Meyers to figure out X's identity before she had a chance to safeguard herself, but Victoria had to wonder about the quality of the policework going into this investigation if this was the best line of questioning. An affair? There were other ways to address infidelity that didn't involve multiple stab wounds. People killed for more than love.

"It's just a question. I'm not judging one way or the other. Hell, I had a case last year where the wife and girlfriend of the victim not only knew about each other but supported their respective relationships. They planned the funeral together. Polyamory is much more common than you'd think."

Victoria closed her eyes. She wasn't offended, but she could see Meyers stretching the truth to fit a narrative, some modern, progressive idea of marriage. It was an admirable attempt, but like hell would she play into the Black Widow motive.

"I never cheated on Warren," she said. "Neither of us had boyfriends or girlfriends or whatever other . . . arrangement you're getting at. Why are you asking?"

It was Meyers's turn to withhold her emotions, slipping beneath a veil of practiced disinterest. "Yesterday morning we interviewed Scott Morton."

A calculated pause grew between them as Meyers waited for her reaction, to which Victoria had none.

"Okay? And? I still don't know who that is."

"Mr. Morton was hired by the Connors as an entertainer for the Gala." She glanced down at her notebook, a performative glitch if Victoria had ever seen one. "A jester."

Victoria ran through the memories of that night with a silent groan. The clown with the grabby hands? "Yes, okay, I remember him. He was sending people inside to greet Margaret and Barnaby. Telling gross jokes and dancing."

"This was your only interaction with him?"

"If you can call that an interaction."

"So you didn't attack Mr. Morton?"

"Attack?" Victoria said, unable to hide the note of aggression. She breathed deep and forced her voice to remain calm. If Meyers was trying to provoke her, it wouldn't work. "That man blocked my exit and shoved his head into my lap; if anything, he assaulted me. Somebody in line helped to pull him off, and, yes, as we separated, I hit him with my purse. Nothing that would leave a mark. I didn't attack him."

"Did you file a police report?"

"I did not."

"Is that how you frequently deal with stressful situations?" Meyers asked, tapping the pen on her knee. "Somebody makes an untoward advance and you . . . lash out?"

Victoria absorbed the pointed edge of the question and the insinuation behind it. Warren had defaulted to this argument style often: belittling her emotions, using her own words against her to highlight that she was either being overdramatic or emotional. Not quite gaslighting, but uncomfortably close.

"I don't put myself in situations where an aggressive man touches me inappropriately to entertain a room full of strangers. I was shocked and clearly didn't react as I normally would. What's next, Detective Meyers? Are you going to ask me what I was wearing? If I'd done anything to warrant the jester's advances? How about my sexual history?"

Meyers raised her hands in defense. "That's not what this is."

"Could've fooled me."

"Look, I've been on the other side of this and know how it feels, so give me a break, all right? I'm sorry if I offended you. That wasn't my intention, but I had to ask."

"Why?"

Meyers leaned slightly onto the armrest. "This morning, before we met with Mr. Morton, another witness came forward with new evidence. They claim that this was a lover's spat."

"What witness? Who told you that?" she asked. In hindsight she probably should've denied the accusation before countering with her own questions. "They're lying."

"I can't disclose my sources."

"Well, your sources are bullshit," she said defiantly. "There was no lover's spat. I'm not sleeping with Mr. Morton. I hadn't met him before the Gala, and I truly hope to never have reason to meet him again."

Meyers reached into her pocket. She presented Victoria with a copy of a photo, the colors faded from the printer ink but vibrant enough to make out the details.

The purple of her gown stood out against the black dresses and tuxedos, and if that hadn't given her away, the shimmer of the lynx mask would have. Victoria leaned against the wall, head tilted as if she was searching for something.

Or someone. She recognized the hallway between the bar and the Connors' throne room. This was taken before she'd found Warren. Approaching her was a man in a familiar red-and-green costume, much too close and staring. From the angle, it looked like their eyes were locked. His hand slightly brushing against hers.

It wasn't damning, by any means, but Victoria could see that with the wrong person dictating where to look, this moment between them could seem like more. A torrid love affair in the wings. It wouldn't take much to fabricate a story like that in Kent Wood Manor.

"You said you didn't know him." Meyers pushed the picture closer.

"I don't know him. We were passing in the hall; I don't even remember seeing him before I got in line to greet the Connors. This is circumstantial, at best."

"Circumstantial?" Meyers asked, amusement tinging the word. "I swear, you watch one episode of *Law and Order* and suddenly you're an expert?"

"That picture proves nothing because there is nothing to prove. I do not know Scott Morton. I was looking for Warren. Who took this photo?" Victoria asked.

"Again, I'm not at liberty to—"

"Was it the same person who gave it to you?"

"I can't tell you that either, Mrs. Tate. The investigation is—"

"Was it Betty Knottier?" Victoria cut in. Meyers had a decent poker face, she gave her that, but the spark of recognition played across her features before she could hide it. That didn't necessarily mean anything; Meyers could've been responding to the name itself, but it was hard to dismiss the knot forming in her gut.

Was X Betty? Or was X using Victoria's distrust to trip her up?

Victoria's phone vibrated beside her on the desk. The text box made her stomach drop.

Congratulations on your first day back! :) Enjoy your welcome gift.

Had smiley faces always been so ominous? What did X mean by "welcome gift"? It had to be Meyers accusing her of the affair, right? To make her look bad.

". . . whatever it takes to find the person who murdered your husband. Victoria?"

"Hm?" Victoria didn't look up as another message came through. A gray box with a stopwatch icon appeared beneath the words. Tap to Download, it commanded.

Well, no way in hell was she opening that. Nope. Victoria wasn't stupid.

She tapped the screen.

A glutton for punishment, she was. Nothing good was going to come from this, but the fear of the unknown trumped whatever X had planned. A virus. Spyware.

The progress flew from one to twenty to ninety-nine percent before freezing. Victoria hit the home button, the power button, tried to force a restart, but nothing worked. The screen stayed stuck. She was about to smash it into the wall (and come up with an explanation for why she'd Hulked out in front of Meyers like a hypocrite or flat-out liar) when the buffering circle vanished.

At the same time, from somewhere down the hall came a shrill scream.

36

S tartled and confused, they ran toward the source of the scream. Judy and several other members of the administrative team were huddled around the conference room where Victoria had left the Connors.

This couldn't be good.

"Is everyone all right?" Meyers asked, hand hovering around her waist. Victoria wondered if she had ever fired her weapon before. Her voice was calm, a commanding presence in the unfolding chaos. She searched the growing crowd for signs of distress before finally entering the conference room. Margaret was curled up into Barnaby's chest, muffling her cries. "Mrs. Connors, are you—"

Meyers halted mid-sentence as her eyes landed on the projector screen. Victoria stared, unable to move.

Her husband's severed eyes sat on an ivory silk pocket square. It had been a gift from his mother before his junior prom. She'd stitched his initials into the corner of the fabric with the caveat that every gentleman worth his salt had a proper kerchief. Victoria had lost track of how many times he'd told that anecdote over the years.

Warren wore it to every formal event. In the aftermath of the murder, it hadn't occurred to her that it might be missing. She hadn't seen his suit under the robes he'd been wearing that night. And even if she had, who notices pocket squares anymore?

She shouldered past Meyers, her limbs numb and buzzing. Meyers's voice was nothing more than a hollow sound, the distant wail of an animal, as she barked orders into her phone. Drawn to the screen, Victoria raised a hand into the light and brought it to the image.

A gif appeared above, a winking face but with the eyes scratched black. The words WELCOME HOME, VIC blinked in time with the action, the letters plain but no less threatening.

X was making his position clear. The picture was a warning. It was time for Victoria to make her move.

37

The sun had already dipped below the tall pines standing sentry at the gate of Kent Wood Manor when Teagan pulled into Victoria's driveway. The sky wasn't quite pitch black yet; a smattering of clouds was still visible against the sapphire backdrop. The hazy transition between twilight and full dark was Victoria's favorite time of day. Good or bad, anything could happen in the shadows.

Victoria sat waiting on the porch with a thick shawl wrapped around her shoulders, her eyes moving from house to house on the quiet street. Every lamppost, porch, and security light blazed, as if the illumination could shield those within from danger. One of their own had been murdered, those lights revealed, and they were afraid. Afraid that death was contagious, that the real world was a little too close to their filtered existences.

Maybe they should be afraid, she thought. The illusion of safety was more comfort than she had.

Teagan was red-cheeked and shivering as she walked up the path. "What are you doing out here?" she asked. Her breath puffed out in white clouds.

"Needed some fresh air," Victoria said, standing to wipe the seat of her leggings. She'd neglected her usual chores because of the added time spent at Livingston—and the whole killer-stalking-her thing. Dead leaves crumpled and skittered across the porch. The HOA would have a field day with fines if she didn't find time to sweep in the next few days.

"I'm all for cryotherapy, but can we get me a cup of coffee first?" Teagan asked.

"Afraid your ass will fall off?"

"More like your face'll get stuck in that horrible scowl."

"Cute," Victoria said.

"I think I'm adorable." Teagan followed her into the house, dropping her coat and scarf on the occasional chair and kicking off her boots. "What's with the running gear?"

Victoria hung up her shawl and frowned at the gift basket. "Betty," she spat, as if the name was explanation enough. "Sympathy leggings."

"That's not a thing."

"It is when you're a nosy neighbor hell-bent on spreading half-truths disguised as kindness." Victoria padded to the kitchen, setting a pot of water on the stove. "You got here fast."

"Finished my consultation twenty minutes early," Teagan said, tugging at the hem of her oversized sweater. Pastel pink wasn't a color she chose often, but Victoria thought it was a nice change of pace from the rigid black-on-black Teagan preferred. "What do you mean 'nosy neighbor'? What did Jessica Rabbit's sketchy understudy do?"

"Caught her snooping through the house when she thought I was preoccupied." She hoped her body language read nonchalant because she really didn't want to get into this with Teagan before she laid out everything else. "You know how it is here; everybody in each other's business. Anyway, it's handled. How'd your consultation go?"

"Huh." Teagan looked like she wanted to say more but rolled with the flow. "Ah, you know. Egotistical husband who's super on board with his wife's lipo but doesn't want to listen to me about her aftercare. I swear to god, the next man to ask me if 'I'm *really* a doctor' is going to get my credentials stapled to his dick."

"That'd be a sight," Victoria joked, fiddling with the hair at the nape of her neck. The ends had started to grow out and it was a little less choppy than on the night of the Gala, but the scratching sensation still surprised her.

"I don't know if it's because I'm pretty or because I'm a woman, but the guy tonight expected me to Vanna White through the op room in a bikini holding a cigar and bottle of brandy while his wife's anesthesia wore off. Like I'd ever sleep with a patient or their spouse."

"Teagan."

"Again. Fine. You know what, Christ, I told you that in confidence, and it was one time. Doesn't even count. Anyway," she said, abruptly changing the subject. "What's going on? What do we need to talk about that's so important I had to rush here in person?" She sat at the table and stretched her lower back with a satisfying crack. "I'll be pissed if this could've been an email."

"And here I was thinking you were enjoying being a pain in my ass."

"I mean if you want to talk Brazilians . . ."

"Where should I begin?" Victoria asked loudly so Teagan would drop this ancient argument.

"How about, why are you boiling water for tea in a saucepot? Might as well put it in the microwave," Teagan said.

Victoria shrugged. "It works."

"Heathen."

"Flatterer." Victoria winked, sticking two bags in matching ceramic mugs.

"First snark and now a tea party. Wow, we really are acting like sisters."

"Even a broken clock." Victoria poured the steaming water from the pot to the brim of each mug, ignoring Teagan's chides about their mother rolling over in her grave. "Do you want milk and sugar?"

"Will that make it semi-tolerable?"

"Shot of Baileys?"

"I knew you were my favorite sister," Teagan said.

Despite the banter and Teagan's chipper mood, Victoria couldn't shake the feeling of stress lurking beneath the surface. Jaw clenched and shoulders taut, she offered a weak excuse of a smile. "You're ridiculous."

"You love me."

"Remains to be seen," Victoria said. "Baileys is on the bar cart in the office if you want to grab it. Otherwise, you get what you get."

Teagan saluted and padded down the hall, leaving Victoria to once again sort through her competing thoughts. On the one hand, she wanted to be able to confide in someone. At least when Warren was alive she'd had a sounding board. Talking to herself was a poor substitute because her every instinct was to go on full offensive until X was found and destroyed.

Because destroy him, she would.

On the other hand, how could she trust someone who'd had an entire lifetime to earn it and had routinely disappointed her? Victoria had been confident in her ability to handle Warren on her own. X, however, was a wild card.

Teagan returned a minute later with the wide-eyed stare of someone who'd just witnessed a hit-and-run. "When were you going to tell me that you turned Warren's office into page forty of a Pottery Barn catalogue?"

While she'd been negligent of the outdoor chores, rearranging the home office had been necessary—and not just because Betty Knotticr had taken it upon herself to play Nancy Drew. She'd taken inventory as she'd cleaned out the room, but nothing had jumped out at her as missing. Being surrounded by Warren's scent and awards and photographs in the midst of everything else was too distracting. Not because she was overly sentimental, but because those things served as a constant reminder of her shortcomings.

Warren was dead, but she hadn't pulled the proverbial trigger.

Victoria pinched her lips together. "I wasn't aware I needed your approval to redecorate my own home."

"Where's all of Warren's stuff?"

"Packed up."

"Isn't that a little soon?"

Victoria blew steam from her mug, increasingly irritated by her sister's blunt line of questioning. "You tell me since your nose job certificate apparently came with a degree in grief management. What's the *appropriate* amount of time to wait before I can set up my own workspace after my husband is stabbed to death at a party?"

"It just seems rushed," Teagan said. Her "doctor voice" was meant to be placating but pissed Victoria off even more. She didn't want to be dealt with like one of Teagan's fragile patients, but her sister leaned into it, a mask of professionalism acting as a barrier. "You know, they say you shouldn't make any major changes for the first two years after a significant loss. I don't want you to do something you'll regret."

What was it called when you regretted the thing you didn't get to do?

"Maybe you should try minding your own business," Victoria said.

"Figures that's your response for everything."

"Parentification doesn't look good on you. I'm a grown woman and your big sister, and I'm mourning. None of those are qualifications for you to shrink me."

Teagan sighed. "I wasn't trying to start a fight, Tor. I just want to make sure that you're not pushing too hard. You tend to go balls to the wall when you're stressed."

"I do not go *balls to the wall*," she said, affronted.

"You keep baby wipes in your desk in case you stay overnight, which means: one, it happens enough that you know you need baby wipes, and two, you'd rather run numbers at work than go home and shower."

"It's practical," Tor said defensively.

"It's insane."

"You're insane."

"The comeback queen, ladies and gentlemen." Teagan deflected. "As enjoyable as this has been, can we skip to the part where you tell me why I'm here?"

Right. Every muscle in Victoria's stomach tightened as she grappled with the decision. To confide or to hide? *Shakespeare, eat your heart out,* she thought.

Teagan looked at her with naked curiosity, and in that second Victoria found herself reciprocating. She leaped with her gut and tucked her chin against the fall.

"I think someone's trying to kill me."

38

They were too old for scary stories, but that didn't keep the
déjà vu from washing over Victoria like a salty wave. On
cold October nights when their father refused to turn the heat
on, Victoria and Teagan would curl up together under a large
flannel blanket, a flashlight casting shadows across their faces.
Trading stories like that became a tradition, a ritual of sorts,
each sister trying to out-scare the other by upping the blood or
gore. They had nothing to gain from the fear but their pride.
Still, Victoria believed that was reason enough.

She wasn't sure X wanted her dead, but she needed Teagan to
be afraid—to not brush her off as overreacting.

"You're joking," Teagan said, mug frozen halfway between
the table and her mouth. When Victoria twisted her face in exasperation, Teagan's mood turned serious. "What do you mean
someone's trying to kill you?"

Better. Victoria let a measured silence give weight to her words.
"I got a message today."

"Are you going to continue to be vague? From whom?"

"He calls himself X."

"How original," she deadpanned to the unamused audience of
Victoria's impatience. "Okay . . . and what did this X have to say?"

What didn't he say, was perhaps the better question.

Instead of removing herself from the suspect list, Victoria had managed to secure a spot in the maybe murdered Warren Tate lineup. Following the projector incident at Livingston, she'd been forced to admit to Meyers that she'd been targeted by someone she believed to be Warren's killer. She'd managed to withhold the original messages, deleting the evidence from her inbox, but her story was flimsy. Meyers had seen right through her lie when she'd said X hadn't contacted her before the picture appeared on the projector. Sooner or later, she would have a whole different set of questions to answer. Why hadn't she come forward with the threats? Why had X come after her?

What was she hiding?

And that was the question, wasn't it? What *was* she hiding? She hadn't actually murdered Warren.

It was the appearance of guilt that worried her. After X had sent the first picture, Victoria had searched her bedroom top to bottom and had come up empty-handed. Googling for answers had been as useful as WebMDing a headache. Spytech had come a long way since the 007 days. Even teddy bear cameras were a thing of the past. Apparently, they made lenses as small as pinheads, and anyone could buy them.

Victoria had diligently inspected every book, picture frame, and knickknack but found nothing. If there had been a camera, it was gone now. Which meant that not only had X been watching her for longer than she cared to imagine, but he also had most likely been in her home since Warren's death.

Unfortunately, that implicated pretty much everyone in Kent Wood Manor and the surrounding areas. Not to mention Betty, Margaret and Barnaby, Jeff—why hadn't she been more selective?

She really needed to install a security system. Invest in one of those doorbell cams at the very least. That was a problem for later, however. Right now, Victoria had to deal with her sister.

Victoria crossed the room and yanked her phone from the charger. Unlocking the screen, she shoved the phone at Teagan, who slow-blinked like she'd never seen a phone before. "You saved him to your contacts?"

"Meyers told me to, but it's probably a burner, so it doesn't matter," she said dismissively. "Just read."

"Fine."

Victoria knew the moment she'd seen the image. Teagan turned the phone over and pushed it across the table. Unscrewing the cap, she drank directly from the Baileys, her throat chugging the sweet liqueur.

"You okay?"

"You could've given me a heads up."

"Don't you get elbows-deep in entrails every day? Didn't think you'd need a content warning."

"Do you ever stop?" She drank again and released the bottle with a loud smack, wiping her mouth with a shaky hand. "You said they'd been cut out, but you didn't . . . you didn't tell me his eyes were *missing*."

"I didn't know. Meyers didn't say anything, so I assumed they were stored in evidence or whatever medical examiners do with body parts after autopsies."

"Medical waste." Teagan hunched into herself, rubbing her temples.

Victoria took the seat across from her. Of the two, she'd always had the best posture, straight as an arrow, but now exhaustion pummeled her bones. She plopped down and slouched, too tired for dramatics but eager to keep the momentum going. "They think he kept the eyes as a trophy. Killers do that sometimes. To relive the "*thrill*" moment later. X is also apparently some sort of tech genius. Not only did he send—" She cut herself off, not wanting to divulge anything about the previous texts. Not yet.

"Send what?" Teagan asked, drowsily raising her head.

"That photo," she said quickly. "Of Warren's eyes. He sent that, but he also somehow hacked into Livingston's system and put it on the projector in the conference room. You should've seen Margaret."

"Margaret Connors? What does she have to do with this?"

"I had an account review with Barnaby and they were in the conference room when X broadcasted his horror show."

"Jesus. Everyone's going to know about this, you realize that, right, Tor?"

Victoria sucked her teeth. "I've gotten a handful of texts from neighbors already. Also, luckily for me, Detective Meyers was already there. Didn't even have to wait for the cops to show up."

"Why was Meyers there?"

"That's not important; I handled it. Either way, she saw the photo and knows about X, but she's clearly not one hundred percent convinced that I'm not behind it."

Teagan scrunched her nose in confusion, leaning an elbow on the table. "She thinks that you, what? Texted it to yourself to prove a point? Did you even know she was coming?"

"No, but it was a weird coincidence. Too convenient."

A noise of agreement, and then, "Is this the only time this X has contacted you?"

Victoria took the phone back and held it in her lap. *To confide or to hide.* Admitting this wasn't the first text opened a can of rotting worms she wasn't ready to deal with yet. "Yes, this is the only time."

"Wonder how he got your number."

"Even with the firewalls and protective measures, he managed to hack Livingston's system. I doubt finding my info was that hard."

Not to mention he was in my home watching me, she thought with a shudder.

"So . . . what happens now?" Teagan asked.

Deep breath and do it, she thought. This wasn't her third-grade science project where she'd tricked Teagan into licking a battery. The stakes were higher than a spark. "I need your help."

Teagan sputtered, clearly as surprised by Victoria's admission as she was. "Sorry, you need *my* help?"

"Forget it," she backtracked. "Forget I said anything."

"No, no, no—this is—this is good, Tor. Whatever you need. What can I do?"

There was no humor in her response that time, but the urge to withdraw was powerful. Victoria held tight to her earlier instinct to keep from unraveling altogether. "The police think that Warren knew his killer. If X is the killer, and I think that's a strong possibility at this point, then odds are I know him too. I need to make a list of suspects."

Teagan tapped a beat on the table, leveling Victoria with an intense stare. A kaleidoscope of emotions worked her face. "The police are investigating," she said.

"I can't wait for them to figure it out, Teagan. Warren is dead. I've got severed eyes in my inbox." And a killer creeping through my bedroom without a trace. "What about any of this says *take your time and trust the police to do their job*? I have to find him."

"Hold up, Vicki Vigilante," Teagan said. "It's one thing to want justice for Warren, but skirting the police to search for a murderer is reckless. And dangerous. Someone could get hurt. *You* could get hurt."

Victoria shook her head and pressed back into the chair. "We can take care of ourselves. We always have."

"That doesn't mean we should."

"And from what Meyers said earlier, the leads are dead ends. They're going to analyze the photo and try to trace the IP, but X isn't stupid. He's careful and meticulous and clearly three steps ahead of any of us."

"You're talking about him like you know him," Teagan said. "But you don't. Leave it alone, Tor. Let the cops do their job. You don't need to get tangled up in this."

"I'm already tangled. If you were married you might understand."

Teagan winced but recovered quickly. Victoria knew the words would sting. She wanted them to. The need-to-please aspect of Teagan's personality, her desire to be a good daughter and prove her worth to their mother, took the hit.

It was that loyalty to their dead mother that burned Victoria. Teagan kept choosing to pick anyone but Victoria, so if she wasn't going to help, then she wanted Teagan to feel the pain.

"I may not be married," she finally said, "but last I checked, marriage isn't the be-all and end-all of love. You don't have a monopoly on grief here, Victoria. Having a husband doesn't make you better than me. Doesn't give you the right to lash out."

"I don't have a husband," Victoria said. "Not anymore."

"No," Teagan said, her voice increasing in volume. "Warren was stabbed to death. *Mutilated*. His killer is antagonizing you. How are you not getting this? People who go looking for trouble find it. You're lucky this asshole only sent you a picture. What if it had been the actual eyeballs, Victoria? How do you know that won't be next? How do you know *you* won't be next?"

Victoria sipped from her mug and decidedly did not look at her sister.

"What about Livingston? Who's supposed to run the damn company if you get sliced and diced on your quest for vengeance?"

"Jeff would be more than happy to take the reins. Maybe we should start there."

"Tor," Teagan sighed. "Listen to me when I tell you to leave it alone."

"You don't have to help me find him," Tori said. "Just help make the list."

"That's the same damn thing and you know it." Teagan stood and walked away, shaking her head in frustration. With one boot on, she was reaching for the other when Victoria approached: composed and practically brimming with defiant energy.

"You owe me," she said.

Teagan scoffed. "Bullshit."

"You do," she said simply. The truth was rarely simple, but when it was, it was a beautiful weapon. "You were one of the last people to see Warren alive. Maybe the last person. And until now, I haven't had a reason to mention that to Detective Meyers."

Teagan let the boot drop, an unreadable expression crossing her face. She leaned against the doorframe. The window glass must have been cold through her sweater; goose bumps raised on her forearms and she rubbed at them absently.

"We never did talk about where you were that night. What happened after I left the Gala?" Victoria pressed.

"Fine," she said, sounding tired. "I'll help you."

39

Teagan needed to *fortify*, as she put it, so Victoria directed her sister to the basement where she could pilfer their wine reserves to her heart's content while Victoria went upstairs to change. Glasses poured, they set up on the couch in front of a fire roaring and watched the flames dance, each lost in her own thoughts.

"I don't think I've ever had an occasion to think about who would want me dead," Victoria said.

"Congratulations, you've entered your Taylor Swift era." Teagan sipped her wine and clicked the home screen on her phone. She'd done it five times since they'd sat down and Victoria wondered if it was just nerves. The need to do something with her hands.

"Maybe I'll get a snake tattoo to commemorate this outstanding milestone," she joked, drawing a looping line along her wrist with the tip of her finger. "Isn't that what people do? Memorialize their suffering in ink and stories?"

"Someone's been reading poetry again," Teagan hummed. "I swear you were one skull and a little black eyeliner away from being an emo English major."

"This is why half of America is illiterate: people like you shaming others for liking to read."

"Okay, before you start soapboxing your presidential platform, can we refocus? It's getting late and I have a full schedule tomorrow."

"Fine. Okay. So. We need to . . . think about . . . who we know that could've wanted Warren dead."

The good-natured ribbing deflated and they reverted to their quiet reflection, the only sounds the crackling from the fire and the settling of the house.

"It's funny," Teagan said after a moment.

"What is?" Victoria asked.

"Well." Teagan drew her knees to her chest. "Okay, I know this might not be the nicest thing to say."

"Never stopped you before."

"But before Warren died, you guys didn't seem to be on the best terms. Sometimes it seemed like you didn't even *like* him."

"And?"

"*And,*" she continued, "if you had asked me to do something like this before, you know, think of people who'd want Warren dead, I would've put your name at the top of the list."

Victoria tensed. Perhaps Teagan was more observant than she gave her credit for. "Every marriage has issues, Teagan. Couples fight and make up. Go through periods where they can't stand each other and then remember why they fell in love."

"So, love. That's why you're going to all this trouble?" she asked.

Love had little to do with it, she thought, but love was complicated. Had her feelings for him worn thin throughout the years? Sure. Was her desire to find X solely based on self-preservation?

A sliver of doubt worked its way through her tough exterior like a splinter. She wasn't heartless after all.

"Warren didn't deserve to die like that," she said.

"That doesn't exactly answer my question."

"Maybe you're not listening hard enough."

"Victoria," Teagan huffed.

"You're not going to let this go, are you?"

"When have I ever taken the easy way out?"

Victoria curled her legs beneath her on the couch and balanced the glass on her knee, carefully choosing her words. "Warren and I . . . we may have been in a rough patch, but that doesn't mean I didn't care—that I didn't love him."

"Okay, so you loved him, and that's great," Teagan snapped. "But you can love his memory and stay away from danger now. Seems like a no-brainer. You don't need to chase down a killer to prove anything. Nobody's expecting you to do that, Tor."

"I want answers," she said. Oh, how she wanted answers, just not to the questions that Teagan wanted to ask. "I have so many things I'll never get to say to him."

"But . . . you still won't get to say them," Teagan pressed. "Unless X is a psychic medium."

"I need to know, one way or the other. There's no other option. I need to know who killed him. Period."

"What are you going to do if you find him?" she asked.

Victoria fixated on the flames. That was an interesting question. "Kill him of course."

Teagan's glass faltered on the way to her mouth. "Victoria."

"I'm totally kidding," she said.

"Right," Teagan said.

"I am."

"I believe you," she said quickly.

And yet it didn't sound like Teagan believed her.

She pushed that doubt further into the recesses of her mind. Paranoia lingered at the edges, and Victoria's burgeoning insecurities threatened to engulf her. She didn't like being on unsteady ground. Teagan had no reason to be suspicious. Victoria had done nothing wrong.

"I don't know what I'm going to do when I find him," she admitted. "I haven't gotten that far yet."

"Right," Teagan said. "Sounded like you were serious for a minute."

Their eyes met again, the unspoken words remaining unsaid, carefully tucked away in the dark. Victoria chose to keep them hidden. Sometimes it was better to pretend.

Victoria had already been mentally compiling a list of suspects. The entirety of Kent Wood Manor could make the cut. Between the funeral reception and subsequent drop-ins, everyone had made their way through the front door. The Sparrows. The Knottiers. The Connors. Not to mention the Livingston staff.

But she wanted Teagan's take, so they worked through anyone who might have held a grudge against Warren too. "There's a reason I said we should leave this to the cops," Teagan groaned, stretching the stiff muscles in her neck.

"By your reasoning, aren't they on the list too?"

"A cop would have been smarter about the whole thing."

Victoria tapped her nose. "That's what they want you to think. Maybe it's an elaborate setup."

"What's that saying about the simplest solution? Take off the tin hat and join me on level ground."

Teagan did have a point.

At the end of their brainstorming session, however, they weren't any closer to a viable suspect pool, and Victoria's head was swimming with wine and motives.

Teagan checked her phone and yawned. "It's late, I'm going to head out."

"Could just crash here."

"As much fun as a sleepover sounds, I'm good. Wouldn't want to push my luck. We'll pick this up again tomorrow night. Don't worry."

Victoria walked Teagan to the door and watched her silently put on her boots.

"What?" Teagan asked, shaking into her coat.

"You're a good sister," she said. "I don't tell you that often. Ever, if I'm being honest. I could try harder with us, I know that. I'm sorry. It's just . . . hard. I don't give you enough credit. Thank you for tonight."

With that, she stepped forward and slowly wrapped her arms around Teagan.

A hug. Victoria was hugging her and not spontaneously combusting. Craters didn't open up beneath their feet. She wasn't swallowed into oblivion.

She couldn't remember the last time she'd initiated a physical act of affection with Teagan. With anyone really. When had Warren last hugged her?

It was . . . nice. No, it was fucking strange. But it was also nice, like petting a lion.

"Anytime," she said, patting her back and separating. "Get some sleep, all right?"

"Sure."

"Victoria."

"What?"

"Promise me you'll try to sleep." Teagan opened the door and stepped onto the porch, tightening her coat against the cold.

"Will do."

"Good girl. Drink some water. I'll—"

Teagan's voice dropped off as her gaze settled on the side of the house.

"Teagan? What's wrong?" Victoria was in motion before her head could catch up. The wind cut through the thin material of her leggings, but she hardly noticed when she saw what had drawn Teagan's attention.

Scrawled across the siding in black spray paint, the word KILLER couldn't be missed.

Beside her, Teagan cursed under her breath and paced, ordering Victoria to get back inside. To not touch anything. That she was calling the police.

She stared at the accusation until the outline floated behind her eyelids every time she blinked. It took her a second to realize that the vibration against her leg wasn't anger thrumming through her system but her phone.

One new message from X.

We're only getting started.

40

S leep was something that had never come naturally to Victoria. Either she fell asleep quickly and woke three hours later, or she was unable to quiet her mind to let exhaustion take hold and watched the minutes tick by until the sky lightened the horizon.

Warren's death had exacerbated the issue, but it wasn't guilt keeping her awake. She didn't long for what she and Warren had had, or dwell on what-could-have-beens.

It was X.

The photo. The eyes on the projector screen. The threat at her door.

A tarp covered the damage on her porch until she could hire someone to repaint—the irony hadn't been lost on Victoria as she'd pulled the plastic cover from her murder supplies—but word of the graffiti had already spread. Meyers had shown up within half an hour of Teagan's call. Victoria answered every question and took no comfort in Meyers's reassurance that the neighborhood would be canvassed for security footage or witnesses.

KILLER might as well be tattooed on her forehead. Gossip was as good as scientific fact in Kent Wood Manor.

Victoria counted side-eye glares like sheep as she drove to work. Because there was no time for wallowing. Losing an entire day to police inquiries and statements the day before had already put her behind. The Livingston lawyers had been eager to step in when the employees were interviewed about the hack of company systems, but that meant an hour of additional meetings to jam into her schedule today.

She yawned and texted Judy to double her usual Starbucks order.

Caffeine wouldn't solve all her problems, but it was a damn good place to start. Livingston was a mess, and X wasn't keeping himself a secret anymore.

As she turned off her street, Victoria's thoughts wandered to how X was pulling off these elaborate taunts.

We're only getting started.

He'd probably used a burner to spoof her number, Detective Meyers had said. She didn't understand all the tech lingo they'd thrown at her. Their theory boiled down to the fact that they hadn't gotten a trace. They had no idea who or where X was, and it wasn't likely he'd use the same phone to contact her again.

Victoria assumed that Meyers was also considering the possibility that she'd sent the messages to herself, but she set that aside for the time being. X might have been working with a burner, but Warren's phone was still missing. It hadn't turned up in his car or at the office, or anywhere else since his body was discovered.

Victoria hadn't taken him off the service contract yet. His phone might be switched off, but she could still try. Scrolling her messages with cursory glimpses at the road, she stopped at Warren's thread and tapped out a text.

I'm going to find you.

Why'd you do that, Tori? It's not smart to antagonize the killer, Tori. Don't poke the bear, Tori, Teagan's voice nagged at the back of her mind.

If she wanted a face-lift, she'd listen to Teagan's advice. Until then, Teagan and her subconscious manifestation could kindly screw off.

As she rounded the corner at the end of the block, her phone buzzed in the cupholder.

Warren.

Not Warren, she reminded herself. No matter how hard she tried, a part of her would always whisper truth to the darkest corners of her imagination. Teagan had her scary movies. Victoria had Warren.

Had being the operative word. Warren was dead.

She rolled to the curb and tapped the message, reminding herself that Warren couldn't hurt her. *Dead.*

That would be a mistake, but you're welcome to try. Give it your best shot. Keep your EYE on the prize, amirite?

"Asshole," she muttered. *Why are you doing this?*

Minutes passed. She refreshed the feed. Wrote fifty different follow-ups and deleted them all. X was good at casting his hook. As Victoria set the phone in the cupholder and resigned herself to rejoining morning traffic, X gave his response.

Wait.

41

Teagan's practice was part of an old nondescript brick medical facility ten minutes from Livingston. The interior had been renovated, all clean lines and sterile furnishings. Geometric mirrors dotted the walls in between promotional posters for various cosmetic procedures.

Victoria waited in the lobby as a bleached-blonde receptionist with a swan neck and collarbones so sharp they'd cut a diamond alerted Teagan of her arrival. It was still early, so only a few patients occupied the seats, filling out forms on clipboards while a morning show playing on a mounted flat-screen droned in the background.

As a welcome distraction from her warring thoughts about X, she considered each of them: the circumstances that had brought them to this place, their insecurities or desires. Her own situation with Warren wasn't so different.

There was a flicker of motion from the corner of the room and Teagan appeared, her white jacket flapping and her auburn hair tied neatly in a signature low ponytail. Her makeup was pristine, but the subtle shadows under her eyes betrayed the late night they'd had.

"Tor, what's going on?" she asked, concern flooding her voice. "Come on, we can talk in my office." She motioned for her to follow, leading them down a corridor that smelled faintly of antiseptic and vanilla.

Teagan's office was bright and welcoming. Her framed credentials behind the desk served as the only personal touch that Victoria could see. No pictures, no books, no artwork. Comfortable chairs anchored her desk, which she no doubt used for consultations, but there was also a settee beneath a row of windows that overlooked the city center in the distance, the steel sheen of the Livingston building at the heart of it all.

"I'm surprised you were able to see me," Victoria said, taking the seat closest to the door.

"A few minutes later and I'd be elbow-deep in fatty deposits. What's going on? Everything okay?"

"Yeah, fine. I mean, not fine, but nothing else has happened since you left."

"How are you feeling in the light of day?" Teagan asked, shrugging off her jacket and pulling at the fabric of her pants until they were comfortable.

Jilted. Off-kilter. Pissed. "Okay."

"Obviously," Teagan said with a roll of her eyes.

"I don't know what you want me to say. I'm fine."

"No, you're not."

A knock at the door saved Victoria from having to delve further into that. The thin woman who opened it wore blue scrubs and her corn-silk hair was tucked beneath a patterned cap. "Doc Teags? We're just about ready for you. Are you going to need the extra ring light attachment on the phone today?"

"No, we should be good with the stadium lighting," Teagan said. "Thanks, Tina." With a timid wave, Tina retreated and Teagan focused on Victoria. "Newbie. Basically a groupie, but Glen insisted I hire her."

"Your boss has a type," Victoria said.

"Don't fucking remind me. Whenever I mention the word *diversity* he glazes over until I give up or he can interrupt with a speech about his two black friends from Albany."

"Glen's a dick, Teags. Why do you work here again?"

"Believe me, I'm trying not to," Teagan said. Victoria tilted her head in interest, but her sister pushed on. "Listen, you have every right to be upset about last night. I would be, too, and if I didn't have so much on the books today, I'd say fuck it and take you out for a boozy brunch, but I'm going to be late for surgery."

A clear dismissal if Victoria ever heard one. "I just wanted to tell you that I'm not going to search for X," she said.

"You're not?"

"No."

"Any particular reason?"

"Yes."

"Okayyyy . . ." she said, drawing out the word expectantly. "Care to share with the class?"

"No. At least not yet."

Teagan nodded as she checked her watch and threw her jacket back on. "I'm not disappointed with this turn of events, but what changed?"

Wait. How loaded could a single word possibly be? "We can talk about it later. What are you doing after work?"

"I'm supposed to meet up with this animal doctor for a romp—"

Christ. "You know most people would just call them veterinarians, right?"

"I'm sure they would, but I'm not most people—and I wasn't talking about his profession."

"God, you're gross."

Teagan's tone morphed into faux outrage. "Don't shame me, Victoria Tate, there's nothing wrong with a good dicking."

"How progressive."

"You know, sometimes you sound like Mom," Teagan chided.

"And sometimes you sound like Dad."

Teagan sighed. "Truce."

"Are you coming over or not?" Victoria asked.

"All right. It probably won't be until later-later, though. I really need to release some pent-up energy, if you know what I mean."

"I think a rock would know what you mean. Just be careful. Don't swipe right on someone you haven't already talked to, or agree to meet someone in an alley."

"Sure thing, Dick Tracy."

They headed to the lobby, but Victoria stopped in her tracks, lowering her voice when the blonde ostrich at the reception table looked up. "X is dangerous, like you said. He was a couple feet away from us and we didn't hear a thing. We don't know what he's capable of."

"Right," Teagan said. "He could paint-by-numbers the kitchen next."

"Teagan."

"Okay. Fine. No random trysts. I'll keep to the disco sticks I know."

"You're crazy."

"Lightening the mood," she said with a wink. "I'll call you when I get off. Well, maybe a little after."

"Okay, I'm going to bleach my brain now."

"Have a good day, dear sister," Teagan chuckled.

And she walked to her car, Victoria was determined to do just that.

42

D amage control.

Victoria could sum up her current state of affairs in two words: damage control. When she wasn't running interference against X, she was mopping up the catastrophic tsunami of bullshit that Warren had left in his wake.

His death had sent a ripple through the financial world far beyond sympathy. Although, Victoria wasn't above using that card to her advantage. Former clients paid their respects, and Victoria used those olive branches to lay the groundwork for a fresh start. She mended contracts and sent out proposals, reigniting relationships with finesse and confidence. By noon, thoughts of X and his KILLER branding had faded as Victoria scheduled two closure meetings, arranged lunch presentations with half a dozen new ventures, and drank her weight in coffee.

Damn, it felt good.

After a delicious lardon salad and an order of homemade potato chips from Lorenzo's, Victoria decided it was time to cut the deadweight. She called up HR to expedite approval, and any account executives who weren't on track to make goal by the end of the year were put on performance reviews. It didn't eliminate the perpetual rock in her shoe that was Jeff Blevins, but she figured it was only a matter of time before she drummed up a reason to cut him loose.

Comfort bred complacency, and Victoria had no patience for anyone willing to drag down the company.

Her company.

As the last exec left her office on the brink of tears, Victoria stopped to check in with Judy. For lack of a better word, she looked wrung out. It had been a long day, but she'd never seen the woman look so disheveled: wrinkled shirt, a rip in her stockings, and makeup caked in her forehead creases.

"How's my day tomorrow?" Victoria asked.

"Sales training for the inbound team in the morning, and your afternoon is pretty stacked. You've got two interviews scheduled for the vacant field AE positions and that call with the Austin office."

She nodded, noting her own calendar to review everything before then.

Before she could save the information, a text from X dropped, complete with a photo attachment. Victoria's breath hitched as she opened the message.

DON'T TRUST HER.

The picture was dark but sharp. The background lighting was blurred at the edges, giving the ballroom an ethereal glow as tuxedos and gowns twirled together. The focus, though, was the couple at the high top.

Warren had his hand wrapped around a tumbler. The horrible plague doctor mask pushed slightly aside to reveal part of his face. His too-handsome-for-his-own-good face. On his left was a woman with fiery red hair and a cocktail dress that was out of place amongst the black ties. Her arm was around Warren's waist, her head thrown back in laughter. They looked close. Cozy.

"Judy, can I speak with you for a minute?"

"Of course."

The question sat heavy on her tongue like old grease, but the doubt taking hold in her chest was worse. She assumed that was what X wanted. His endgame wasn't clear yet, but Victoria knew a smear campaign when she saw one. Betty. Victoria. Judy.

Was it possible X wasn't the killer? That he had dirt on whoever the real murderer was? If that was the case, why wouldn't he go to the police? Keeping anonymous hadn't been an issue.

God, Victoria hated mysteries. Riddles were one thing. They had a definite answer. A logic. Mysteries required no such distinction. No promise of being solved or getting closure. She was putting together a puzzle upside down, and someone else was holding the pieces. Finding X should've been as simple as getting from A to B not navigating a pothole filled back road with a poorly marked detour.

The big, flaming arrow was currently pointing at Judy.

Judy, who had access to Warren's calendar—who wasn't invited to the Gala.

Victoria stared at the photo a second longer, studying the way Judy leaned into Warren, seemingly content to be smooshed against his space heater, polyester-clad body.

Maybe she'd fallen in love with Warren, a walking cliché lost in the trope of a Hallmark movie. Judy seemed the type who would really fucking love Hallmark movies.

"I've been reflecting on the night of the Gala," Victoria said. "Trying to remember if I saw anything suspicious. And I was wondering if you could help me fill in some gaps."

"Me? I'm sorry, I don't know how I could be of any help."

"You weren't at the Gala?"

"Uh, no. The Connors keep an exclusive guest list." She snickered and reached under her desk for her purse, taking out a container of breath mints. With a pinch, Judy popped one into her mouth and laughed again, but the sound was dry. Mirthless.

As if Victoria was being ridiculous. As if Judy hadn't been caught practically groping her husband on camera.

"Really? Could've sworn I saw you."

Judy's lips curled into a frown. "Maybe I have one of those faces. No, no. The only dancing I did that night was with a rerun of *Step Up*. Channing Tatum is something else, isn't he?"

Lying didn't automatically mean guilt in Victoria's experience. People lied for any number of reasons, herself included. Guilt. Avoidance. Pleasure.

She could show Judy the photo and demand answers, which would inevitably lead to a confession that may or may not be true. Or she could hold onto this card until she had a chance to dig around a bit.

"Mm-hm, my mistake. A heads up, though, Detective Meyers might be stopping by in the next few days," Victoria said. Just because she wasn't putting Judy on the spot didn't mean she couldn't make her sweat. "Apparently new information has come to light about Warren's case."

"That's great news," she said, eyes widening. She twisted a strand of hair as she spoke. "Any idea what she's discovered?"

Interesting choice of words, Victoria thought. "Not yet, but she seemed optimistic. Asked a lot about Warren's schedule outside of work the last few months. It's scary, isn't it? How you think you know someone, but none of us really know each other at all. Keep this between us, all right?"

Judy gulped. "Of course."

"Unless you feel you can't handle that responsibility." She let the statement curve into a question.

"I can do that," she squeaked. "No problem."

"Good," Victoria said. "Feel free to take off once Finance gets those numbers over. I'll see you in the morning."

She turned toward her office then, tapping out a response to X.

I don't trust you either.

The dots appeared immediately, and the response arrived before she reached her door.

You shouldn't.

43

L ong hours had been a part of the job for as long as Victoria could remember. In school, her father had given her extra homework assignments. He'd wake her up an hour early to read a particularly complex analysis of the market, the scent of his aftershave sharp in her nose. Her first years at Livingston were a blur of fourteen-hour days and all-nighters. She'd push until fatigue collapsed into exhaustion, investing in espresso beans, energy shots, and an ergonomic chair.

Coffee addiction and the lack of proper sleep didn't bother her anymore, and as Victoria knocked items off her agenda, she settled into the familiar rhythm with a warmth in her gut. In her office, classical music played softly in the background while she sent out the last emails of the day, prepped documents, and approved contracts to her heart's content, the antithesis to those torturous nights when Warren gaslit her into believing that runner-up was just as good as first place.

Who needed to be CEO when her trajectory was locked into a future as Warren's happy housewife and incubator?

Children were wonderful. She loved watching the kids in the Manor trick-or-treat and hunt for Easter eggs, and the Christmas pageants in the clubhouse were delightful. If she ever went down the mothering route she had no doubt she'd be one of those moms organizing matching outfits for photo shoots, doing that little bit extra.

But for Victoria, that possibility remained hypothetical. She had no desire to be in the same position.

And that was okay. Warren should've known that forcing the issue would end in nothing but disaster.

Victoria was not meant to be a mother. She knew that in her bones. But for this? she thought, closing the file for the night. For the satisfaction of her hard work coming to fruition? For this, she would gladly sacrifice sleep.

Because if Victoria's roots were planted anywhere, it was at Livingston. This was more her home than the house in Kent Wood Manor or the brick behemoth where she'd spent her childhood. Finishing up at the office that night, she no longer dreaded the hours until she'd be able to return. Whatever pressure she'd put on herself to live up to Warren's expectations—of motherhood, of having the white-picket-fence wife—had slowly dissipated.

Who needed therapy when an anonymous psycho could murder your husband for free?

She'd just shut down her laptop when a sharp rap made her look up. Jeff leaned in the doorway, shirtsleeves casually rolled to the elbows, tie askew. His hair wasn't gelled today, she saw, and he kept running a hand through it as if the free-falling strands were foreign to even his own fingers.

"Hey, I'm on my way out," Victoria said, shoving her things into her carrying case. "If it's not an emergency, can it wait until tomorrow?"

"Did you have a chance to look over that hiccup with the Peterson account? I emailed you this morning but didn't hear back."

"I cc'd you on my response; I sent it over to Lauren, and she'll have it handled by Monday."

"Ah," he said. "Must've missed that."

Bullshit, she thought when he didn't move. "Was there something else you wanted, Jeff?"

"Do you have plans for this evening?" he asked.

Victoria stopped fussing with her bag's zipper. "Plans?"

The woodsy scent of his cologne suddenly filled her nostrils as he came toe to toe with her. "Tonight. Are you free? We could grab a late dinner at Lorenzo's or that new fusion place downtown."

"I don't think so."

"A couple of drinks at the very least. Come on, don't leave me hanging. I want to run some ideas by you."

Her bingo board had not included a thinly veiled attempt at a pickup line, but there they were. He hadn't actually believed she would say yes to that, had he? "I'm sorry. That's not going to happen."

Jeff's face hardened. "Vic. It's one dinner. You have to eat, don't you?"

"I do, but I'm under no obligation to do it with you." *Dick.* "And it's Victoria."

"All right." He took a step back, scoffing and wiping at his lips as he made a show of gathering his thoughts. "I urge you to reconsider."

"Submit your comment card to HR."

Her sarcasm hit the mark. Jeff's cheeks reddened, his nostrils flaring slightly. "You know this power trip you're on really isn't a good look. This—" he motioned in a wide circle, "—doesn't belong to you."

"And yet here I am telling you to get out of *my* office."

"People talk, Vic. Warren talked. He wasn't happy with the way things were—with you—and then he winds up dead and you have the corner view."

He's guessing, her subconscious argued. *A shot in the dark because his pride is hurt.*

Warren and Jeff hadn't been close. He couldn't have known about the leave. The margin of error was slim, however, and she couldn't be one hundred percent sure.

Even if Warren had spoken to Jeff about his dissatisfaction with their marriage, would he have entrusted Jeff with the details of his plan?

The accusation ignited a flame in Victoria's gut. "We're through. Get out."

He skulked away, pausing at the door to meet her gaze. "The board's going to call an emergency hearing. They don't want anyone with a nefarious reputation running this company. Bad for the brand, bad for business. I'd say 'suspect number one in a murder investigation' falls under that umbrella, wouldn't you?"

Victoria didn't speak, seething at the threat.

He was bluffing.

Jeff's smile was filled with daggers in the shadows. "Have a good night, Vic."

44

With the cold came the kiss of the holidays in Kent Wood Manor. Trading pumpkins for pines, the residents adorned their porches with wreaths dotted with cranberries and fat plastic snowmen. In a week there would be another party—not a Gala, thank god; Victoria couldn't have handled that. This would be a quieter event with hot cocoa and ice skating. Holly-jolly families would travel the block, caroling and casting votes for best decorations.

Life, as they said, was indeed moving on. Everyone was fighting so hard to maintain normalcy. Sympathy cards had waned, and the meal train had expended its supply of air-fryer friendly packages. The neighbors actively avoided mentioning her dead husband while planning cookie swaps and Secret Santa assignments. Outward appearances of mourning were packed away neatly in totes and stored in attics alongside Halloween decorations and outgrown clothing.

Fear remained, but they dressed it in a bow and called it a gift. The gift of *appreciation*. Of *not taking a single day for granted*. Of *holding your loved ones tight*.

Victoria hadn't sold her soul, but she might as well have rented it out.

And the more she thought about X and his ambiguous motivations, the more she realized that she was fine paying that price—as long as he stayed out of her way.

Whoever he was.

That was part of the issue. It was difficult to stay the course when she didn't know who was building the obstacles.

She'd stayed an extra half hour in the office, wanting to avoid another run-in with Jeff. Finally turning onto her street, Victoria's mind bluescreened as she took in the chaos unraveling in front of her. Police cars. An ambulance. The perimeter around the Knottier house was crawling with activity.

Betty's husband stood at the base of the stairs. His usual composure abandoned, he ran a hand through his hair and gestured wildly at the house while an officer motioned for him to calm down. For some reason it was his glasses that Victoria focused on, slightly askew on the bridge of his nose. It would've taken all of two seconds to straighten them out. A twitch of his nose. Instead, he left them crooked.

The flashing red-and-white lights cast shadows over her face as Victoria parked and joined the group of neighbors huddled around the scene.

"What's going on?" she asked.

Mary Sparrow blew into her wrinkled hands with tears in her eyes. "Oh, it's horrible," she said, her voice thick with emotion. "Just horrible."

"Did something happen to Chelsea?"

Betty's daughter was a junior in high school and it was no secret that she'd been struggling with drug addiction. Breaking her wrist stealing a base during a softball game had allegedly led to a reliance on painkillers, of which there was no short supply in the Manor. Although Betty had done her best to tamp down the rumors, shielding her daughter from the worst of the stigma by organizing fundraisers and anti-drug awareness campaigns, Chelsea was a teenager. Breaking rules was what they did.

A wail erupted into the night. Victoria turned to the source, absorbed in the collective gasp that issued around her. Two paramedics emerged from the house, stretcher in tow. A white sheet was spread over a lifeless form. Victoria's vision doubled, and when she blinked she was in that small room in the basement of the hospital. The closed-circuit screen fuzzy yet the body, *his* body, so incredibly crisp.

The dry rasp of the sheet as the ME peeled it away from his lifeless form.

She bit her cheek and winced as her mouth filled with the iron taste of blood. The jolt of pain broke apart the image in her mind, but the paramedics remained, as real as the flap of skin she tongued at in her mouth.

Whispers carried in the wind as the paramedics carefully navigated the stairs and path. The officer speaking with Dave put a hand on his shoulder and shook his head when he started to move forward. Dave crumpled, elbows on his knees and fingers buried in his hair, convulsing next to an LED Santa with rosy red cheeks and a burlap sack.

Poor Chelsea, Victoria thought.

A second cry echoed through the crowd, breaking her concentration. Victoria craned to see who had lost it, but everyone seemed equally confused. Moments later, a disheveled, fair-haired girl stumbled through the doorway into her father's arms. Moans heaved from her chest in heartbreaking arcs, ebbing and flowing with her breaths.

Oh shit, she thought. Chelsea wasn't on that stretcher.

Her phone vibrated against her leg. Victoria felt every nerve freeze in anticipation as she slowly drew it from her pocket. She'd come to associate the buzz with X and was dismayed to see Warren's name on the screen.

A single word, loaded with venom.

Whoops.

"It's Betty," Mary said, gripping Victoria's forearm. "Betty's dead."

45

The Kent Wood Manor fitness club was a small but well-stocked facility on the south side of the development. Popular with families in the summer, the outdoor pool was closed for the season, which meant most of the patrons were in the back classroom for Zumba. A woman with face-framing highlights and stiletto nails took approximately three thousand selfies in the mirror before her weight-lifting narration commenced. Teagan explained that she was probably trying to get various angles recorded for a TikTok, and Victoria had subsequently suggested they avoid the free-weight section like the plague.

Her original plan had been to meet at a café halfway between their offices, but Teagan had been too jittery for coffee and Victoria had zero appetite. At least at the gym there was a chance she'd work off some tension.

Stuffing their bags into some cubbies, they chose two ellipticals next to each other and set their own paces. The temperature had dropped below freezing overnight and cranking the heat hadn't taken the chill off. Victoria had only stayed a few more minutes after they'd wheeled Betty's body out, but she felt like she'd never get fully warm again. Arms pumping hard, she worked her heartrate into the target zone and turned up the volume as the local news started its main segment.

"The residents of Kent Wood Manor are reeling this morning following the death of another of their own. Betty Knottier was found late last night in her home on this quiet cul-de-sac." Coverage flicked from the anchor to footage of the scene, bright lights and confused faces swimming in and out of focus. "Details are scarce as the investigation is ongoing, but in a statement from Kent PD, Detective Briana Meyers says the police want to assure the public that there is no cause for concern."

Coverage shifted again to a circle of phones and audio recorders surrounding Meyers, bags heavy and dark under her bloodshot eyes.

"We can confirm that Betty Knottier was found deceased inside her home. While we are not releasing any additional information until more conclusive data has presented itself," she said, chewing gum visible in her back teeth, "we are following up on several leads and encourage anyone with information to contact the number at the bottom of the screen."

"If you're asking for help, does that mean Kent PD is operating under the assumption that this was a homicide?" one of the reporters asked.

"Cause of death will be determined by the medical examiner."

A non-answer, thought Victoria.

"Two deaths on the same street in less than three months, Detective. Is this a pattern? Do we have an actual serial killer on our hands?"

Meyers frowned. "No, and suggesting that we do does more harm than good. Might I remind you that everything you see on *CSI* and *Criminal Minds* is dramatized for entertainment. At this time we have no reason to suspect that the community is in any danger."

Voices clamored over each other to be heard next, but Meyers abruptly raised her hands. "I'll let you know when we know more. No further questions. Thank you." Disappearing into the team of officers and men in suits waiting in the wings, Meyers shook her head at whatever was said and stomped out of the shot.

"So, Betty brought you a sympathy gift," Teagan said, wiping her forehead.

"She did," Victoria agreed.

"Then came up with a bullshit excuse to get you out of the room so she could snoop around."

"I think so, yes."

"But you have no idea what she was looking for and don't think she actually took anything."

"Correct. I mean, it's Betty. For all I know she was just stirring up gossip for the hell of it."

"That's a lot of suburban espionage just to start a rumor," Teagan said with a dry laugh.

"Well, she was asking about Warren. About his work. That was weird to me. She's never taken an interest in Livingston before."

"And now she's dead."

"And now she's dead."

Victoria was feeling better about her decision to confide in Teagan with every dot she connected on her own. For all their numerous differences, sometimes it paid to have a sibling who was raised under the same cutthroat conditions.

The Zumba class finished with a round of applause. A few women trickled out, laughing and sipping from their water bottles before gathering around the flat-screen closest to the changing area. Another station was covering Betty's story. The delivery was a little more sensationalized—the focus being on the shock and heartbreak of a daughter losing her mother in such a tragic manner—and included a slideshow of selfies from Chelsea's Instagram.

"I can't believe she'd be so selfish," a redhead with matching Lulus commented. "I don't care what anyone says: suicide is the most selfish decision a person can make."

"You think she killed herself?" her friend with a complicated braid replied.

"That's what I heard. Mike from the hospital told Chris that she hanged herself. The daughter found her in the living room with a belt knotted in the ceiling fan."

A gasp from the perky brunette to her right. "No, that's terrible!"

"Mike's as trustworthy as a two-headed coin," the friend with the braid scolded. "They haven't even finished the autopsy yet."

"Why would they need an autopsy if what Mike said is true?"

"Exactly my point," the brunette said with a flick of her ponytail.

Teagan increased her incline, a slight tilt of her head the only indication she'd been listening. "What are the odds that Betty I-can't-believe-they're-not-real Knottier offed herself? Wasn't she just bragging about securing another ultra-supreme-mega-senior brand ambassadorship for one of those MLMs?"

"Yeah, but it's possible she had more going on that we don't know about. Her daughter was having a hard time."

Teagan scoffed. "I have it on good authority that Betty Junior was supposed to start an in-patient program at The Elms next week. Voluntarily. I'm not saying the road ahead of her is sprinkled with marshmallows and gold, but chalking this up to guilt over being a shitty parent isn't cutting it for me. We had shitty parents and look how we turned out."

That was a whole trash can of worms Victoria refused to open. "How do you know that and I don't?" Victoria asked. "About The Elms?"

"I have my ways."

"By *ways* do you mean a mattress and a garter belt or . . ."

"Bitch," she sniped, smacking Victoria on the shoulder hard enough to sting. Clearly her remark was still in the joking category but bordering on offensive.

The Zumba group approached, walking slowly, in the midst of their own heated argument. The brunette gestured, cutting off her friend. "Listen, I'm not saying Mike's a bad guy, but he's a huge drama queen who wants to be the center of attention. Hal heard they're looking at the husband."

"Why the husband?"

"It's always the husband," complicated braid said.

"Well, you heard Piper saw her at the Thai bistro downtown like a month or so ago with that guy."

"Which guy?"

"Piper couldn't see who he was; his back was to her, but she said it definitely wasn't Dave. This guy was built with dark hair. Dave's bald. Anyway, they think he found out she was cheating on him and killed her when she said she was leaving."

"How is this any more believable than what I said?" red hair asked.

"Dave's as passive as they come. Last summer, they came to our Fourth of July barbeque. He caught a wolf spider in the bathroom and instead of killing it like a normal person he trapped it in a cup and released it into the woods. If the man's not squashing spiders, he's not strangling his wife in a jealous rage, I'm sorry."

"Aren't we excluding another obvious scenario?" The woman with the complicated braid locked eyes with Victoria, a sneer on her lips. "Kent Wood already has its very own resident killer."

46

Although Victoria had contemplated hundreds of ways to murder her husband, she'd never actually been in a fight. Middle schoolers would form circles in the halls and roar as two girls went at each other, yanking hair and screaming about any number of ridiculous offences. Shit talking, boyfriend stealing, wrong looks—sometimes there wasn't even a reason. Bored rich kids were willing to go to crazy lengths for entertainment.

Her father had demanded that she learn how to hide her true feelings. It wasn't that she couldn't feel, he'd said, but to truly succeed in this world she had to be impenetrable. Unflappable. A cool blank slate.

Years of practice. Hundreds of heated negotiations and show-downs with executives who wanted nothing more than to put her in her place. All of it meaningless when one woman with a stupid braid made a pointed comment.

They were just words. Words didn't have power unless you let them, and even then, that power could be redirected. Victoria's anger rushed through her, a familiar warmth she both loathed and welcomed. Instead of pushing it down, however, she let it consume her. Climbing off the machine, she stepped directly in front of the woman.

Suburban showdown, she thought briefly, and indulged in a ridiculous moment of fantasy about twinsets set against wild west imagery.

"Do you have something you wanted to say to me?" she asked, more statement than question.

"Tor." Teagan was at her side in a flash, delicately touching her elbow in warning.

The woman scrunched her face in mock confusion. "Not sure what you mean."

"Anne, don't." The brunette's face filled with fear.

"No, I'm sorry, she should know," she said. "For what we pay in fees we should feel safe wherever we go in the Manor, and I am definitely speaking for the silent majority here when I say we don't feel comfortable sharing a space with a murderer. Maybe you should find another place to work out from now on."

"And maybe next time don't go to Mexico for cheek implants," Teagan said. "Are you bitches done, or are we about to have a dance battle like the good old days?"

"I didn't murder my husband," Victoria said, her tongue finally unsticking from the roof of her mouth.

"Sure," Anne said, pushing past her. "Let's ask Betty if she agrees." Victoria did a piss-poor job of hiding her surprise—again caught off guard by the insinuation that she was also responsible for Betty's death—and Anne reveled in the upper hand. "Interesting design choices you've been making lately, by the way. The three-foot-high mural announcing your proclivities really hits the nail on the head."

"Did you do it? The graffiti?" Victoria didn't know these women from a hole in the ground. The chances of one of them being X seemed slim since he was hell-bent on making this personal. Everything about Warren's murder had been a statistical anomaly.

Anne smirked, the same half-mouthed twitch of superiority that actress from *Game of Thrones* had built her career on. "The HOA board is meeting tonight," Anne said. "Emergency vote to have you removed from the committee. We're a tight-knit, wholesome community. We have values that you are clearly unable to adhere to. They might not have enough to arrest you yet, but it won't be long. If I were you, I'd make yourself scarce. *Killer.*"

First Livingston and now her own home?

Victoria bristled and stepped right into Anne's personal space, inhaling her sweat and strawberry body spray. She studied the pulse point under her jaw, the subtle *lub-dub* and visible veins running just beneath the surface of her pale skin. How hard would she have to squeeze before the woman's skin turned scarlet and those veins protruded from the pressure? What would it feel like to have those muscles tense in her bare hands?

"And if I were you," she said through clenched teeth, "and I truly believed that my neighbor was a dangerous, murdering crazy person, then I wouldn't dole out ultimatums. Seems like a solid way to dig your own grave."

The other women gasped.

"Victoria," Teagan spat. "Don't say another word."

"Stay away from me," Anne said, but the bravado was gone from her voice. She waggled a finger, repeating the warning as she turned for the exit. The Zumba women followed her, looking anxiously over their shoulders at Victoria. Two had phones aimed in her direction.

Shit, she thought. *Shit.*

"That was literally the dumbest thing you could've done," Teagan said when they were gone. "What the hell were you thinking?"

"She was provoking me. They think I killed Warren. And Betty. We don't even know if Betty was murdered."

"Of course they think you killed Warren!" she near shouted, reeling it in a notch just in time to avoid causing another scene. "Of course they do. You're the wife of a wealthy financier who stands to gain a boatload of cash, a multimillion dollar company, and the freedom to stretch your cougar paws. The tabloids write themselves."

"I'm not a cougar, Teagan!"

"And I'm not saying you are, but I'm your sister. My word doesn't count for shit when it comes to the Reddit threads analyzing your fight with the clown at the Gala."

"This is insane."

"This is the age of digital warfare, and social media is king."

Victoria groaned. "Why aren't you mad at them? I didn't do anything." She knew she sounded like a petulant child, but as her adrenaline ebbed the rest of her emotions overwhelmed her.

"Tor, it doesn't matter. None of it matters, all right? Whether you killed him or not is irrelevant. The accusation is out there. You can't stop it. People are going to be awful; you can't stop them, and trying to defend yourself by picking fights with the Stepford Wives in a discount Gold's Gym isn't going to change their minds."

"What do you mean whether I killed him or not? You don't believe them, do you?"

"Are you not listening?" Teagan asked. "It doesn't matter." She punched a fist into her palm to emphasize each word. "The court of public opinion is an entirely different ballgame. The gossip and speculation about what happened at the Gala is nothing compared to whatever videos those witches are probably uploading to Facebook as we speak."

Victoria's muscles tingled and her head spun. She stumbled to a bench near the cubbies and plopped down heavily. What was happening to her?

Teagan approached a minute later, handing her a water bottle. "Drink," she said. "Just drink the damn water."

She took several small sips while staring at her feet, replaying the events of the last few minutes. The stress was getting to her. She was making rookie mistakes and destroying every method of damage control in her book. When was Victoria going to start being smart about this?

Defending herself against X had been her main priority. She'd assumed he was the only one working to make her look guilty. She wondered if he would be pleased with this turn of events. If this was what he'd wanted all along.

47

Never had a day dragged so long before. HR was pushing back on the incentive program she wanted to run, Judy was more skittish around her than a newborn kitten, and back-end issues with filings kept being escalated to her desk. Little things on their own, but Victoria felt like she was being crushed by an invisible boulder. She couldn't breathe. She couldn't think

Why was this so hard?

When the office cleared and the janitorial night crew arrived, Victoria still hadn't been able to find her groove. She'd struggled through emails and meetings, short-tempered and distracted. At one point, with Judy crowing about how Warren had done things *this* way, and Warren would've wanted *that* account, Victoria's patience had snapped.

"Do me a favor, Judge Judy. Google the nearest psychic and book yourself a séance since you're so interested in my dead husband's business practices. I'm sure he'll be delighted to hear from you."

Judy hadn't stuck around long after that, thankfully; with a dirty look and an under-the-breath comment, she was sounding the alarm with erratic click-clack nail taps on her phone before

Victoria had logged out of her email. But the empty office offered little reprieve. The silence was thick, the heat dry and itchy. By the third draft of a simple request to the legal team, Victoria gave up. Sloppy wouldn't save Livingston. She would go home, sleep off her bad mood, and start fresh in the morning.

Tomorrow would be different.

It had to be.

She drove on autopilot, stopping and signaling when prompted but mostly coasting while a murder mystery podcast drowned out her thoughts. Voices clanged around her head like the kid she'd never have bashing pots and pans together on the kitchen floor: Warren telling her she was done at Livingston. Teagan insisting she didn't know how to be happy. X's texts. The First Wives Club calling her out at the gym.

Killer.

Victoria wasn't a killer, though.

She clicked the garage door opener as she approached the house, but nothing happened. Rolling closer she pushed it again, but the door stayed shut. Wonderful, she thought. Did these things even have batteries? She'd never had to replace one before.

In the driveway, Victoria locked the car and dragged herself up the path. The front door was reserved for guests and deliveries, and it felt strange fumbling with her key ring for the one with the little blue house tag.

Footsteps slapped the pavement behind her as Victoria stepped onto the porch. Ears pricking in alert, she turned as a dark-coated figure appeared on the porch. "Detective Meyers," Victoria said. "Scared me. I didn't see your car. Everything all right?"

"Sorry, I tried calling out to you but you must not've heard me."

The astringent odor of fresh paint lingered. The workmen had finished covering the graffiti, Victoria was relieved to see, but even if no one else could see it, she knew it was there. Shadows of accusation. Forgetting was easier said than done.

No holiday lights or garland would distract Victoria from the memory. She hadn't even considered decorating. Juggling false holiday cheer with the chaos of navigating Warren's death didn't seem apropos. Mourning was a fine excuse for being the sole dark and dreary house in the Manor. No one had given her grief about her reticence to celebrate.

But someone had attached a sparkly crimson bow to the doorknob.

Sweet, was her first thought. Exactly the kind of feel-good behavior the Manor community was known for. They'd made a balloon arch for the graduating seniors one year. When the little girl across from the Connors had been diagnosed with leukemia, they'd staged a carnival in the common area. Dunking booths and popcorn and a petting zoo.

And Victoria . . . got a ribbon. Huh. On second thought, it was strange that there was only one ribbon. The bare minimum would've been an entire box of ornaments and a six-foot tree.

Not sweet. *Weird.*

Maybe they were trying to be subtle without hurting her feelings. A reminder that she had a responsibility. Okay, it was petty, but Victoria had overseen a claim committee about allowing children to use sidewalk chalk. Congenial and petty often went hand and hand.

Criticizing her lack of holly-jolly spirit was one thing. Spray-painting slander and openly accusing her of murder, however, didn't sit well. Heat prickled under her skin. She glanced at the bow again, the blood-red velvet and the intricate knot. Had it been there when she left this morning?

"Mrs. Tate, can we talk?" Meyers's face was serious; the wrinkles around her eyes hardened with concentration.

"About?"

"I just have a few quick questions and then I'll be on my way."

A few quick questions. Code for *doubts about Victoria*. "Okay. I haven't had a chance to shop, but I could probably rustle up some tea or decaf?"

"That won't be necessary," Meyers declined.

Even better, Victoria thought. "What's going on? Any leads?"

Meyers nodded. "Possibly."

"That's good. Possibly's good, right?"

"Depends on who you ask."

Way to be vague. "What did you need to ask *me*?"

The detective shifted her weight and leaned closer, puffing stale coffee breath in Victoria's face. "I'm sure you've heard by now about Betty Knottier."

"I did. News spreads fast."

"I used to think that was a symptom of small towns," Meyers said. "Country gossip. People knowing everything about each other's business. Turns out it's not a geographical thing. It's a human thing. We're programmed to be curious. We need to know what's going on, but more than that, we've developed this sense of entitlement. Like we need to know, but we also deserve to know. Secrets are a privilege."

This was the shittiest time for an after-school special tangent, but Meyers was on a roll so Victoria let her go on. If she wanted to wax poetic about the dark side of human nature, and it maintained her amicable ties, then so be it.

"I like to think it comes from an altruistic place, but if I've learned anything since Warren's death it's that people are self-motivated pricks. Kindness has become a commodity."

"Mm," Meyers said absently. Her favorite noise, Victoria theorized. Why else would she constantly sound like she was playing a kazoo? A placemark for agreement, dissent, and consideration. "I'm glad you mentioned kindness. Rumors have a way of getting twisted, like a macabre game of telephone. For the record, we are pursuing Betty Knottier's death as a homicide."

"Oh," Victoria breathed, fighting the onslaught of questions rising in her mind. Were they killed the same way? Had Dave been arrested? Was there evidence? "Oh. That's—I'm sorry to hear that. Do you think it's connected to Warren?"

"Now why would you ask that?"

"Because we're neighbors?" she suggested with a hint of irritation. "Maybe someone targeted them based on location or—"

"Where were you yesterday evening?"

Victoria spoke slowly and chose her words carefully. "The office. Always at the office. I have a company to run."

"Sure." Detective Meyers nodded, looking off into the distance. "And how's that going?"

"As well as can be expected."

"Any more contact with the anonymous texter?"

"No," Victoria said automatically. "I would've called you."

"Glad to hear it." She shifted her weight and stuffed her hands deeper into her coat pockets. "Mrs. Tate, I've received several reports about an altercation between you and Mrs. Knottier."

Victoria's stomach lurched. "There was no altercation."

Meyers winced at the cold but flipped open her notepad, her knuckles pink but her fingertips white. "Witnesses claim Betty visited you to pay her respects but you, quote, *chased her from the porch, threatening to hurt her if she ever came back."*

Maybe it was time to move, Victoria thought. "I never threatened Betty."

"We were provided with Ring footage from a neighbor who happened to catch the incident. The angle isn't perfect, so I'm eager to hear your side of things, but you were seen following her out of your house. Words were exchanged. Mrs. Knottier left in a hurry, and I have to tell you: I watched it myself several times. She looked scared. Seems like maybe this is becoming a pattern with you."

"This is ridiculous," Victoria said, crossing her arms over her chest. "Standing up for myself doesn't make me a violent person. Hell, being aggressive doesn't make me the bad guy. If I had a dick, then would it be okay for me to *run her off my property*?" She threw up air quotes and put a little more space between them. "Would you even be here? I highly doubt it. Betty lied her way into my home so she could sneak around, and now I'm being accused of—what exactly are you accusing me of, Detective?"

Meyers shook her head innocently. "Nothing." *Yet,* the implication remained. "But I am curious about what happened when Mrs. Knottier visited you."

As if on cue, Victoria's phone vibrated. She glanced at the screen and bit the corner of her lip.

Get rid of her.

Victoria glanced down the street in both directions but saw no movement. Her skin itched, a tingly hot-cold sensation that left her feeling raw and exposed.

X was here, and he was watching.

48

"**M**rs. Tate, are you all right?"

Meyers's voice cut through the fog of Victoria's anxiety. "Long day," she replied, giving Meyers her best everything's-fine smile.

Meyers looked uncertain. "Do you want to explain what happened with Mrs. Knottier?"

No, she really didn't. "She brought a gift and asked for some HOA papers, and when I went to get them she took it upon herself to go through Warren's things."

"Not yours?"

"She was coming out of his office."

"I see."

"She tried to leave as soon as I gave her the HOA materials. I could've pretended I hadn't caught her, but I prefer to have things out in the open. Being blunt works for me, and honestly, I wanted her to know she couldn't pull that kind of move and not be held responsible for it. I don't know what she was looking for—if she was just snooping or hoping to find dirt—but she was rattled."

"Mrs. Tate, how would you describe Betty's relationship with your husband?"

"Cordial?" she said distractedly. "We've been neighbors for five, six years? The Knottiers come to all the social events, and Dave used to golf with Warren's crew when they were short a guy."

Meyers scratched something down in her notepad and then met her gaze. "Had you noticed any unusual transactions in your bank account prior to Warren's death?"

"Unusual how?" she asked.

Ding. Get rid of her. Now.

"Large sums being taken out? A pattern of withdrawals you didn't approve but Warren might have?"

"I, uh . . ." Victoria fumbled, glancing in both directions again, trying not to appear as flustered as the texts were making her. "No, nothing like that. Why?"

"Do you feel comfortable granting us access to your financial records?"

Victoria frowned. "I'll need to speak with my lawyer, and it would be best to handle that in the morning. I'm sorry I can't be of more help right now, but I am exhausted."

Meyers held up a finger. "Just a few more things."

Victoria sighed. "Quickly, please, it's cold."

X wanted her gone. Victoria had to play along to get that done without raising suspicion.

"The night of the Gala. Did anything seem out of the ordinary?"

"Everything was out of the ordinary, Detective Meyers. It was the Gala. Not your run-of-the-mill night. We've been over this. You have my report."

"Give me a break. Just walk me through the party one more time. You said you got ready with your sister?"

"Yes, Teagan and I got ready and drove over together. It was easier for her to leave her car here, and Warren was going straight to the Mansion from Livingston. We chose our masks then split up so I could find Warren. I stopped at the bar, had a quick drink, then got in line to greet Margaret and Barnaby."

"Where you spoke to the jester."

Ding. NOW.

Where are you? she tapped. Then to Meyers, "Yes. No, I mean, we didn't speak in the sense that you're implying. I wasn't having a chat with my good friend or paramour, or whatever unsavory label you tried sticking to him before."

Meyers agreed halfheartedly. "Do you need to take that?"

"Sorry. Work stuff. You know how it goes."

"Damn, that's some dedicated customer service. I can't even get my bank on the phone during regular business hours "

Do not take the bait, she told herself. "I have a lot of catching up to do."

Her phone buzzed again. Closer than you think. You really want to find out what happens if you don't listen?

"Maybe it's best if we do finish this inside."

"'That won't be necessary." Victoria shoved the phone in her pocket.

"What time were you in the greeting line?"

"I have no idea."

"Did you chat with anyone else while you waited?"

Victoria huffed. "Yes? I'm not rude. If you'd ever been to one of these events, then you'd know that it's impossible to go more than six feet without being reeled into a conversation."

Meyers sucked her teeth. "Alas, my invitation seems to get lost in the mail every year. C'est la vie. Can anyone vouch for your whereabouts?"

"At the Gala? Where I was photographed repeatedly and, as I just told you, spoke with several people over the course of the night?"

"From the time you left the Connors until you were notified about Warren."

"Are you asking for an alibi?"

Meyers held up her hands in defense. "Getting a little ahead of me."

Victoria pushed the door open a crack. Notes of ginger and cinnamon hit her full force, but there was something else beneath it. Like wet pavement after a heavy rainstorm. "I have been incredibly cooperative with your investigation, Detective Meyers. You have my statement, witness reports. I have nothing to hide."

Meyers wrote something else down in her notepad. How could she have so much to write? Was it deliberate? A calculated tactic to make Victoria nervous?

Another noise, somewhere between a *hm* and an *ah*. The ambiguity was really starting to get on Victoria's nerves.

"One last question then, Victoria, and we'll call it a night."

Fine. "Go ahead."

"What happened in the red room?"

She paused. "Red room?"

"Yes."

Victoria answered tentatively. "I wasn't there very long."

"You were alone."

"No."

"Who was with you?"

"That's where I found Warren."

"Had you seen Betty or Dave Knottler at that point?" she asked.

I was a tad preoccupied planning Warren's murder, Victoria thought. "No. I don't remember seeing Dave at all, actually. I'm not sure he was there. Betty gave me the bandage in the lobby before I left."

The notepad shut with a clap and an easy smile. "Okay. That's all I need from you for now. Thank you for your continued cooperation."

"Are you going to explain what this was about at least?"

"Better get inside before you catch cold," Meyers said, jogging to where a blue sedan was parked a few houses down the street. No wonder she hadn't seen it when she pulled in.

Victoria waited until the taillights disappeared around the corner before going inside. The visit wasn't an automatic call for alarm, but she didn't like it.

She didn't like it at all.

49

Victoria's thoughts raced as she entered the house and started to take off her coat. Was she a suspect? Like, a legitimate suspect, and not just a due-diligence-because-it's-always-the-spouse type suspect? Gossiping wine moms was one thing; she could handle side eyes and social-pariah status. X was in his own category, the catalyst and the stimulant, but until the off-putting conversation with Meyers, Victoria had been confident in her ability to handle him. Identify the source. Isolate the source. Eliminate the source.

She froze, one arm out of her coat. Something wasn't right.

The air was static, as if someone had recently left but their energy was still floating around. She toed out of her boots and did a double take looking down at the spot where her shoes should go.

Another pair of shoes sat on the doormat. Black dress shoes. Victoria was willing to bet that if she looked inside she'd find a tag for Gucci, size twelve.

The last shoes Warren wore while he was still alive. The ones she'd packed up herself when she'd emptied his side of the closet. They were supposed to be in the basement with the rest of his wardrobe.

Dropping her stuff on the floor in an uncharacteristically messy pile, Victoria yanked out her phone and scrolled through her missed notifications from X-as-Warren.

Good girl.

Beneath your tough-love demeanor, you always were a glutton for praise.

Welcome home.

Imagine if she'd gone upstairs.

Had X been inside the house the whole time?

Was he still in the house?

Something rustled upstairs. Victoria snapped to the sound, ears straining in the silence. A thump in the walls. The whir of air through the vents. Were these the normal noises of her house? Fear had the ability to transform a familiar setting into a nightmarish terrain, and Victoria suddenly questioned the safety of every corner and dark hallway.

"You've got this," she exhaled under her breath. Yeah, she was talking to herself. Sometimes it helped ground her, and this was one of those times where she'd use any trick in her arsenal. "If he wanted me dead, X has had plenty of occasions to kill me already. I'm good, I'm good, I'm good."

Victoria had to be smart. She wasn't going to run. Or hide. Or rely on Briana Meyers to get her lumpy, prying ass back to the house to help. Whichever door she picked as her prize, the ending would be the same.

Tiptoeing to the kitchen, she set her phone down and silently opened the island drawer grabbed the first utensil that screamed *weapon*: a filet knife with a sleek handle. She twisted it in her grasp, testing her ability to hold it should her hand get sweaty. Or bloody. She could wield it if someone—not someone, X—got too close.

Because this was real. Victoria had to start thinking outside of hypotheticals. X was in her house, and X was dangerous.

What X didn't seem to understand was that Victoria was dangerous too.

The scratching sound grew louder as she climbed the stairs, which did absolutely nothing to calm her frayed nerves. The noise made her think of wasp wings, paper thin and raspy. Or the dry tug of a cotton shirt rubbing against flat paint, a noise that always sent chills down her spine.

She reached the landing and gagged. God, the *stench*. Dense and wet with something earthy. Like the protected swamplands on the outskirts of the Manor. She covered her mouth with her shirt, taking shallow breaths through her mouth, and pushed forward.

At the end of the hall, a sliver of light seeped out from beneath her bedroom door. Victoria didn't sense movement; no shadows shifted, but the noise continued, and the smell was terrible.

The smell was strongest outside the door. She gagged again and dropped her collar. It wasn't helping anyway.

Do it, she urged herself. *Don't be a baby. Do it.*

Adjusting her grip on the filet knife, Victoria turned the knob. Counting down from three, she braced herself and pushed the door open.

50

Victoria choked back the urge to vomit.

The room was covered in blood. She stepped forward carefully, realizing the sound she'd heard was the plastic drop cloths scratching against the furniture in the breeze from the ceiling fan. X had laid out the sheets exactly the way she had done the night of the Gala.

A pained groan escaped her lips as she took it all in. Bloody streaks and drips broken by congealing clots and yellowish lumps of gelatinous blobs. Stumbling backward, Victoria's chest heaved. She coughed and leaned heavily on her knees as the floor tilted.

In through the nose, out through the mouth, Victoria blocked everything else out, shrinking her world to the air in her lungs and the hard wall behind her. The worst of the dizziness slowly receded, and as she raised her head her gaze landed on the dresser.

Avoiding the largest of the blood splatters like a kid pretending the floor is made of lava, Victoria crossed the room. The plastic sheets covering the drawers were smeared with blood, dark and rusty, the pattern forming two words.

OPEN ME

No.

From downstairs, a phone blared to life, making her jump and almost drop the filet knife on her foot. That couldn't be her phone. She hadn't turned the sound on. Not since 2003.

The ringing stopped. She waited. For what, she didn't know. X to come barreling up the stairs. An axe-wielding psycho in a Ghostface mask. Warren's liquefying zombie corpse. It didn't matter that his body had been cremated, the ashes spread under the bridge of a waterfall in the Adirondacks.

But the house remained quiet. Victoria resolved to concentrate on the message on the dresser.

OPEN ME

Tracing the letters close to the surface, dread pooled low in her gut. If X had seen her laying the plastic, he'd also seen the mahogany box.

They'd never found the murder weapon.

Victoria dropped the filet knife and tore at the plastic sheets covering the bottom drawer, not thinking about the blood scraping beneath her fingernails and the matter sticking to her skin. Whatever reservations she may have had about getting dirty were quickly forgotten, replaced by a burning need to *know*.

She breathed a sigh of relief when the outline of the box became visible, but it was too much to hope that X hadn't found it. Wishful thinking would get her killed.

Victoria gripped the side of the box, thumbed over the brass latch, and opened the lid.

"*Shit*," she hissed, shoving the box out of her hands. It hit the back of the drawer with a hard thunk and jostled the contents.

Victoria gagged. The hunting knife was gone. In its place were Warren's eyes. The opaque whites had taken on a beige tint.

The irises were black marbles set in the center of overcooked egg whites. Pink strands of muscle dangled from the back like tentacles.

How were these the same eyes she'd stared into over dinner on date nights? The same eyes that had cast judgment on her decision to stay on at Livingston. Warren wasn't here; his ashes had been spread and his soul, if there was such a thing, was long gone. But that didn't stop the swell of emotion from bringing tears to Victoria's own, very much alive, eyes.

The phone rang again.

Victoria jolted at the sound and stumbled like a newborn calf toward the hall, stopping briefly to peel off her socks to avoid spreading blood throughout the rest of the house. At least her common sense hadn't completely abandoned her.

In the kitchen she found her phone, but there was no incoming call. The lock screen remained the same, the time covering Warren's face as they posed for the photographer after Warren's keynote last winter. She turned it over in her hands, thumbed into the home screen and flicked back and forth in the menu. No missed calls.

A phone was still ringing. Victoria swiveled, following the sound from the kitchen, past Warren's office, to the door that shouldn't be open.

Perfect, she thought. *Only good things come from basements.*

51

Victoria crept into the darkness, step by step, straining to see. She wasn't thinking about severed eyes or a crazy person who may or may not be feeling particularly stabby, or the angry ghost of her husband lurking in wait. Nope. Victoria wasn't scared of X, and she certainly didn't believe in ghosts.

Many people wished for the dead to come back; it was natural to mourn for someone you'd lost and long for them to return. Victoria, however, had never been one of those people. Not once. Not when her mother died, wasting away in her pink satin nightgown until her collarbones protruded and her cheeks sunk in. Not when her father had followed a few years later after a stroke.

Not when Warren was murdered.

She wanted answers, to confront X and deal with her unresolved issues about how Warren had died—of which there were plenty. A therapist would have a field day. But getting Warren back would've meant sacrificing more than she was willing to give.

It was best if the dead stayed dead.

Victoria flicked on the lights at the bottom of the stairs, her mouth dropping in a wide oh of surprise. Warren's boxes were upturned, their contents thrown everywhere. Button-downs and ties—some knotted because Warren hadn't been able to do it himself—laid haphazardly across the couches and overstuffed chairs. Wedding photos and copies of old files were strewn about like confetti. Several of the frames were broken; glass glittered under the recessed lighting, prettier than it had any right to be given the chaos.

Warren had kept hard-copy notes on every major client, one of the only things he'd ever done correctly in his tenure, but now that they were contributing to the disaster zone, Victoria was reconsidering her position.

Ringing diverted her attention. She approached the source close to the bar in slow motion, expecting someone to jump out at her at any moment, but she was alone. And on the stool, in a bright rectangle of light, was Warren's phone. She examined it like a new, dangerous specimen of insect, turning it over as the ringing abruptly cut out.

A notification flashed on the screen. Victoria tapped in Warren's passcode and flicked through the list, ignoring the missed calls from relatives and golf buddies. As she slid into the messages, the phone dinged in her hand with an incoming text from a restricted number.

She read it quickly, lingering on the one taunting word.

Answer.

Answer. Was that . . . did that mean X was going to call?

A second of doubt, and the phone rang again. Victoria gripped it tight and pushed accept. "Hello?"

52

There is a reason true crime is so popular. Dramatics aside, at its heart is truth. Real people whose lives are irrevocably changed by a horrible event. That is what separates fictional monsters and immortal serial killers from the guy next door with a cage in his basement.

Both are scary. Only one has the ability to crack your foundation and swallow you whole.

Victoria shifted as she heard the telltale sign of life on the other end of the line. X's breathing was harsh and shallow, and when he spoke, his voice distorted and mechanical, déjà vu hit her hard. The red room at the Gala. Warren's hideous mask.

And the executioner.

"Good girl," he said. "You take directions well for someone who claims to be a leader."

"Didn't leave much of a choice."

"We always have a choice," X said matter-of-factly. "What you do once the options are presented is entirely up to you."

"Technicalities; we both know that's not true. Why don't you come out so we can have this discussion in person? We're overdue a heart-to-heart, don't you think?"

X chuckled. "There she is, trying to take the reins when the cart's not even attached. Let me tell you something, Victoria: You have choices. What you lack is the discipline to execute."

Execute. "I've never had a complaint about my performance."

"How's your stamina?"

"Better than yours, I assure you."

Another robotic chuckle. X wanted her to think he was enjoying this—that he was carefree and fully in control. Maybe he was. The confidence ploy. She used it herself.

And damn it, it was working.

"Enough with the foreplay," X said, laughter abruptly tucked away. "Check your phone."

Victoria's phone vibrated before he finished speaking. A link from a blocked number flashed on the screen. "More torture porn?" she asked.

"Open it."

"If I say no?"

"Don't."

She considered being difficult, throwing the phones out altogether, but ultimately, X still had the advantage. He knew what he wanted to happen. He knew Victoria wouldn't say no. Didn't mean she had to make it easy.

"You want me to get a virus? Because this is how you get viruses."

"I'm patient, Victoria, but I am not a saint."

"A sinner, if I remember correctly. No way the executioner mask was a Gala Good Guy."

"Open the link."

Curiosity won out over defiance. Victoria tapped the link. A new window opened in the browser, loading slowly as she listened to the faint rasp of X's breath.

"Do we need the pomp and circumstance?" Victoria asked. "Can't we sit down and hash out whatever grievance you ha—"

The page finished loading, revealing a crisp shot of the basement. A time stamp ticked in the corner. Victoria turned toward the source of the video as the image on-screen moved with her, the effect dizzying.

"Do I have your attention now?" X asked.

Warren's movie posters hung along the far wall, framed stills of his favorites. *Cinderella Man*. *The Shawshank Redemption*. *Rocky*. Every man had a *Rocky* poster. Light reflected off the glass in spidery bursts. She could probably find the camera, but it would take time.

"What do you want?"

The screen flicked to the foyer. Another camera.

"Go upstairs," he said.

With leaden feet, Victoria lumbered up the stairs, leaving the remnants of Warren's life behind. She watched herself come into the shot, imagining X doing the same. "Okay."

"Keep going. The bedroom."

The screen flipped to an aerial view of her room, then a view from a side angle by the door, and then from the far window. X had multiple cameras set up, broadcasting the bloody mess.

She continued to the bedroom, not bothering to check for intruders this time. Real life or not, this was a game, her own personal Jigsaw, and distracting Victoria with jump scares didn't seem like X's style. Emotional terrorism, however . . .

The smell permeated the thin material of her shirt, but she covered her mouth anyway. "I'm here, but you already know that. What's next, Simon?"

The laugh came again, curdling in her veins. "Always trying to be *the man*, Victoria. Whiskey-swilling, pants-wearing, take-no-bullshit Victoria. Cratering relationships and cutting ties to anything or anyone stupid enough to get in your way. Warren tried to stifle you, though, didn't he? Smothering you like a campfire that's burned for too long, gotten too close to the brush. He could see that in you—the flames. Knew you were dangerous. Hubris, however, wasn't a good look for him."

"Wow, look at you putting that word-of-the-day calendar to good use."

X ignored her quip. "Pride goes before a fall. He was too proud of his plan—so sure you'd go along with it. How many children do you think he would've demanded of you before you voluntarily gave up the ghost? Each birth breaking off a tiny piece of you until there was nothing left. A shell. A void. My guess was three, but we'll never know, will we? I made sure of that."

She couldn't breathe.

X spoke, laying bare Victoria's darkest secret. The wall she'd built around the truth crumbled. "H-how—" she fumbled, clearing emotion from her throat. "How did you know?"

"The how doesn't matter; not even the why concerns you. Growth requires reflection, Victoria, and I am your mirror."

"I don't understand."

"You will." The screen split into four, showing live shots of the basement, foyer, kitchen, and bedroom. "You once asked what any of this had to do with you. Why didn't I disappear with Warren's ashes? Have you considered that eliminating Warren wasn't my core objective—that my interests are more varied and complex than his continued existence?"

Her hand trembled as she readjusted her grip on the phone against her ear. "Is that a rhetorical question?"

"You fool yourself with sarcasm, but I see what that mask hides. I see your doubt, your fear, how hard you fight against it. Admirable. By now you've come to your own conclusions, tried to find me, and asked yourself: Who is X? Where is X? Not knowing makes you look at everyone in your life through a different lens, doesn't it? You've begun to evaluate the people who surround you and found reasons to distrust them all when only a few are deserving of your scrutiny. Let me take some of the guesswork out of it. I want you, Victoria. At my mercy, one way or another. So, here's how this is going to go. I give you a task. You complete the task. If you are successful, then we meet, and I will tell you everything."

"What do you want me to do?"

X's voice was soft but firm. "Clean it up."

"I'm sorry?" Victoria asked.

"Clean. It. Up."

"I don't—"

"You built your career on the belief that you can handle everything on your own. Independence is a good place to call home, but a house would be nothing without a solid foundation. An unshakeable core. Show me that's you. Prove it. Clean the room. You have two hours."

Victoria surveyed the mess. "Wait, you want me to get rid of this in two hours?"

"If the room isn't back to its original neat-freak glory before the last second strikes, I will notify the police. The footage—from the Gala, from tonight, from the little private moments I've captured when you thought no one was watching—your search histories, Warren's search histories, GPS data, purchases—every piece of damning evidence will go straight to Detective Meyers.

They won't have you with a smoking gun over Warren's body, but they'll have enough breadcrumbs to follow the trail, which will undoubtedly end with you in a jail cell."

"There's nothing to give to the police!" she shrieked. "I didn't kill Warren, I didn't kill Betty, I didn't do . . . whatever the hell happened here."

"That's the fun part," X said, a smile clear in his voice.

"Can't we skip all this and go straight to our meeting?"

"Life's about balance, Victoria. All work and no play never went well for anyone."

"Seems to be coming up aces for you."

The smile was evident. "And I intend to keep it that way. There are rules, but they are simple. One: This has to be done alone. You can't ask for help from anyone. Two: Don't get caught. Goes without saying how important that is. I'd hate for this to end prematurely because one of your nosy neighbors needs to borrow a cup of sugar when you're knee-deep in body scraps."

"What if I refuse?"

"I thought the whole Detective Meyers angle would be enough to convince you of how serious I am, but, sure, plan B. That's where the cameras come in. If you refuse, I'll not only involve the cops, I'll go live and immediately alert the media. You thought Warren's memorial was bad? Everyone in your life will get a front-row seat to this bloodbath, Lady Macbeth. I won't ruin the surprise and disclose exactly how I made the masterpiece that is your Olympus just yet. You might be able to survive an investigation, but would you want to? Livingston would oust you faster than your own father did. Who'd be left when the stone cracks and your castle falls?"

Defiance threaded her nerves, but Victoria was already mentally mapping out the logistics of what it would take to accomplish the task in time. There was a lot of blood. "Most of your leverage hinges on the cameras, but you're not actually here, are you?"

"I'm close."

If she located the source of the feed, there was a chance she could knock everything offline. It wouldn't solve all her problems, but it would give Victoria the advantage she needed to make a move against X.

X, however, was on the same wavelength. "This isn't *Speed*, and you aren't Keanu. Attempt to disable the cameras, tamper with the footage, call for help, or alert Meyers, and I will end you. Social media, police, the entire world will know you're a murderer. You have two hours. I'll be watching. Good luck."

The line disconnected. Powering down Warren's phone, Victoria tossed it on the bed. Hopefully Meyers hadn't figured out that it had been active. Hopefully she was only working against one clock.

She stared at the security footage playing on her phone a little longer, tempted to throw up a middle finger and go to Meyers anyway. Call X's bluff. He didn't have evidence because she didn't kill Warren.

Teagan's words echoed through her mind, though. How quickly would Kent Wood condemn her if a stranger offered them proof with a pretty shine?

"Fuck," she spat, leaning the phone against the mirror of her vanity.

Hands on her hips, Victoria evaluated the challenge. Floors. Walls. Furniture.

So much blood.

It was time to get to work.

53

Victoria was well-versed in disasters, from the downfalls of major corporate empires to the slow decline of her marriage. She never tired of the thrill of coming out of them unscathed.

But she'd never handled anything like this. In the many, many nights that she'd laid awake as Warren snored beside her, blissfully unaware that her jagged thoughts were meandering dangerously close to the edge of homicide, Victoria had let her imagination roam. Death was a chameleon, a revolving door of options, but in the end, she'd preferred the idea of a quiet, contained bathtub of blood.

Not this massacre. Not the permeating stench of rot.

Squeamish wasn't a word she used to describe herself. Her father hadn't taken her on his hunting trips; those were only for men. Tough, manly men who shot big guns and got dirty, never mind that Jeremy Livingston's uncalloused hands and perfectly creased slacks cast serious doubt on his definition of masculinity. But when he'd return from a weekend in the woods it was Victoria he called to his side.

His reservations about the act of hunting didn't extend to the handling of the carcass. He'd had no qualms about Victoria watching him hang a gutted deer from the garage ceiling, narrating as he worked to break it down. Granted, it had been years since those delightful life lessons, but Victoria hadn't forgotten.

She knew what it meant to get dirty.

As she peeled away the disgusting drop cloths and rolled them into sticky piles, however, the years since those Sunday mornings with her father grew exponentially. Warren was supposed to have died peacefully in the bathtub and a crime-scene team was supposed to dispose of the aftermath while she played the part of Stunned Wife.

A red glob flapped off a sheet and slid down her forearm. Victoria grimaced and batted it away with a few choice words that were not playground approved. And Warren had wanted her to be the mother of his many children?

She wasn't going down that road again, not when the point was irrelevant and the more pressing issue was someone else's blood staining her bedroom. Lost in thought and arms full, Victoria tripped and went sprawling to the floor. The blood-covered plastic sheets smeared the carpet with a sickening slurp.

"Son of a—" she groaned, head thrown back in exasperation. She was tired and sore. Blood had soaked into some of the soft-fabric surfaces. Clots had hardened in the places where the carpet had been inadvertently exposed in her efforts. A third of the bedroom was a still from a Rob Zombie movie.

And through it all, X was watching; she was acutely aware of the rolling video feed, ignoring the creeping sensation of a being a bug under a microscope.

Victoria checked her watch. An hour and thirty-seven minutes.

There was also the matter of Warren's eyeballs decomposing in the drawer.

Victoria yanked off the dish gloves she'd grabbed from the kitchen and opened a private browser on her phone. The security footage slid to the corner as she typed in her search parameters of how best to remove the stains from the carpet. The top result was a blog from a mother in Indiana raising three kids with her three favorite men (husband, God, and Jesus). Flowers and blubbering pink hearts with chipper dimples danced along the byline. Archives devoted to preschool activities, toddler lunches in fancy boxes, and aligning secular readings with the Bible were arranged on the left menu.

"Wow," she said, scrolling through paragraph after holy-dripping paragraph of anecdotes and allegories. Warren probably would've loved for her to make a mommy blog.

He probably would've liked for her to go to church, too, come to think of it, but potato, tomato; it was too late for Victoria to redis-cover Catholic guilt. She'd made her own peace. If she'd learned anything about religion from her upbringing, it was that the worst sinners were often the ones pointing fingers the hardest.

The louder you were, the easier it was to blame someone else for your crime.

Victoria was experiencing this firsthand.

Somewhere in between teaching your dog to sit for Jesus and a how-to on constructing the perfect grievance letter to your way ward neighbors, Victoria found a section on household chores and deep-cleaning solutions.

She skimmed down to a suggestion of Dawn dish soap and a steel brush. "Because even the Devil's afraid of Dawn," she read aloud. "Praise be."

She let loose a dry laugh and dropped her chin to her chest. Victoria was *exhausted*. Racoon rings was an understatement. The bags under her eyes had bags. She couldn't remember the last time she'd ever felt the buzzing need to rest.

One hour and twenty-nine minutes.

No rest for the wicked, she thought, closing the browser. No rest for the wicked and certainly not for her, wherever she fell on the morality spectrum.

She didn't have any Dawn. Warren insisted she buy the fancy soap that smelled like brambleberry and moisturized. God forbid he use an extra squirt of lotion.

The longer she took, the deeper the stain would set. The harder it would be to remove. She could almost feel it clawing into the fibers. X's mechanical laughter echoed in her ears.

Don't ask for help.

Don't get caught.

Her keys and purse were by the front door where she'd left them after Detective Meyers's surprise visit. A quick glance at her clothes reminded her that she couldn't go out in public looking like Carrie at the prom. Getting to her closet the way it was, however, would be an enormous pain in the ass and a waste of time.

Victoria instead turned to the basement.

Skirting around glass from a broken picture frame, she wove through the chaos of Warren's things in search of something clean and close to her size. It wasn't like he'd be wearing them anytime soon. She put her dirty clothes into a pile and grabbed a pair of his old joggers and an oversized gray hooded Syracuse sweatshirt.

Victoria smoothed her hair—good enough—and headed toward the stairs when her foot caught the edge of a box, upsetting a massive container of files. Warren had insisted on keeping multiple copies of their important documents: expired IDs, passports, car titles, birth certificates, marriage license. He'd even kept duplicates of their tax statements going back five years. *Just in case*, his only explanation.

Just her luck to knock over a paper trail of their relationship when her future was on the line, she thought.

She bent to scoop them up, ignoring the voice in her head telling her to leave it for later. Old habits die hard. As she shuffled the stack together, the words on the top caught her attention. CERTIFICATE FOR THE DISILLUSION OF THE ENTITY.

That was strange. The rest of Warren's client files were either digital or stored at the office. The date was listed as the week before his death. Warren hadn't mentioned anything about shutting down one of their clients recently. That many were leaving for different agencies, she knew. But willingly terminating any of their entities would have involved her consideration.

These documents hadn't been filed, nor was the information complete, she gathered from a brief scan of the fields. She wanted to delve further into the contract notes but decided to bring them with her instead. Getting sidetracked by Livingston business was exactly what X would want.

Whatever deal Warren had been working on could wait for the light of day. X, however, could not.

54

An in-and-out trip, Victoria told herself. X hadn't sounded an alarm as she drove away, which she hoped was a good sign. He hadn't explicitly forbidden her from leaving the house, but she also didn't want to break an arbitrary rule and return to a bazaar of bad luck.

The phone buzzed. *Where are you going, Victoria?*

Milk run, she responded.

The footage flickered in the corner. A figure dressed in black and wearing the executioner's mask appeared in the foyer. Victoria gasped as a gloved hand waved slowly back and forth before disappearing from view.

Remember the rules. Tick tock, the message warned.

The idea of X in her home no longer made her feel slimy. Violated, yes, but it left her simmering in anger instead of anxiety.

A horn beeped, yanking her concentration away from the feed as the headlights of an oncoming car blinded her. She swerved in time, having crossed the double yellows, but turned the phone away for the remainder of the drive.

Her thoughts turned to Warren.

Their relationship hadn't been just a marriage. They were business associates. Competitors. She knew his freckles and his faux pas. The things he was afraid of (failure) and the things he was *really* afraid of (bugs and clowns). Before she'd found those files, Victoria would've said he was incapable of getting a lie past her, not when it counted. When you were with someone in that capacity, on all fronts, for as long as they had been, the fathoms only ran so deep.

You had him fooled, though, her mind offered up. *He wouldn't have seen you coming.*

Suddenly, she wasn't so sure about that.

The Walmart sign was half-dim and as depressing as that mental lightbulb. Victoria checked her reflection quickly for signs of blood. Satisfied, she ran inside, grabbed a basket, and squinted at the aisle signs in the fluorescent lighting. Crafting materials. Linens. Dorm futons. Flip and fucks, they'd called them in college. Warren had a black one in his common room junior year. It stunk of boys and was filthy, covered in spilled beer and god knew what else.

"Victoria?"

She skidded to a halt at the sound of her name, hairs prickling on the back of her neck. Son of a bitch, she did not need small talk right now.

"Victoria, I thought that was you."

Shit. Margaret Connors. Seriously? What were the odds of running into her, of all people, at this store, at this hour?

Margaret radiated beauty and Parisian chic in her silk scarf and dark glasses, tapered black pants, and long-sleeve black shirt with a soft boat neck. Dressed to impress, even at Walmart in the middle of the night.

Victoria turned slowly, a small smile already plastered in place. "Margaret!" They pecked cheeks and embraced. She hoped Warren's lingering cologne masked the slaughterhouse odor. "How are you?"

Margaret spoke fast and kept her sunglasses lowered. "I'm well, thank you. Busy, you know. With the Gala and—and everything after the Gala and my mother. I haven't had a minute to catch my breath in weeks; it's just never-ending."

"I can imagine." Victoria peeked in Margaret's cart. A package of European outlet adapters, a wireless charger, and a petite carry-on suitcase in a muted floral design. "Going somewhere?"

"Ahhh," Margaret spluttered, unsuccessfully shielding her cart. "Yes. Barnaby has to leave in an hour. Red-eye to Venice. I'm joining him tomorrow, maybe the day after, once I finalize some things with my mother's care. She's feeling a bit better. They say it's the calm before the storm. She won't make it to the new year."

Venice. Margaret and Barnaby were leaving the country.

"I'm sorry to hear about your mother. Seems like you'd want to stay closer to home, not jet set to Italy."

Beneath the contours and foundation, the color drained from Margaret's face. "Yes. Well. We don't always have a choice, do we. Or maybe we do, but neither option is what we truly want."

"Like you know anything about not getting what you want."

Margaret ignored the dig. "Have you spoken with Dave since Betty passed? He mentioned the lovely gift basket she put together for you. Never would've guessed it would be one of the last things she did."

A dam broke, some long-held tension between them. They shed their pretenses like snakeskins, the remnants of decorum forgotten.

"I know what you're doing." Victoria snapped.

"Can't say I appreciate your tone. What are you suggesting?"

"I didn't do anything to Betty."

"Exactly what a guilty person would say. Tell me, Victoria, would you be more willing to tell the truth if we were alone? Without the crowds and the cameras?"

Cameras.

All at once, Victoria was certain that she was missing a vital part of this conversation. Apprehension sat heavy on her chest, the same dense dread she felt when X texted.

And that was something worth examining.

"What do you know?" she asked.

Margaret shrugged. "More than you want me to. I just think it's funny what people will do when they think no one's watching."

Victoria was too tired and angry for sugarcoating. Her bones ached. Her head was pounding. This was supposed to be a milk run. She had an hour and change before X went to the police, and Margaret's I-know-something-you-don't-know attitude wasn't going to fly with her.

"Are you following me?" Victoria asked

"Darling, you sound paranoid."

"How did you know I was here?"

"Victoria, I honestly have no clue what you're talking about. I came because Barnaby—"

"Yeah, Barnaby's impromptu wanderlust." Victoria said with a sarcastic wink, growing more confident by the second. Margaret had been in her home. She knew about Betty's gift. Mentioned cameras. Who else had easy access to surveillance equipment and ample opportunity?

"You know, when I heard about the incident at the clubhouse, I didn't want to believe it. I said, Victoria Tate? Level-headed, logical, above-the-drama Victoria Tate? No way would she threaten anyone without provocation. But then I remembered the night of the Gala, and it made me rethink all the other things I'd brushed off as circumstance. Your clipped behavior with Warren. Allowing your sister to make a mockery of herself with a saucy gleam in your eye."

"Did you say 'saucy gleam'?"

"I know what you are," Margaret said, keeping her voice conversational but unable to control the razorblades beneath her words. "That horrible show at your office—I know what you did."

Victoria scoffed. "How long have you been spying on me, Margaret?" Margaret angled the cart and moved to pass. Victoria grabbed her elbow. "We're not through."

"Let me go," she said, tugging at Victoria's grasp.

"How long?"

"I swear I will scream."

"Go ahead," Victoria said. A dare.

Margaret's perfectly sculpted eyebrows knitted together. Victoria stepped closer and released her arm, enjoying the flinch of pain as she plucked the sunglasses from Margaret's face. Without the lenses to protect them, her gray eyes were red-rimmed and haunted, which only spurred Victoria on.

"You look terrible. Guilty conscience?" Margaret scoffed but remained silent, so Victoria pressed on. "Why are you doing this? Did you think I wouldn't find out it was you?"

"I—" She put the cart between them and loosened the knot on her scarf, fish-mouthing as she failed to come up with an answer.

"Destroy the footage and we can discuss this like adults."

Margaret groaned. "I'll have her badge for this."

Victory. Yes. She knew trusting her instincts would—wait. *Her?*

"X is a woman?"

"X?"

"He—she—has been texting me for weeks," Victoria said her mind racing.

"Weeks."

"Yes, since the service. Well, technically since the night Warren died."

Margaret waved a manicured hand in the air as she spoke. "Hold on. That's impossible. We didn't even know about the camera until this afternoon."

"Who is we? And what camera?" Margaret's face filled with horror. Victoria waited for her to explain but grew impatient as when answers came. "What camera, Margaret?"

"Shit," Margaret said, a breath of a word. She closed her eyes and slid to the floor. Brushing away dust bunnies and crinkled candy wrappers in disgust, she drew her legs to her chin and wrapped her arms around her knees.

From court queen to temper tantrum. Oh, how the mighty had fallen.

She almost felt sorry for her.

Almost.

Victoria pushed the cart out of the way and stood akimbo over Margaret, who removed a slender gold box from her bra strap. It clicked open to reveal an ornate lighter and a sleek row of hand-rolled blunts. She tapped one against the case, lit the end, and inhaled deeply.

"I don't understand."

Wisps of smoke rose around them, the sweet-skunk smell of weed. "Detective Meyers."

Victoria startled at the name. That was not what she'd been expecting. "What does she have to do with a camera?"

"She thinks you murdered Warren, and honestly I think you did too." She leaned back against a shelf, the delicate gold chain around her neck glimmering under the harsh lights. "The graphic message at your office. We all saw the graffiti. Your erratic behavior at the clubhouse and with . . . with Betty, may she rest in peace. Did you do it, Victoria? Did you murder your husband?"

"No," she said. Victoria snatched the blunt from Margaret, crushed it into the metal edge of the shelf and dropped the remnants in her lap. "I'm out of patience, so please start making sense. What camera? Why does Meyers think I murdered Warren?"

Margaret wiped away the ash, her tired eyes now lit with fury. "We have video of you in that conference room."

55

That X had been watching her outside the house wasn't surprising. It's what she would've done had she been in X's position. Victoria had more in common with X than she wanted to admit.

They'd both wanted Warren dead. They both loved the thrill of the takedown. Victoria racked her brain, retracing her scattered memories of the days before Warren's death, but came up with nothing.

"Conference room?" she asked. "At Livingston?"

"At the Gala."

The Gala? "You'll forgive me if my memories of that night are somewhat skewed by the traumatic loss of my husband, but I have no clue what you're talking about."

"Yes, you do," Margaret said. "Barnaby received an email this morning and clicked on the link before I could dissuade him. Man's never met a porn site he could say no to, unfortunately."

"Not my business."

"Imagine his disappointment when he discovered that it didn't lead to the *interesting threesome* as was promised in the hyperlink, but rather a recording of you with two other people.

One of whom turned out to be Warren. In some sort of strange standoff."

The red room. That's how Meyers had found out about it. "Why would you give that to Meyers without asking me about it? We may not be the best of friends, but I thought our relationship would've warranted common courtesy."

"Please, Victoria, save your melodramatic antics for your primetime interview. I didn't need to ask you what happened because I saw everything play out with my own eyes. Why on earth you decided to hash out your revenge plot in a public forum, I don't dare to guess, but you reap what you sow."

"You put that together," Victoria said slowly. "Warren said it was your idea."

"Well, he was lying."

That was becoming a common theme. "Who sent the email?"

"It's unimportant. The police have it now, and I've been assured the matter will be dealt with discreetly."

Victoria shuddered, the plague doctor and executioner getups imprinted on the back of her eyelids, the off-putting crimson walls pulsing like a beating heart. They'd demanded a name, and she'd given one. "I can explain what you saw. Not all of it, but most of it."

"Like I said, Victoria, I don't need to hear any of your excuses or lies. You ordered a hit on your husband. Cold blooded."

"But I was talking to Warren," Victoria argued. "I knew it was him; that's why I called him out in the first place!"

Margaret shook her head. "I didn't see Warren—just you and the hitmen. And a few hours later, Warren was dead."

X hadn't sent the whole video. Of course, he hadn't.

Shit. That interaction would look bad for anyone, but for Victoria? A guilty spouse, no-brainer.

All work and no play, X had said. This was his play. He was the disturbed child and she was the live butterfly being pinned to the collector's board.

Victoria's expression darkened. "If you didn't see Warren reveal himself, then you don't have the full story, and anything you gave to Meyers is circumstantial."

"Not my problem or concern."

"Where's Barnaby?" Victoria asked. "Hiding in the next aisle? Trying to get more 'evidence' for Detective Meyers?" They were the angriest air quotes she'd ever used in her life, and damn it, they were warranted.

Margaret stood abruptly, wiping her pants. "You're insane. He's not here. He was too nervous to leave the house because he was convinced that you'd find out we'd gone to Meyers. And apparently, he was right."

"Because you just told me."

"A likely story."

Victoria would not slap Margaret. She would not. "I've had a very long, very *trying* evening, and—"

Margaret snatched her sunglasses from Victoria and primly slid them back into place. "You don't scare me, Victoria Tate, and one notch on your belt isn't impressive. You think Barnaby and I got where we are by sticking to the clean side of the street? Normally, I wouldn't be so direct, but really, dear, what are you going to do? Kill me? Warren may not have had the guts to stand up to you, but make no mistake: we are not the same, and I won't hesitate to—"

"For Christ's sake, I didn't kill Warren!"

But she'd wanted to. Was going to.

"I guess we'll see, but between you and me, if it looks like a duck and quacks like a duck . . ." She shrugged, the gesture so effortlessly banal it set Victoria's teeth on edge. "I'm sure Detective Meyers will be in touch soon, so if I were you, I wouldn't leave town."

No. *No.* That was unacceptable. Margaret couldn't drop that in her lap and then waltz off to a sun-soaked villa for tapas on the piazza.

Victoria stepped in front of the cart. "Why did that door have a Gala logo? The red room from the video. It was marked for the party."

"I don't know. We had nothing to do with that. I probably shouldn't be telling you this, but Meyers has already spoken to the event planner, design team, and decorating crew, and they've all attested to the fact that there was no red room on the party manifest. A velvet rope should have cordoned off that hallway, leading you directly into the banquet. Everyone else was able to make it there without an issue. Everyone except you."

"I never saw a rope," Victoria said.

"How you ended up in there is a mystery. But I watched the video dozens of times before we turned it over. The clues add up. You said you wanted Warren dead, and then he ended up dead."

"That's not . . ." Victoria fumbled. "Look I know you think you've got this figured out, Margaret, but there's a lot about this situation that you're missing, and honestly, I don't have the mental fortitude to get into it with you. You want the truth? Mask or not, I knew it was Warren the second I heard his voice. I was trying to beat him at his own game. Because I was frustrated. He'd canceled our lunch date, and we'd been having some personal issues—nothing that would warrant extreme violence," she added, because that's what a wife who hadn't been planning on murdering her husband would say. "Just . . . issues. We were working through them, but I hadn't seen him all night and then found this sketchy setup and him in disguise. I couldn't believe he'd play such an awful prank on me, thought he'd had too much to drink and . . ."

"Issues," she said, nodding as if in mutual understanding. "Right. So, this *was* a revenge thing. Warren could be mean when he was drunk?"

"No—" Jesus, it was like reasoning with a toddler, she thought, "—this wasn't a revenge thing. There was no *thing*. He was my husband. I cared very deeply for him, and yes, you saw a video that looks very suspicious, but I didn't kill Warren. Someone wants you to think that I did, though."

They'd moved closer throughout Victoria's outpouring of emotion. She watched Margaret's hard edges melt into sympathy with every admission. The whole world was a stage, and apparently Victoria's star performance was set in a dirty aisle of a run-down Walmart.

"Poor love," Margaret said, stroking her arm.

"Don't touch me." Victoria scowled, looking pointedly at the hand moving up and down her arm.

Margaret withdrew slowly, lifting a finger at a time until the connection ended. "Sugar and vinegar, didn't your mother teach you the difference?" Margaret asked. "Too often kindness is rewarded by kicks, don't you agree?"

"You know only douchebags wear sunglasses inside," she said.

"Vulgar." Margaret heaved an exasperated sigh and clucked her tongue in disapproval. "And proves my point. Listen, we've had some good times together, yes? I'm willing to overlook your little outburst. You're under inordinate amounts of stress. I'm probably the last person you want to hear this from, but it's . . . obvious you're struggling. If you need anything, help with your bills, anything, we'd be happy to lend you the money. We know a wonderful realtor who could—"

"Hold on. I don't need money," Victoria snapped. "Why would you think that?"

She paused. "Since we're being honest . . . after our meeting, Barnaby told me about Livingston's . . . staggering downward trend, we'll call it."

"Livingston is solid."

"Warren botched that big deal with Harpers, and then the issue with the Knottiers—I just heard that things were precarious." She cocked her head, as if to state the obvious. "Sweetie, you're shopping at Walmart. At *night*. Wearing *that*."

The audacity of this woman, Victoria thought, but found the words ringing true like church bells in her head. She'd been drowning in account management for weeks but hadn't gotten the full rundown because her power still came with an asterisk.

"You're here, too, Margaret," she said.

"Yes, dear, but out of necessity. Barnaby *cannot* miss this flight, and Amazon doesn't deliver that quickly. Plus, I'm incognito." Margaret slid the sunglasses up her nose before swiftly retying the scarf around her head. "You're not even trying."

Do not slap her, she thought. *It's not worth it.*

She checked her phone and staggered at how many minutes she'd lost arguing with Margaret. "I should get going," Victoria said, her thoughts reeling. There were too many strands. She needed to get home and contact X.

Margaret called out a few seconds later as Victoria spotted the bottles of Dawn on an endcap. She selected three and dropped them unceremoniously into the basket, pointedly ignoring Margaret's repeated attempts to get her attention. Livingston going under. She knew nothing about nothing.

"Honey, this is poor form, but I have to ask," Margaret said, stepping into her space. "Since we're having a moment. We are having a moment, right?"

"No, we're not."

"We definitely are," she said dismissively, inching even closer. "Victoria, if you didn't kill Warren, then who did?"

Victoria ran a hand through her hair. "I don't know."

"You said someone's been texting you?" Victoria held her tongue. The cart squeaked closer and Margaret appeared beside her. Vanilla notes invading her bubble. "I can call Meyers if you'd like. Tell her we made an error. Better yet, why don't we go down to the station together? I'll drop this stuff off at home, and we can go to Meyers—"

No cops. "Who was the executioner, Margaret? The person with Warren."

She curled her lips in. "I have no idea."

"They were your costumes."

"That wasn't one of ours."

"It had to be," Victoria said.

"I've talked to every guest. No one remembers an executioner. If I hadn't seen it for myself, I would've said you'd made him up."

"You had professional photographers. People took pictures all night. Someone had to have seen him. I can't be the only one."

I wasn't, she thought. *Warren saw the executioner too.*

"I wish I had a different answer, sweetie. Warren had flaws, but he was a good man," she said, resigned to the acknowledgment. "I'll let you know if my security team finds anything. We still haven't located the camera, and the whole Mansion was swept before the Gala."

They wouldn't find anything, Victoria knew. X was careful. "Sure."

"Victoria, it doesn't look good for you right now. I'm saying this as a friend. Well, maybe not a friend after this, but as someone you should respect, at the very least. I'd speak to an attorney. Just in case."

Moment's over. "Piss off, Margaret," Victoria said. "Tell Barnaby the same."

Her reflection tilted in Margaret's designer lenses as she settled into her queen energy once again. "Goodbye, Victoria," Margaret said deftly, heels clacking on the linoleum.

Victoria waited as long as she could to avoid an awkward checkout encounter and then raced through the line without meeting the cashier's inquisitive stare. As she unlocked her car, however, Victoria heard frantic clacking footsteps approaching.

"Victoria! Victoria, wait!"

How she managed not to topple over on the slick pavement in those shoes was a miracle. Impressive or not, Victoria was in no mood for anymore chats tonight. The blood wasn't going to clean itself. She slid into the driver's seat and slammed the door as Margaret barreled forward.

"Margaret," she said, rolling down the window. "What's your problem?"

"Victoria, your house!"

Her house?

Margaret held her phone between magenta fingernails. A news broadcast panned to follow the flashing lights of emergency vehicles in a residential area. A blue banner ticked updates across the bottom of the screen. Letters and numbers, one after the other. A hashtag and email address. None of it made sense.

It was the Manor. It was her house.

Oh, shit, X had turned her in.

Margaret shook the phone in bowtie arcs. "Barnaby called. Everyone's trying to reach you. They think you were trapped in the fire."

Her mind was stuck on the crime scene that was her bedroom. There was so much blood. How was she going to explain that? Not even Livingston's best lawyer could—

It took a moment for Victoria's thoughts to catch up to what Margaret was actually telling her. "Did you say fire?"

56

Her texts to X went unanswered. Victoria grew warier the longer Warren's phone stayed on and in her possession. It should've been with his body. Meyers might've had an alert set up in case it was reactivated. They could track the location. The true crime podcasts probably talked about this, but she hadn't paid attention.

Rolling down the window, she tossed the phone onto the highway and watched it shatter into sparkling pieces in the rearview mirror. The security feed on her phone had gone dark, but if X wanted to contact her, he could find her in person.

No more games.

Dilapidated houses gave way to the crumbling facades of old factories and warehouses as Victoria wove toward downtown. The streets were empty at this hour, the trendy eateries and gastropubs in the renovated spaces dark and quiet. Twinkle lights shimmered in the storefronts; her headlights reflected off the glass and Victoria strained against the glare.

Christmastime in the city was beautiful. Serene. The exact opposite of her night.

She couldn't go back to Kent Wood Manor. X had made sure of that. Had they found the bedroom before the flames spread?

By now, she assumed that Margaret had informed the police that she was alive and well and hiding out at a nearby Walmart. The look on her face before Victoria sped out of the parking lot spoke volumes.

Margaret believed Victoria had started the fire, and if she believed it, everyone in the tri-state area was going to be hunting her before Starbucks brewed its first venti.

Even on the off chance the police weren't trying to arrest her, they'd have questions that she couldn't answer.

She needed X. Teagan would help her. One way or the other, Victoria wasn't leaving her sister's condo until she found him.

Turning into The Heights, the upscale condos where Teagan lived, Victoria ignored the dozens of notifications on her phone and dialed her sister. She answered before the end of the third ring.

"Victoria? Tor!" She raced on before Victoria had a chance to respond. "I've been calling you for like an hour, and now your mailbox's full, what the hell? What happened? Are you all right? Were you in the house? I've been going out of my mind."

"My ringer wasn't on, I'm sorry. And no, I'm not home. I ran into Margaret Connors. She told me about the fire."

"You weren't home when it started?" she asked.

"Clearly not."

"Clearly not," she mimicked. "It's astounding you've made it as far as you have when you lack the fundamental skills of communication."

Victoria tripped on a mental snag. Why had Margaret been the one to break the news about the fire? X had never been shy about his moves before. Taunting her, testing her limits. Yet she'd received no warning, no ultimatum or big reveal.

"I've got two fingers and a four-letter word for you," Victoria said. "How's that for fundamental?"

"An improvement. Why weren't you home? Too late for you to be at the office still, isn't it? And why the hell were you with Margaret Connors?"

Teagan sounded like she was in a tunnel. "Am I on speaker?" Victoria asked, pulling into a spot in the far corner of the parking lot.

"Yeah, sorry, I'm making some tea," she said.

"I thought you hated tea."

"I meant coffee." A bell pinged monotonously in the background. "That's the microwave. Popcorn fix."

"You thought I died in a fire and stopped to make popcorn?"

"I was waiting to hear back from that fireman from the summer. The one with the nice calves?"

"I remember." *Unfortunately,* she thought, blinking away the memory of walking in on her sister riding the man with nice calves on top of the patio table on the back deck. She'd triple bleached her brain and the table until Warren had complained about the odor.

"Mm-hm, well, he called to give me a heads up. Said that if you were inside, odds were low that you would've been able to survive the blaze because it spread so hard and fast. Last I knew, they were still trying to contain it but had managed to catch the worst of it. He said . . . Victoria he said I should mentally prepare myself to identify your body but to wait for someone to contact me first. That there was nothing I could do and going there wouldn't be good for anyone. I thought I lost you. I needed a distraction."

"I'm sorry I made you worry."

"You and me both," Teagan said. "Where are you now?"

Victoria watched a dark sedan roll up to a resident's spot in front of the building. The door opened and shut quickly. Her attention narrowed, trying to discern the driver's identity "Coming to you. We need to talk. *I* need to talk."

Scratching noises, and the echo-effect faded. She wasn't on speaker anymore. Teagan's voice suddenly filtered into her ear, calm and reassuring. "Okay, good. God, Tor, I'm so relieved, you have no idea."

"I'm okay."

"I mean the texts. Betty. The fire it's not safe for you to be alone. I don't want you running around with a crazy person on the loose. I told you this would happen."

"Uh-huh," Victoria agreed. "You did."

"I know, I know; I won't rub it in. Listen, I've got some extra coffee pods. I'll get a cup on for you, and we can figure this out. I'd say we could open a bottle of wine, but I think we're better off sober tonight. We're going to get through this together."

"Couldn't agree more. Thanks, Teags. I'll be there soon."

The call disconnected but Victoria didn't move. Didn't breathe A figure finally emerged from the car, a woman with her hands full. She was unloading several duffel bags from the backseat. Her long auburn hair was swept in a high ponytail and it bobbed in the faint light of the building's recessed panels.

The woman, focused on getting the straps of the bags situated without dropping anything, didn't see her. Victoria saw *her*, though. Watched her fumble with her keys and bound down the sidewalk into the building.

Teagan.

Teagan had lied. Warren had lied. Victoria needed to know why.

57

In the low light from the dashboard, Victoria thumbed through the disorganized pile of Warren's secret papers. Because that's how she was thinking about them now: the thing he was hiding. The talk they were supposed to have after the Gala. Her gut screamed that these were dots worth connecting, and that intuition hadn't steered her wrong yet. The red flags were waving too hard for this to be dismissed as coincidence.

So she read the documents.

And she read them again.

And still, she couldn't believe.

Hands shaking, she stared unseeingly out the window, one thought throbbing in her mind: How?

How had this happened?

How had Warren *let* this happen?

How had she been so obtuse?

Margaret, that bitch, was right. Livingston was on the brink of bankruptcy. Past the brink. A breath away from full-on crisis.

The truth was there in black and white. Warren had done an excellent job covering his tracks, fudging reports to hide the real numbers. Expense accounts and initial assessments. A draft of a lender contract with a company she recognized as one of Barnaby Connors's investments.

They were drowning.

How could he have done this to her?

"You're lucky you're dead," she gritted. *That lying, deceitful dick.* Victoria warred with a strong desire to reincarnate his lying corpse and kill him again. Maybe three times. Painfully. She gripped the wheel and squeezed. Squeezed. Squeezed.

Rage reduced to a simmer but didn't dissipate completely. It wasn't just that the financials were screwed, and she'd probably been days, a week tops, away from discovering this without the hidden papers. Warren's investments were . . . suspect. First-year stats class failure-level suspect. She'd have to fine-tooth-comb it, but he'd made rookie mistakes—careless, unvetted errors in judgment.

Victoria reviewed months' worth of bank statements, her finger grazing over the account number and a list of outgoing transactions. She flipped pages and took another proverbial bullet when it turned out to be a statement for an offshore account in the Cayman Islands.

"What the hell," she said, utter disbelief draining the adrenaline from her system.

Warren had a Cayman Islands account.

Warren was using Livingston to maintain a shell account—maybe more than one; she wouldn't know for sure until she dug deeper, but one was one more than he should've had.

And she hadn't suspected a goddamn thing.

The last item on the activity list was a pending transfer that yanked the floor out from beneath her feet. Warren had been preparing to send almost a quarter of a million dollars to someone just days before he'd been murdered.

The recipient's name wasn't listed, and the identifying information was incomplete. A PO Box. A local number that she didn't recognize and a generic email address. Wasn't much to go on, but this wasn't an accident, nor was it a client taking advantage of a legal loophole.

Because despite appearances, Warren knew exactly what he was doing.

"*Really* lucky you're dead," she said.

It was like she'd slipped into an alternate reality. Warren hadn't just fooled her once. He'd been lying to her every day. Deceiving her on a level she would've said he wasn't capable of. This was the same man whose mother had done his laundry until he was twenty-three. The man who'd put a metal tin of leftovers in the microwave and almost blew up the kitchen. Those weren't the traits of this cunning and ruthless and—wait.

She'd tossed page after page on the floor as the revelations became apparent, but now came to a stop at the sheet in front of her: a scanned contract between Livingston Corporation and a medical company.

What was Warren doing meddling in the medical field?

Livingston had a health-care division, but they rarely, if ever, interacted on the same accounts. They were run by different executives, followed different federal and state guidelines. A medical practice was outside of Warren's purview. According to this, though, Warren had promised a substantial sum to a startup of a private practice.

Copies of emails followed, and Victoria came untethered. For months, Warren had been putting out feelers—nothing egregious, just testing the waters. Keeping his proposals hypothetical. Expressing interest in an independent venture, which was bullshit speak for screwing Victoria over. Starting fresh, he'd written. *A new opportunity.*

Victoria trembled with anger.

Warren had intended to ground Livingston—and destroy her in the process—so he could invest in a . . . private medical practice?

Madness.

No one in their sector would've advised him that this was a good idea. If she'd had any inclination before he died that this was his intention, Victoria would've quashed it before it had even left the gate.

This was—

"No," she moaned, dragging out the word in horror as everything finally clicked into place. The answer was so glaringly obvious in the space between the lies.

Only one person could have convinced Warren to make that move.

58

In fairy tales, siblings were always strongest when they were together. Hansel and Gretel. Tweedledum and Tweedledee. Hell, even Cinderella's stepsisters were unbeatable before their heels were chopped off to prove a moral. Real life, however, hadn't been that kind to Victoria and Teagan. Not with a mother whose love remained surface-deep and a father who would pit them against each other to better teach them the definition of defeat.

At best they were teammates, competitors.

At worst they were rivals, sworn enemies who knew each other to the core: every strength, weakness, and point of vulnerability. Warren's death had created a bridge for them. A space to nuture a new kind of dynamic. It had widened their common ground, opened a door of communication that had previously been dead-bolted and boarded-up. But as Victoria approached her sister's building, a new truth settled in her bones, and she disassembled the bridge brick by traitorous brick.

She ignored the festive boutique window displays, grateful for the deserted street and eerie yellow glow from the streetlights. To her right, walking paths wound through the rocky rifts along the Hudson. The guardrails were low. It wouldn't take much to push someone Teagan's size over the edge, just a little shove at the right angle.

Gravity would do the rest.

She crossed to the entrance with her head bent against the wind. A sign outlined the rental office's business hours, but the door was locked. She only had to wait a few minutes for someone to exit, but she paced against the cold and her nerves, pretending to fumble with her keys to not draw suspicion as she thanked the couple before slipping inside. She shook off the cold in the silence of the lobby, pressing the elevator button before circling the waiting area.

It was nice. Trendy. Victoria hadn't been to The Heights since Teagan had moved in, circumstance or work schedules keeping her from making the trek downtown. A tubular vase of flowers cozied the harsh lines. Chic lounge chairs flanked geometric tables, all white, and floor-to-ceiling windows looked out on what was a fabulous view of the Hudson during the day. All she could see now was murky blackness, occasionally interrupted by industrial streetlights.

Victoria pressed the elevator button again and then dipped to the side where a tiny room was lined with mailboxes. She noted a security camera in the upper corner, the red light focused on her as she meandered casually back and forth. She pulled the hood of her sweatshirt over her head and swiveled back toward the elevators.

The doors opened with a puff of hot air. A woman with earbuds emerged, focused on her phone and humming a song off-key under her breath, unaware that she was barreling into Victoria.

"'Scuse me," she said with a hurried nod as they danced around each other.

"Sorry," Victoria said at the time, groaning when she was hit with a slap of recognition. In black workout gear and with her hair twisted in a loose braid, Judy's face filled with surprise.

Judy. As if the night could get any worse.

"Victoria, hi!" Judy said, hand to her chest as she looked up. She hit pause on her playlist and gave a confused smile, the ghost of eyeliner dotting her lids as if she'd wiped her face in a hurry.

"Hi."

"What are you doing here?" she asked. "Are you looking for me? I know we had a rough day, and I just want to say that I'm sorry if I overstepped any boundaries. I was going to apologize tomorrow, but if there's something you need in the meantime, I'd be more than happy to—"

"Judy," she said firmly, hoping to stopper the awkward ramble. She either hadn't heard about the fire or she was good at pretending. And from what she'd seen, Victoria leaned in favor of the former. Judy wasn't an actress. "Relax. I'm visiting my sister. I didn't know you lived in The Heights."

"Yeah, going on six months now. A studio—you don't pay me that well," she tittered nervously. "I love it, though. I'm surprised I haven't run into Teagan. Small world."

You have no idea. "I was just thinking the same thing."

"Well, I won't keep you. It was good seeing you. I'm on my way down to the gym, so . . ." Judy said, offering a timid smile and shaking her water bottle in explanation.

The picture that X sent of Judy and Warren at the Gala flashed through her mind. There wouldn't be a better chance to get her alone outside of a work setting. "Can I ask you something?"

"Of course."

"You lied to me."

Judy twisted, the color draining from her cheeks. "That's . . . not a question. I'm sorry, when did I lie?"

"When I asked you about the Gala. You said you didn't go, but I know you were there. With Warren."

If she'd looked pale before, Judy turned positively ghostly at the mention of Warren. "Okay, I don't know what you heard or who you've been talking to, but I wasn't there. I wasn't *invited.* I couldn't have even gotten through the door. The Connors would've kicked me to the curb before I'd raised my bony, unpolished hand to show my poor-person ID." She tugged at a flyaway, her eyes flitting around the lobby. "Not that I think I'm poor—never mind, I didn't go to the Gala. I worked late that night."

"You left early," Victoria countered, recalling their discussion when she'd phoned the office. God, that seemed like a lifetime ago. In many ways it had been. "I can pull video from security if I need to, but I'm hoping I won't have to involve the authorities."

"The *authorities*? Little overkill, don't you think?"

"Why are you still lying?"

"I'm not, I'm . . ." Judy's bottom lip trembled. She took a shaky breath and looked toward the ceiling, tears gathering in her eyes. "I . . ."

Victoria forced her face into a neutral expression, neither condemning nor welcoming. As a child, Victoria's mother had taught her that a woman's power rested in her grace, in her ability to maintain composure. If someone sensed negativity—impatience, unhappiness, displeasure—they took immediate offense, lashing out and locking down.

Women should be grateful. Appreciative. To parents first, and then to husbands. The obvious progression. Real women, the ones who survived the batting order of social hierarchies, didn't bite the hands that fed them or turn their noses up at what they were given.

"It's all right," she said. "I won't be mad."

Judy whimpered. "He made me promise not to say anything."

Nailed it, she thought. "Who made you promise?"

"Warren."

The way she said his name, like he was the sun and she was a flower turning toward his warmth. Jesus, she had it bad. Main character in a Hallmark movie hadn't been far off the mark.

Judy took a deep breath and met Victoria's stare, tears streaming down her cheeks. "You're right. I was at the Gala. Not for long, but Warren asked me to meet him there. Said it was important."

"You and Warren were *together.*"

Judy's eyes widened. "No! No, it wasn't—it wasn't like that. He was, Warren never would've been with someone like me. He was . . ."

"Married."

"I was going to say out of my league, but—"

"But?"

Judy chuckled flatly. "I mean, there are all kinds of marriages. At first I thought you must've had an arrangement. He started scheduling lunch meetings or evening consults, and it was fairly obvious what was really going on; and you didn't bat an eyelash. I wasn't going to ask my boss for specifics, though. What happens in the bedroom, stays in the bedroom, that's what I always say."

Unless you have an audience, Victoria thought, but she pushed the pettiness aside. "So, you thought we had an open marriage and started sleeping with him."

"Not me," she said. "Warren was seeing someone, yes, but it wasn't me. I wouldn't have done that to you, Victoria. I could never betray your trust."

"Uh huh."

"I thought it was your neighbor," Judy whispered. "The one with the bright colors and, um." She motioned at her chest with a *you know* expression.

"Betty Knottier?"

"Yes, Betty."

"Why did you think Warren was having an affair with her?"

"I saw them arguing at her car one night. I'd stayed late to finish the West Coast account lists. I think it was the weekend you had that benefit for children's cancer research."

Victoria thought back to early summer when the benefit had taken place. She'd been hot and irritated. Warren had wasted half the morning trying to convince her that redistributing territories would shake things up for the execs, bring in more revenue, when the real result would've been chaos and uncertainty among the ranks—and she would've been the one who had to handle the fallout when their best people started looking for jobs outside Livingston.

He hadn't shown up for the benefit. A stomach bug, if she remembered correctly. But Judy wanted her to believe he'd missed the event because of a tryst with Betty.

Who was also dead.

A tragedy, or an awfully big coincidence.

"Okay, but arguing in the parking lot doesn't prove they were sleeping together," Victoria said. "Unless you heard them discussing private matters?"

"You're being unbelievably calm about this."

Was she? It felt like her skin was on fire. "Yes, well, I keep my therapist rolling in summer vacations, so I should be."

Judy clucked her tongue. "Cliff's Notes version: I couldn't hear everything they were talking about, but Warren mentioned Dave. And being discreet. He emphasized how *no one could find out*. Then Betty saw me heading to my car and put on a big show of handing over an envelope she said was full of HOA receipts, but Warren looked mortified. Stuffed it into his jacket and gave a stiff wave before turning back to her. I thought it was random, but of course, I wasn't about to start asking questions. You know how gossipy everyone around here can be."

Everyone else.

"Sure."

"The afternoon of the Gala, he had a lunch date."

A jolt ran through Victoria. Hadn't the women at the gym mentioned Betty being out with a man who wasn't Dave? Tall with dark hair. That could very well have been Warren.

"I remember."

"Betty had called that morning asking for Warren. He was in a meeting, and she didn't leave a message. After the meeting, though, he asked me to put the lunch on his schedule. I may have put two and two together."

Math wasn't her strong suit. "I can see why you'd make the leap."

"Thank you," she said, vindicated, some unspoken argument with someone else settled in her favor. "He went to lunch and came back angrier than I'd ever seen him, which was strange because before he left he'd been in a terrific mood. Warren's basically Grumpy Cat in the mornings, but he'd been friendly and polite. He even asked Pauline from Marketing how their newest campaign was going and if there was anything he could do to facilitate the roll out."

"Warren offered to help Marketing?" Victoria buzzed. Warren hated Marketing. Said the entire department could be eliminated and outsourced to teenagers with smartphones (since people were glued to them anyway—his competing views on technology had never ceased to astound her).

"Right? So weird. Just super happy. He said good things were coming."

Like her resignation. Victoria tried that idea on for size, picturing Warren tap dancing around the office because she was going to leave.

"And after lunch?"

"Like night and day. He was furious and doing a *really* bad job of hiding it. He asked me to send over half a dozen dead files and wanted the exact amount we had available in the petty-cash fund."

Victoria's thoughts raced. The dead accounts could be explained in a number of ways: pulling for review or checking for performance issues. But the petty-cash fund? He wouldn't need to know how much they had on hand unless he'd planned on using it immediately. That fact, compounded with the Cayman Islands accounts? Warren had been making moves.

Backing the medical company still didn't make sense, though, and unless Dave had eschewed his lucrative career as a technological consultant in the private sector to go back to nursing school, then the connection to the Knottiers remained a mystery.

Why Betty?

She could've asked her if she wasn't six feet under. Yet again, Victoria was stuck.

"How much was in petty?" she asked.

"Just over ten thousand. He had me get a certified check made out to cash but told me not to discuss it with anyone. That he'd take care of everything."

Whoosh. "Did he say what it was for?"

"No, but that's why he asked me to meet him at the Gala. He needed the check and didn't have time to grab it beforehand."

"And you have no idea what the check was for?"

"No, he didn't tell me anything. Why would he? I'm his . . . I was just his secretary." A sour look of disappointment flooded her face. Oh, but she'd wanted more. Warren must've known and used it to his advantage.

It was more cutthroat than she'd expect of him, but then again, so was stealing her company and forcing her to resign and become a soccer mom.

Ten grand was a hell of a lot for a date night with a mistress, though. A bigger picture began to form in the gray space between facts. "At any point in the few weeks before he died, did Warren show interest in particular accounts? Maybe he mentioned doing foreign filings for offshore accounts?"

Judy's brow furrowed. "Not that I can remember, but he wouldn't talk to me about that anyway. He had a few lunches with Jeff, but . . . you were the go-to for most of the larger acquisitions."

Victoria made a show of checking her watch. She was well past the deadline X had set out, and even without Warren's phone she'd expected . . . something. A threat, a stab wound. Not this palpable silence. "Listen, can you do me a favor?"

"I guess?"

"Can you keep this conversation between us for a little while? I need to look into a few things in the morning and it would be a big help if I could do that without having to go through official channels just yet."

Judy's eyes lit up. Realistically, chances were good that Judy was going to spill to the first person she saw, but Victoria couldn't do anything to prevent that from happening. And locking Judy in one of the building's basement utility rooms was too harsh.

Wasn't it?

"I won't say anything," Judy said, breaking through the wave of rusty chains and soundproofed walls.

"Thank you." Victoria laced her response with gratitude and slapped on the curled-lip, doe-eyed deer face she thought of as her girl-talk look. "It's refreshing to be able to count on someone again, Judy. Trust doesn't come easily for us, you know? Women are pitted against each other far too often. Look how strong we can be when we work together."

Her shoulders straightened, her chest puffed slightly. "So true, Victoria."

"I have to get going, but I'll see you in the morning. Is it okay if I message you if I think of anything else?"

"Sure, whatever you need."

Victoria moved aside, nodding in understanding. "Thanks again."

They separated, Judy continuing down the hallway where an arrowed sign was marked RECREATIONAL FACILITIES.

Victoria pressed the elevator button and watched the numbers descend, running through all the things she wanted to say to Teagan. When she stepped inside a shiver ran down her spine.

Her reflection in the metallic doors shook as they closed, and she had a moment before the lift started to think about how strange she looked in the light.

How cold, how flat.

How dead.

59

The ambiance on the fourth floor matched the lobby: soft lighting and a chic aesthetic. Victoria scanned the numbers on the doors for Teagan's apartment. She paused outside the corner unit, her hand primed to knock but unable to make her presence known. A feeling of finality settled into her bones. Whatever happened next, there was no going back to the way things were—not to before Warren or X, or any of the moments in which she'd previously defined her old life. Her husband was dead. Her house was gone.

She was on her own.

With a steadying breath, she rapped quickly and listened for sounds of movement. Hot air rattled from the vent above her head as a lock clicked and Teagan appeared. As usual, she could've stepped out of a magazine. Short and fit, all lean muscles and sharp angles accentuated by glowing skin and a thick, messy ponytail.

Even in loungewear, Teagan Livingston was undeniably beautiful, but that wouldn't help her tonight.

She pulled Victoria in for a tight hug. "I'm so glad you're all right."

Victoria reciprocated automatically, cupping Teagan's elbows as she leaned back, the world reduced to them. The flood of emotions overwhelmed her: anger and resentment, fear and loss. She bit the inside of her cheek and exhaled.

"Me too," she said flatly. "Everything's going to be fine, though."

Teagan's head tilted. "Shouldn't I be the one comforting you?"

"I'm okay."

"That's not what Bitch Face #14 says."

"I'm about to unleash Bitch Face #1 if you don't knock it off," Victoria said. "You going to let me in or are we going to chitchat in the hall all night?"

"Oh good, your sparkling humor's still intact; I was worried you might've lost it. Yeah, come on, let's get you warm." Teagan smiled and stepped aside so Victoria could enter, locking the door behind her. She padded to the kitchen and gestured widely. "Make yourself at home."

"Been a minute since I've been here," Victoria said, lazily looking around the apartment. Despite having lived there for over a year, there weren't many personal touches. A couch and two stiff chairs were arranged around a sleek coffee table. The drapes were heavy, the floorboards were dark and wide, and the walls were barren. Not a single picture, knickknack, or piece of art. It had museum vibes.

Or mausoleum.

"Whose fault is that?" Teagan asked.

"No one's. Love the whole minimalist design, by the way. Sociopath looks good on you."

"If I were a sociopath, wouldn't it make more sense for me to overcompensate? Some ugly still life of a bowl of fruit? Those ceramic mugs with words in a skinny font that every suburban twenty-something on TikTok has? Like Dexter bringing donuts trying to fit in at the station."

"Do you have donuts?"

Teagan muttered what sounded an awful lot like *bitch* under her breath. Victoria liked that she was getting riled up. It would make the next part easier, and if she enjoyed twisting the pin in the voodoo doll, that was no one's business but hers.

"Coffee?" Teagan asked.

"Coffee," Victoria repeated.

Teagan grabbed mugs and pods and prepped the Keurig as Victoria sat on the uncomfortable couch. Her reflection grimaced in the mounted flat-screen. She peeled back her hood and smoothed a hand through her hair, watching Teagan glide from one spot to the next, almost floating above the floor. Grace was for dancers, ballerinas who pirouetted for transfixed crowds hungry for perfection or disaster.

But apparently, grace was also for plastic surgeons with a penchant for lying.

"Are you ready to talk about what happened tonight?" Teagan asked, rummaging in one of the drawers without looking up. "Thought I had those fancy swizzle stick things you like, but I can't find them."

"That's fine."

"Fine's never fine. You deserve a cup of coffee the way you like it."

"Teagan, I said it's fine." Why was it that whenever they had something important to discuss, they always ended up arguing about the little things instead?

"Okay, princess, don't complain when it sucks, though. Milk?"

"Black. Thank you." She strode to the kitchen and accepted the mug from Teagan with a curt nod. The chill finally receding, she wrapped her fingers around the warmth and leaned against the counter.

They blew on their drinks in silence, almost mirroring the last time they'd shared a moment like this. When X had threatened her and Victoria had in turn confided in Teagan in the hopes of finding the person responsible for Warren's death. The distance between them was deeper now, and Victoria reminded herself to keep it that way.

She'd let herself down in the past, put blind faith in the altruism of others, but she wouldn't do it again.

Teagan perched against the counter opposite her, her auburn hair almost fiery in the light. "So," she said, dragging out the word before firing off a barrage of questions, "can we start with the obvious? Tell me everything about the fire."

"You probably know as much as I do."

"How did you wind up with Margaret Connors?"

"That's . . . complicated."

"Vague," Teagan said.

"Processing."

"Have you talked to the police yet? Does anyone know where you are?"

Victoria held up a hand, hoping her mood read as unbothered and not hanging on by a silken thread. Once she started speaking, however, the words tumbled out. "Yes, we can talk about the fire. I'll tell you about how I'd only been gone for twenty minutes at most before my house must've gone up in flames. We'll talk about how I have a sneaking suspicion that X was behind it. How Margaret accosted me in a Walmart. How my entire world ended in a trashed basement and an empty downtown parking lot. We can talk about all of it," she said calmly, "but first, you're going to explain why you killed my husband."

60

T eagan flinched like she'd been slapped.

Good.

She should be scared.

"Why would you . . . you're joking." A big, relieved grin spread across Teagan's face. "Wild. Morbid and maybe too soon, but we'll run with it."

"I don't have a sense of humor, remember? What was it you said? I don't know how to have fun. Why did you kill Warren?"

The smile dropped. "Tor, come on."

Victoria didn't waver, the epitome of confidence, which only served to shake Teagan more. Coffee spilled onto the counter as Teagan set her mug down. She hissed as the hot liquid hit her skin and rubbed at the spot before sopping it up with a dish towel.

"Careful," Victoria said. "You've made enough messes as it is."

A switch flipped, the familiar shaking-off of polite expectations as Teagan's nostrils flared and color flooded her cheeks.

"That's rich. Maybe talk to me about messes when you're not a slob-kabob wearing Warren's ratty old sweatshirt." Teagan arched her eyebrow and patted her stomach for emphasis.

"Bun in the oven, or packing on the pounds by grief-eating your way through the pantry? I seem to recall you having a soft spot for Oreos."

Victoria's face flamed, shame burning low in her gut. They weren't children anymore, but sisters never lost the ability to provoke each other, regardless of age.

Victoria hummed in response. A few shitty remarks from her sister weren't going to break her concentration. She had to stay focused. "Now that that's out of your system, think we can have this conversation like mature adults?"

Teagan flung the dirty dish towel into the sink with a shrug, her tone petulant. "I can control myself if you can."

She doubted that very much but held her tongue. Teagan reclaimed her coffee and followed Victoria to the living room. They sat at opposite ends of the couch and sipped in silence, the calm before the shitstorm

How theoretically idyllic.

As peaceful an image as they made, the air was thick and electrified. Victoria maintained eye contact, taking the opportunity to study her sister. Outwardly, her body language was as stoic and poised as Victoria's. Teagan stared back just as hard, unaffected and confident, but Victoria knew it was an act.

Inwardly, Teagan was reacting like any predator being backed into a corner by a worthy adversary.

"I can't imagine what you're feeling right now," Victoria said, testing the waters.

"Because you don't have a creative bone in your body."

"And you do?"

"I'm an artist, Tor. No paint brushes or colored pencils, but at my most basic level, I create beautiful things. I give people a sense of self-worth, like they're living masterpieces. It's . . . it's special. You, on the other hand, destroy everything and everyone in your orbit. A walking, talking black hole."

"A lot of frilly words for *I'm full of shit.*"

"You wouldn't understand. That stick in your ass is the closest you'll get to out-of-the-box thinking. Warren wasn't good for you in that respect. Before you met him, you at least had a sense of adventure. Remember that night we snuck out for NSYNC tickets? Four and a half hours in a line downtown without coats in February. Would've gotten away with it if the news hadn't recorded us dancing in the background. Who knew Dad would pick that day to give a shit about local events? I can still hear him shouting from the car when he found us, red as a goddamn tomato. Grounded for weeks but we didn't care. We didn't shut down and hide behind *rules.* After you married Warren, I couldn't even get you to double dip your chips. He had some vision, but on a small scale. Micro desires when I was aiming for the macros."

Victoria shook off the monologue, picking out the important notes. "Artistic differences? That's why you killed him?"

"All right." Teagan slid her mug onto a coaster and leaned forward, elbows on knees. "This shouldn't need to be said, but I didn't kill Warren. That's crazy."

"Absolutely."

"But you don't believe me."

"I know the truth," she replied simply, abandoning her own mug on the table and clasping her hands together primly. Proper lady-in-a-church-pew etiquette.

"And what truth would that be?"

"Where should I begin?"

"Maybe we should take a step back for a second," Teagan said. "You've been through something incredibly traumatic tonight, and you're having trouble processing the loss. Making decisions based on intense experiences never works."

"Seriously, Teags? Quoting *Speed*?"

"What? Classic Keanu. Can't go wrong with Keanu."

Echoes of her earlier conversation with X came to mind. "Don't try to change the subject," Victoria said, shaking off the tangent. "Burnt down house or not, for the first time in months I'm seeing things exactly as I should be."

"I'd appreciate it if you'd stop speaking in riddles and tell me what's going on."

"You killed Warren. Is that straightforward enough?"

"Wow. You're—you're serious." Teagan's face crumpled into outrage. "You think so little of me? I knew we had a fucked-up relationship, but that's low, even for you. You honestly think I could kill your husband and act like nothing ever happened? Just continue living my life while you suffer? That I could do that to you?"

"Yes."

It wasn't that black and white; life rarely was. But for this conversation, it was warranted.

"Why?"

"Million dollar question."

"I'd settle for the dollar menu if it means you'll get to the point sooner."

She was committed, Victoria thought. Believable. Putting the appropriate gravity into her voice. It might've worked on someone else, but not her.

Teagan was good, but Victoria was better.

She shifted on the couch to face Teagan head on, when her gaze landed on the bookshelf in the corner. Spines were organized by color, the titles themselves unimportant. Teagan read widely and criticized harshly, only holding onto books that spoke to her. Victoria had gone through them herself when she'd moved in, arguing over the moralities of both Stephen King and Shakespeare.

It was the box on the bottom shelf that caught her attention. To anyone else, that box wouldn't look like anything special, nondescript and simple as it was. Victoria, however, would've recognized it anywhere.

And just like that, the rest of the pieces fell into place.

"I came home from work tonight after an altercation with Jeff."

"Jeff Blevins? That tool's still around?"

"Not for much longer. That's beside the point," Victoria said, brushing off the distraction. Jeff was a pain in the ass and had a misogynistic streak a mile long, but he could be dealt with later. "Anyway, X started texting because he saw Meyers questioning me outside my house."

"Saw how?" Teagan asked carefully.

"Cameras, it turns out. Multiple cameras. He's been watching for a long time—and he'd been inside my house. The basement was totally trashed; Warren's things were everywhere."

Teagan schooled her reaction, but her lip twitched. A slight blink-and-you'll-miss-it blip of uncontained nerves. "How scary. Clothing strewn about haphazardly? Your worst nightmare."

"The upstairs was worse," Victoria said through clenched teeth.

Here, Teagan smiled, sly and mischievous. "Did X rearrange your spice rack? Delete your Netflix queue? Alert the police."

Victoria went along with the abrupt change in mood. "Staged a bloodbath would probably be a more accurate description, but I didn't get to check Netflix before I was sent on a fool's errand."

"Bloodbath, huh?" Teagan asked, leaning back and hooking an arm over the back of the couch. She was settling in.

Victoria didn't want that. "Whose blood was it, Teagan?"

She fixed an innocent expression on her face. "How should I know?"

"Because you're X."

61

W hen Teagan blinked in response, Victoria paced to the window and looked down at the Hudson River. In the dark, the water was little more than an impression of movement. On the opposite bank, a thin line of trees stretched in front of the sparkling lights of the city. For a second, she wished they could forget they'd started this whole conversation.

But Victoria wasn't running. Teagan wasn't backing down. They were really doing this—and she'd never felt more alive.

"You think I killed Warren and then created this X persona to . . . what? Why would I do that?" Teagan asked with a hint of amusement. She'd resumed her relaxed posture, not a care in the world. Like they were discussing party favors and not murder. "I'm curious what led you to this conclusion. Walk me through your sleuthing, Nancy Drew."

"It wasn't one big thing. A lot didn't add up. Kept nagging at me. Like a hangnail that keeps getting caught on your shirt until you're forced to clip it off."

"And this is you"—Teagan was off the couch and across the room before Victoria could react. She gripped the back of Victoria's neck and dragged her downward, nails digging into her skin—"clipping it off."

Victoria hissed at the pain. The few inches difference in height disturbed her balance, but Teagan didn't let go. Arms at her sides, Victoria gritted her teeth. Teagan squeezed and pressed their foreheads together.

Her eyes sparkled darkly with a newfound intensity, and in the split second before she tightened her hold, her face transformed into a person Victoria didn't recognize. Someone who wouldn't hesitate to rip her to shreds at the slightest provocation.

"First cuts, right?" Victoria sneered.

"What if I did do it, Tor?" she asked, exhaling stale coffee and mint.

"Not a matter of what if, as far as I'm concerned, but why."

"*Why.*" All at once, Teagan uncurled her fingers and flung Victoria away. "Awfully presumptuous. I'm not the Black Widow of Kent Wood Manor."

"Because you made everyone think that I did it. The graffiti, the rumors, the edited recording from the Gala—it didn't take much. If anyone understands how people talk in this town, it's you."

"Hypothetically speaking, yeah, it would've been incredibly easy. You're the spouse. You had a lot to gain from Warren's death. I said it before: the scandal wrote itself. And then you signed on at Livingston before his body was even cold. Threatened Betty, fought with those women at the gym—if I were X, I could've narrated this arc in my sleep."

"Speaking of Betty," Victoria said, rubbing her neck. She paced to the far corner near the bookshelf. "Why kill her? She was annoying but ultimately harmless."

"Harmless?" Teagan sprawled on the couch, lazily crossing her legs, an easiness to her that contradicted the tension between them. "I thought you had this figured out, Tor. Why does it feel like I'm filling in the gaps?"

"Do you know why Betty was snooping around?"

"MLM research."

"Teagan."

Teagan sat up. "Based on everything you've said so far, I think it's just as likely that you killed Warren and want so badly to believe it was someone else—*anyone* else—that you're seeing things that don't exist. Betty was delivering a sympathy basket."

"I caught her in Warren's office."

"So you say."

The implication being that no one could verify her story. Betty was dead. Having to justify her actions left Victoria feeling like she was on trial. "X warned me. He said I couldn't trust her. You know something and aren't telling me."

"Oh, yes, the mysterious X. A digital phantom. Untraceable. An anonymous villain hell-bent on destroying you. Convenient, isn't it? Who better to take the blame than a faceless bad guy? Everybody loves a good versus evil story. The cathartic explosion when the main character is triumphant in the climactic scene. Come on. We both know that you've concocted this whole X character as an out. A psychological manifestation of your guilt. Your mind's way of coping with the horrific things you've done."

"Stop it."

"With a proven history of sleep issues, a proclivity toward violence, a clear shirking of stereotypical suburban ideals—shit, they wouldn't even question me, a lowly plastic surgeon, about my diagnosis. They'd respect my medical opinion and chalk it up to mental health issues. Face it, Tor, you're just another crazy woman in the attic."

"Stop!" Victoria shrieked, chucking a book across the room. It smashed into the wall with a heavy thud, leaving a dent mark in its wake.

Chest heaving, Victoria fought against the spots clouding her vision.

"You're safe," Teagan said, her hands up in a placating gesture. "This is a safe space. I am your sister. We will get through this together."

"Stop, just stop. No more games," Victoria said. She massaged her temples, her eyes closed against the turbulent emotions coursing through her. "You disappeared at the Gala. We got our masks and split up, which in hindsight should've been impossible. We should've ended up in the same place, but I didn't see you again until the ballroom. Where were you?"

"Dancing. Drinking. Schmoozing—exactly what you're supposed to do on the Connors' dime."

"What about the red room? You couldn't have known I was going to end up in there; Margaret said that area was blocked off."

"Unless you did that yourself and are proving my point." She tapped her chin. "Or you were followed."

"None of this makes sense, Teagan, why—"

"Could you sit down, please?" Teagan asked. The feral creature who'd grabbed Victoria's neck minutes ago was gone, the growl replaced by a soothing whisper. "You're making me nervous, and if we could avoid putting a hole in my wall, that'd be great."

Victoria wasn't going to sit down. "You were the executioner. You and Warren plotted together wearing those sick disguises, trying to screw me over."

"Plotted? Are you hearing yourself?" Teagan asked. "Look, it's late. Why don't you get some sleep and we can revisit this in the morning? When was the last time you had pancakes, huh? Fresh blueberries and real maple syrup? I'll even spring for some bacon. Full fat. No turkeys."

"I didn't see you again after we got to the Gala," Victoria interrupted, talking over Teagan's breakfast rant. Diversions and distractions.

Teagan unleashed an exasperated sigh. "Whose fault is that? You left early. Remind me again why? Migraine, was it?"

That inflection. The hint that she knew more than she was saying. "When I left is beside the point. I was home all night."

"Were you? Perhaps we should ask Meyers. Because the last time we talked she told me that even with the snow you could've had time to return to the Gala after the driver dropped you off."

Was that true?

"I'm not doing this, Teagan," Victoria said, starting to shift her weight from side to side. She needed to burn off some of the excess energy. Adrenaline was great until it overloaded your system. Meyers had raised doubts about the window of opportunity, or lack thereof. Several times. "You didn't come back for your car."

"Because I Ubered."

"And you didn't answer your phone."

"It's not 1998. Rarely do I answer my phone."

"If it's that simple, then what were you doing? Who were you with? Give me the name of one person who saw you after the dinner and I'll drop it here and now."

"Jesus, Mom, relax."

"You can't because there was no one."

Teagan scoffed. "Please. If I was going to murder my brother-in-law and cut out his eyes, I would've made sure that plenty of people saw me before the body was discovered. Only stupid people don't have alibis."

Victoria opened her mouth to argue the point further, knowing she was dangling from the hook. The bait was too enticing. Teagan's gaslighting too reminiscent of Warren's manipulative tactics.

A knock at the door, however, interrupted them.

Both snapping at the sound, they shut their mouths and looked toward the sound.

Teagan pulled out her phone and cursed under her breath. "Fuck," she whispered, tiptoeing to meet her and turning the screen so Victoria could see the Ring footage. Detective Meyers stood in front of the door, hands in her pockets, curiously studying her surroundings.

Fuck.

Teagan tossed the phone on the couch and locked eyes with Victoria. *Hide,* she mouthed. *Now.*

62

Victoria followed her sister down the hall and let Teagan push her into the closet behind the garments like two kids playing hide-and-seek.

"Shut up," Teagan said, holding a finger to her lips and stilling the swinging hangers. "I'll take care of this."

"How?"

"Quiet."

With a pointed look, Teagan wrapped herself in a robe from the hook on the wall and fled, shutting Victoria in darkness. Everything in her mind narrowed to a singular, pounding thought.

Trapped.

She was trapped. Couldn't leave the apartment. Couldn't leave the damn room.

Also, now she had the added stress of Meyers showing up before Teagan had actually outright admitted to anything.

Teagan's muffled voice cut through her thoughts. "Detective Meyers, is everything all right?"

Meyers's response was too soft to hear. Teagan must not have let her inside yet.

"No, I haven't heard from Victoria since this morning," Teagan said. "We spoke briefly before work. Why? What's going on?"

Meyers's answer was reduced to the womp-womp-womp of Charlie Brown's teacher.

"I don't know where she could be," Teagan said. "I could try calling her. Most of Tor's friends live in the Manor. I don't think she'd go to a colleague if she was in trouble. *Is* she in trouble?"

She would be in trouble if Teagan couldn't get Meyers to leave.

Teagan's next dismissal was louder. "I'm sure it's important, but now doesn't really work for me. I have an early surgery and need at least eight hours to be at my best. I'm sorry to say no, but Tor's probably fine. We can set something up for a more appropriate time tomorrow."

Victoria caught snippets of half-formed words. *Sis . . . fi . . . missing . . . concer . . .*

She was telling Teagan about the fire.

"Okay, no—no, of course, I had no idea. Please, come in. Can I get you something to drink? Tea? Cup of coffee? Black, right? Yes, I've got a good memory."

Give her an A-line and a strand of pearls, and Teagan was a clone of their mother.

The next minutes were some of the most frustrating of Victoria's existence. She couldn't hear Teagan and Meyers talking in the kitchen. Being in the dark in an unfamiliar place was disorienting. Was that Teagan banging the cabinets, or was Meyers searching the apartment?

She had to get closer.

Slowly, Victoria opened the door until there was enough space to squeeze out of the closet. Ted Bundy had murdered dozens of women unchecked, and his downfall had been a traffic infraction. Victoria was not about to get caught because she stepped on the wrong floorboard.

Not that she was comparing herself to Ted Bundy.

Victoria tiptoed across the room and repeated the process with the bedroom door. She had an obstructed view of the living room. Teagan had drawn the curtains at some point. The lamp on the end table created a soft, inviting glow.

Meyers's voice got louder, and Victoria withdrew deeper into the shadows. ". . . fire chief has started the preliminary stages of his investigation. His crew are working the scene now, trying to piece together the specifics."

"How horrible. Are they thinking faulty wiring? Tor mentioned a house fire in the Manor a few years ago. Something about the materials they're using in new constructions not being as resistant. The family lost everything."

"It's too soon to say with any certainty what the official ruling will be, but the chief did say that, based on his initial findings, the burn patterns don't look accidental. There were definite points of origin, at least three."

Teagan gasped. "Arson?"

"We haven't ruled out the possibility that Victoria set the fire herself."

"That's ridiculous," Teagan said. "Why would she burn her own house down?"

"A very good question, which is why it's important that we find her. Hear what she has to say."

Meyers sat at the far end of the couch. Teagan extended a steaming mug to her, which Meyers graciously accepted. She blew on it, eyes fixed in front of her, and sipped tentatively. "This is a good blend."

"Death Wish," Teagan agreed.

"Sorry?"

"The brand. It's called Death Wish."

"Ah, yes. Cumbie's is usually as fancy as I get. Most bang for the buck."

I'm under suspicion of arson and murder, but sure, let's continue this discourse on the merits of gas-station coffee, Victoria thought.

Meyers quirked her head to the side as if she were thinking hard. "Ms. Livingston, did I interrupt something?"

"What do you mean?" Teagan's confusion was convincing, but every fiber in Victoria's body was screaming.

She tipped her chin at the mugs on the table. "You said you were getting ready for bed, but there are two mugs." She leaned forward, gently touching each cup. "Still warm."

Shit.

Teagan wrapped her arms around her torso. She sneaked a glance down the hall, catching Victoria's eyes, and with a minute shake of her head, a warning to stay put, she rounded the couch. "They're both mine. Forgot to put the old mug in the dishwasher," she said. "Perks of being single. Don't need to explain my cleaning habits to anyone."

"Is she here?"

"Is . . . who here?"

"Your sister."

"I already told you; we haven't spoken since this morning."

"Care to reconsider your original statement?" Meyers asked.

Teagan shrugged, stuffing her hands into the robe pockets.

Meyers chuckled drily. "Obstructing an investigation is a crime, one I won't hesitate to act upon should you give me a reason."

"Good thing no one here is above the law."

"Your sister is wanted for questioning in connection with *two* murders."

"So you've said. I can't help you."

"Look, if she's asking you to stick your neck out for her, that's not any family you want to keep."

Teagan stared her down. "For all you know, Victoria was trapped in the house when it went up in flames. Maybe you should be there assisting with the search instead of harassing me."

"We know she's alive. We have a confirmed sighting."

Teagan paced methodically. Right. Pivot. Left. Pivot. A pendulum of energy. "Confirmed by who? Margaret Connors? The self-proclaimed Empress of Kent Wood? Forgive me if I don't jump aboard that gossip train. I know the price of the ticket."

Meyers moved to put her mug down and froze, hand hovering midair. "Who said anything about Margaret Connors?"

Teagan abruptly stopped. "You did," she said.

Shit. Victoria gripped the doorframe, losing the fight to *stay put.*

"No," Meyers said. "I didn't."

Suspension of time never felt more real to Victoria than it did in that moment.

"Hell," Teagan spat, moving with the speed of a viper. She snatched something from the depths of the couch cushion and jabbed it at Meyers.

"No!" Victoria cried, a beat behind in processing what was happening as the needle hit its mark.

A blink of an eye and an eternity passed in the space of seconds.

Meyers slapped at her neck, reeling back on the couch as she caught sight of Victoria.

"Victoria, get back," Teagan said, level and calm.

"What did you do?"

"Don't worry about it."

Meyers attempted to stand. She went to steady herself on the table, missed the edge, and fell forward. The discarded needle rolled off the couch and landed between Victoria and Teagan.

"Hnng," Meyers moaned. "Ssss." Stumbling, collapsing, she managed to skirt the couch and claw at Teagan. Disturbing grunt-groans escaped her throat beneath a face much too red to be normal.

Teagan shook her off easily, more irritated than afraid.

Meyers's movements became sluggish and slow. Her half lidded eyes went cross as she patted drunkenly at her torso. The heel of her boot dug into the area rug, like she was trying to push herself away from them. Toward the door. Toward escape. A futile attempt.

It all stopped. One way or another, they'd reached the end.

"Teags," Victoria said, the word a whispered bastardization of a prayer.

Tossing the robe aside, Teagan smoothed her hair neatly off her face and put her hands on her hips with a theatrical sigh before turning to Victoria. "You want her arms or legs?"

63

Victoria had dragged many businesses through the mud over the years, but while corporations might have counted as people in the eyes of the law, they didn't typically collapse on the floor after being injected with a paralytic.

Okay, that was an oddly specific parameter to not have met, but Victoria needed something to rationalize what she'd just witnessed. What she was doing. She'd never had to drag an actual human from one spot to another. When Warren drank, he'd had the decency to pass out on the nearest couch or easy chair, but Meyers was deadweight. Literally.

They'd successfully maneuvered her through the hallway to the guest room. The distance was short but cumbersome. Backpedaling, Teagan knocked the door into the wall and unceremoniously dropped Meyers's legs. "That sucked."

"Maybe don't slam the body down so hard next time," Victoria said, breathing deeply through her nose. "Scratch that—there is no next time."

"Zigazig ahh," Teagan sang. "You in the mood for some nineties throwbacks? I could load up the boy-band flow, throw some Spice Girls into the mix." She kicked Meyers's feet, splaying them wide with an exasperated moan. "Should've laid off those donuts, Detective Meyers."

"Not worried about neighbors?" Victoria asked.

"This isn't the Manor, dear sister. What I like best about The Heights is everyone minds their own damn business. Besides, the soundproofing in this building is excellent."

Victoria lowered Meyers's torso to the floor gently and stretched, the muscles in her lower back straining. Shadows cast half the body in darkness, the light from the other room giving Meyers a waxy half-moon glow of death.

This was bad.

Kneeling, she pressed two fingers into the soft tissue beneath Meyers's jaw. Her breathing was shallow. Pulse seemed weak.

Not dead, but she would be soon.

Teagan crouched by Victoria's side. With a dramatic sigh, she unleashed a fresh wave of frustration. "This is incredibly inconvenient." She patted Meyers's coat pockets and extracted her phone, scowling at the lock screen. "Of course, it's a cat," she said, tossing the phone to Victoria. "Do something with this."

"Like what?"

"You're the criminal expert. What would your precious podcasters recommend?"

"Not murdering the lead detective in an investigation directly tied to your sister, for starters," Victoria said.

"Whoops." She shrugged into a look of false remorse. "And she's not dead."

"Yet. Will she remember this?"

"Maybe," Teagan said nonchalantly. "Everyone reacts to sedatives differently, and I wasn't exactly meticulous with the injection. If we're lucky, she'll stay under while we figure out what to do with her."

"We're going to let her go, Teagan."

"Are we?"

Were they? The logistics of the situation were looking more dire by the minute, but there was a huge difference between planning Warren's death and murdering an innocent person.

Wasn't there?

True, Meyers's death would mean Victoria could walk away from this unscathed. Everything was at stake, and while she liked to believe she was the dragon, that title had mostly applied to Warren. Warren, who had threatened her at a fundamental level, exhausted every other option until the only thing left—the only avenue that made sense—was an untimely death.

Meyers could still be saved.

"It was stupid of you to drug her."

Teagan reeled back, a look of pure anger on her face. "Where's the respect? You've always acted like I'm some kind of burden. Condescending and dismissive, and I'm sick of doubling my effort to make up for your slack. I did this for you, so maybe try a little gratitude."

"You did this for me?" Victoria asked, taken aback. "Murdered my husband, mutilated his body, killed my neighbor, framed me for all of it, and attacked the detective. For me."

"She was going to arrest you. You're my sister. I couldn't let you get carted off to jail in the middle of the night for a crime you didn't commit."

"That is truly an astounding stream of logic."

"We should talk. Game plan," Teagan said, wiping her hands on her thighs as she stood. "What are you going to do with her phone?"

Victoria sighed. "It'll be more suspicious if we turn it off now. We have to assume the department can track her activity or location. Even if they can't, I doubt she would've come here without telling someone, which means they'll be looking for her. We'll have to deal with it eventually, but for now it stays on. I'll silence it." She clicked the button and slid the phone back into Meyers's pocket. "How long will she be out?"

"I only had propofol left, so I'll have to dose her again in a few minutes to keep her under. Hold on." Teagan hurried out the door and returned with a small black duffle bag. The zwip of the zipper was loud in the quiet of the bedroom with the detective sprawled out before them. Victoria tensed, but Teagan presented her with a black kit holding a neat row of syringes, one spot empty. "Good thing I snuck one behind the cushion before I opened the door, huh? I'll give her another dose. And before you ask, no, it won't kill her, but I'm not an anesthesiologist. I can't guarantee she won't have an allergic reaction, so don't shoot the messenger if she doesn't make it."

"Who's the messenger in that hypothetical situation, you?"

"Bitches get stitches, Tor."

Teagan prepped the syringe with professional efficiency, tapping the side to remove the air bubbles in a gesture Victoria had assumed was merely for show. It was unnerving to see it done in real life, but she also found it fascinating how clinical her sister had become in the span of a few seconds. No emotions, no nerves. Cold and detached.

Setting the needle beside her, Teagan lifted Meyers's shoulder and pulled at her coat. The sleeve slid down awkwardly, but once it was out of the way she hiked up the rolled shirt cuff, tapped at the veins in her elbow, and sunk the needle in.

Meyers didn't move.

Victoria found that she didn't want her to.

64

Teagan locked the guest-room door and slid the key into her robe pocket. "The sedative should hold her steady in dreamland, but better talk fast, in any case."

Victoria paced around the apartment, her thoughts scattering like dandelion puffs as she tried to make sense of them. "We'll get through this a lot faster if you'd cut the mind games and admit that you killed Warren," Victoria said.

Teagan rolled her eyes. "Fine. Yes, it was me. I killed Warren."

Victoria's stomach flipped. "And you're X."

"Am I?"

"Teagan," Victoria asserted.

"No fun," she said.

"What part of this is supposed to be fun, Teagan?"

"You shouldn't scowl like that. Peptides can only do so much. Your skin loses elasticity the older you get, and—"

"Seriously?"

"—hydration and—"

"Unbelievable," Victoria said, shaking her head. "We're contemplating a third homicide and you're pushing Botox."

"Oh, we're a *we* now?"

"I see no other way around it, so yes, we're a team."

"Ugh, fine," Teagan groaned begrudgingly. "I'm X."

Vindication settled in her chest like a fuzzy blanket. She cradled the tiny victory in her heart and asked the most obvious question. "Why?"

Teagan plopped onto the couch. "I suppose I owe you an explanation, but for the record, I think this is pointless. My reasoning doesn't change the fact that he's dead, and it doesn't help us get rid of Meyers. You'll have answers, but at what cost?"

"Let me worry about the price of truth," she said. "At first, I couldn't understand how Warren could be so dumb as to willingly proceed with a lopsided deal on a private medical practice that was riddled with red flags. He loses Livingston. Calls in favors from the Old Boys Network and burns those bridges in the process. That was you, wasn't it?"

The heat kicked on, blasting hot air from the vents. The curtains fluttered against the windows, keeping a beat like a metronome.

"He promised that he was being careful, but I should've known better. There's no such thing as careful when it comes to Victoria Tate. What tipped you off?"

"You did actually. Warren was hiding the documents at home. When you trashed the basement, I found them. I didn't dig in right away because *somebody* had me in a choke hold running late-night sanitation tasks, but I saw enough to know they were important. So, when you lied about making popcorn, I started connecting dots."

Teagan stared open-mouthed. "Huh."

"You look surprised," Victoria said.

"I am. That's a big leap. I might've been lying for any number of reasons."

"I'll admit, I wasn't entirely sure, but there were too many coincidences to disregard."

Teagan scoffed. "Again, I underestimated you. Okay. Yes, Warren was helping me, but in my defense, I didn't know he was tanking the company. I never wanted to hurt you."

"Don't do that," Victoria said, pressing a hand to her temple and collapsing into a chair. "We're not sugarcoating our excuses tonight."

"All right," Teagan said slowly.

Victoria gave a curt nod. "Warren was giving you money to venture out, and you weren't going to tell me."

"We would've told you eventually."

"How kind." She paused, absorbing this revelation through pinched lips. "Teagan, why did Warren agree to help you in the first place? It's not like I didn't know you were close. I went to you for help with X because you knew him as well as I did. The deal doesn't make sense."

"It's not supposed to. If we'd wanted to include you in the deal, we would've."

"Are you ever going to give me a straight answer?" Victoria asked. "Like pulling teeth."

"Believe me," Teagan said, "this is nothing like pulling teeth."

Victoria shuddered. "Did he hate me that much? He would've rather destroyed Livingston and our legacy than give me control?"

"What do you want me to say, Tor? That he married the idea of love? He wanted to keep you under his thumb, yes. At least in the beginning. He could feel you getting antsy. Your deals were rock solid, the clients you were roping in were pushing you into the next stratosphere of recognition, and they wanted *you*. Not him. Jealousy was highly motivating, but it wasn't the only factor that got him to help."

Victoria dropped her head, opened and closed her mouth in vain attempts to respond, ultimately landing on an exasperated, tired laugh. She rubbed her face and ran both hands through her hair. "Okay," she said, picking at the chair like she'd find the words in the seams. "Break it down for me. What other factor am I missing?"

Teagan pouted her lower lip, somewhere between sympathy and flat-out pity. "We were sleeping together."

65

The curtains continued to flap and sway, oblivious to the conflict and heartache. Victoria wanted to go to them, run her fingers along the cool glass behind and shield herself in their folds, the translucent barrier between her and the Hudson, the soft fabric at her back. There'd be no room for Teagan to betray her, for her husband to resent her existence.

"Say something," Teagan prompted.

Victoria had turned in her seat, gazing toward the windows. She resolutely would not look at her sister. "No."

"Tor."

"No."

Teagan sprang to her feet, standing directly in her field of vision. Victoria refused to meet her gaze, looking anywhere but at Teagan. Was it childish? Perhaps, but she needed a goddamn minute to process the fact that her sister had been sleeping with her husband. Because while she knew that she should feel hurt, she didn't think that was the emotion clawing at her chest.

"Hey, Tor," Teagan clapped in her face. "If we're going to have this *civilized discussion*, then let's really have it, all right? You couldn't care less about my sex life—or Warren's, for that matter—so stop acting like I pissed in your Cheerios."

She's not wrong, Victoria thought. It would've been easier to stay mad if she were.

Sex with Warren was a passion free fumbling in the light of the TV on scheduled weekends and birthdays. Desire was a perfume on her dresser. And she didn't blame the years. Getting in the mood with the man who expected her to organize PTA brunches in a sweater set didn't come easily. Or ever.

"Fine," Victoria said begrudgingly. "It's not that you slept with him but why you did it that bothers me. Is this some sort of fetish? A thing for unavailable men?"

"This isn't a pattern."

Victoria backed up a step, crossing her arms over her chest and raising an eyebrow.

"*One time,*" exclaimed Teagan, "and I regret every second of my weakness in trusting you with that. Warren wasn't some random patient's unhappy spouse who I made the mistake of falling for, however briefly. Warren said all the right things, made all the right moves. I knew it wasn't ethical, but I also believed him when he said you were in the process of getting divorced."

"You wanted to sleep with Warren, so you slept with Warren. Not every relationship is an epic love story."

"Warren and I weren't in love, idiot. He wanted me. I needed him. Simple math. Not much different than what you do at Livingston on a daily basis. You deal with numbers, but it's basically the same thing."

And there it was again: the steadfast Livingston logic.

"Why wouldn't you have come to me?" Victoria asked. "Why do exactly what Dad did and go to Warren?"

"First of all, Dad was a dick who played you like a fiddle. Don't lump us together. Warren didn't give a shit about Livingston, not if it meant you'd be his boss. The man was good on paper to a lot of people."

"I'd like to think I had a decent understanding of his beliefs since I, you know, married him."

"Then why was it such a shock that he wanted to force you out? Why fight it so hard? You knew what he wanted when you married him, and yet when he pulled the Husband and Provider card, you balked."

"Why do you care?" Victoria was near shouting. "You've been manipulating me from the very beginning. You went behind my back to convince Warren to leave me and torch the company."

"I never tried to get him to leave you," Teagan interrupted. "We weren't absconding into the sunset with briefcases full of money, laughing at your gullibility. I swear, I wasn't trying to hurt you, Tor."

"The only person who stood to gain anything from this messed-up situation is you."

"Intentions don't count, is that it? There have been plenty of people in my life I've purposely set out to hurt, but you aren't one of them."

"Yeah, that makes sense."

"Do you know what my colleagues say about me?" Teagan asked.

"I have several guesses."

"They think I'm seducing patients into the practice to make partner."

"Are you?" Victoria asked.

"Don't be ridiculous. I have standards. I'm a good doctor—yes, *doctor*, don't roll your eyes at me—and secured the TikTok plastic surgery corner early, but my popularity apparently gives the staff free reign to start rumors about my patient list. And when they're not accusing me of sleeping my way to the top, Glen is there to ogle and berate me; it never ends. I'm constantly on edge waiting for the next round of rumors stemming from someone else's feelings of pettiness and inadequacy. And then Glen uses that to his advantage. God, the number of times he's pointed to the Doc Teags account as a justification for his shitty behavior. I'm sorry, but I can't just wait for him to retire or die. I need to get out of there or I'm going to do something horrible and royally fuck my future."

"Drama queen."

"Vanilla bean."

And, oh, how Victoria understood the urge to *do something horrible.* "Why does it matter what Glen says? You could easily find another practice to set up shop."

"Being a content creator isn't as lucrative as it seems. Even if it were, I can't spend the rest of my life posting lipo TikToks to viral song clips. It's embarrassing. And a lateral movement from one practice to another would accomplish nothing. I needed more."

"And sleeping with Warren was the only way to get it?" she asked.

"Like I said before: I didn't know about Livingston when I asked Warren to back me. He knew, though, and he was eager. He was pushing for me to have the proposal set before the end of the year. Everything was moving along without a hitch, but a few days before I had the forms ready he came to me and said he couldn't do it anymore. Refused to tell me why. I think we both know what the hitch was now."

"His change of heart?"

"His determination to get you on board with the family plan." Teagan scooched the other chair closer to Victoria's so they were sitting interview style, knees nearly touching. "The idea of being a father himself—I don't know, I think he was getting lost in the fantasy. He was thrilled by the prospect of you staying home with a baby, all midnight feedings and dirty diapers. That rosy nuclear daydream made him a coward."

He was always a coward, Victoria thought. "So you killed him."

"He didn't give me much choice. Warren was going to give me the rest of the money at the Gala. We met in the woods outside the Mansion, but instead of celebrating with the final check installment, he told me he was having doubts."

"The check was for you? Judy thought it was for Betty."

Teagan chuckled and reclined further into the chair, running her thumb up and down the fabric in a soothing line. "Judy's sense of self-importance is truly a thing of beauty. Betty was an . . . unexpected irritation. Warren didn't give me all the specifics, but Dave somehow let it slip to Betty that he was considering investing in us—me."

"Dave and Betty were backing your private practice?"

"Is it that hard to believe?"

"Dave was one of the first clients that Warren brought in outside of Dad's list."

"Have you learned nothing about the game?" Teagan asked. "Dad, Barnaby, Dave—they're all the same. They make the money, sure, but they put that money where they're told to. Betty wanted more. Her entire life was an Instagram sponsorship, and she was ready for more creative agency. She got greedy, though. Tried blackmailing Warren into siphoning money directly to her instead of waiting for the return on their investment. She threatened to out us if we didn't give her a bigger cut of the profits, and she wanted a lump sum up front for the trouble. Let's just say she was not happy with me when I pointed out how it wouldn't cover half the amount that she'd need to fix her boobs."

Victoria released a rush of air. "So Warren was going to give the money that he'd promised to you to Betty to keep her quiet, but that was also a stopgap. He wasn't going to go through with the investment to your practice, and that pissed you off."

"I mean, yes, I was fucking furious. We'd been arguing for days. Then he went to lunch with Betty, which I knew was a horrible idea, but he didn't listen. Whatever she said to him worked because he lost his nerve. Let me be clear: If he'd have lived, there was no chance he would've let that transfer go through. He was digging his heels in. I knew that if he were to be taken out of the equation, however, the future would become much more manageable. I didn't want him to die, but he had to go."

Victoria wondered briefly if this was how she would've sounded to someone else if she'd tried to explain her rationale for planning Warren's murder. It had all made sense in her mind. It had been foolproof.

"Are you hearing yourself?" Victoria asked. "Instead of asking me for help, you killed him."

"Please," Teagan sneered. "Tor, be real. You would've kicked my ass to the curb before I finished the question. I'm a burden, someone you have to tolerate. You have no faith in me or my career. One big joke. Getting struck by lightning would've been more likely than you offering to support me going solo."

To that, Victoria had no response. It would be easy to say she would've helped, to protest and deny, but ultimately, they both knew it would've been an act.

66

"Meyers needs another dose," Teagan said calmly. "We should wrap this up."

"I know." Victoria cupped her chin in her hand, reflecting on the night. Weighed down by fatigue, her shoulders ached, begging for rest and reprieve. "I know. I just . . ."

What? What was she trying to say? The answers weren't what she wanted to hear, but that was often honesty's brand. It was bitter and rarely sweet, and if tonight had shown Victoria anything, it was that everyone was capable of doing bad things. People were just people. Good. Bad.

It took monsters to affect change.

Who the monster in this room was, though, she didn't know.

"Let's say for a second that I understand why you did what you did. Not that I'm okay with it; it's going to take some time to forgive."

"I don't want or need your forgiveness. You asked for an explanation and I gave it to you. We're losing the cover of night psychoanalyzing the whys and hows, and trust me, we don't want the dead body of a police officer on our hands come morning."

Victoria couldn't make any decision about Meyers until they'd finished, though.

"You could've ended it with Warren's murder," Victoria continued. "The investigation would've run its course. But you didn't stop there. You stabbed him repeatedly and cut out his eyes. That's—that's not just needing him gone to collect money. That's rage. Why? More importantly, why invent X?"

"I was protecting you. Same as what happened when Dad died."

"What does Dad have to do with this?"

Teagan shot her a skeptical glance. "Dad ran on caffeine and adrenaline, sure, but he was a healthy son of a bitch. They thought he'd make a full recovery from the stroke. But he didn't. One day he was asking for the latest account updates, and the next he'd died in his sleep. I heard the doctors were suspicious."

Victoria tapped her foot on the floor. "People die all the time."

"Sure they do," Teagan agreed. "And sometimes they have help."

The hospital walls had been blindingly white. From the green chair on the side of the bed, Victoria had studied the beeping machines that night, watching her father's chest rise and fall.

"Why'd you cut out his eyes?" she whispered.

Teagan sighed at the change of subject. "That was a pain in the ass that I almost regret. You ever tried to scoop out eyeballs with a curved blade? No, clearly not, but it's not easy, take my word for it. That plague doctor mask was fortuitous but also not the best tool for the job. I knew you'd be a suspect, and I was right. Meyers was looking at you from the get-go, but to be honest, so was I. Not for the murder, obviously, but for what happened leading up to the Gala."

"How long were you watching?"

"Warren and I set up those cameras months ago. Quite the voyeur, your husband." Teagan winked, and Victoria's stomach clenched. "Catching you setting up a room that would essentially wipe away trace evidence, though, that was the most interesting thing we recorded."

"Wait. Warren saw that?"

"I showed it to him at the Gala. Thought it would be the push he needed to take my side. You clearly had ulterior motives going on in that pretty, newly cropped head of yours. I merely pointed him in the direction I wanted him to look, and he did the rest." She reached behind the chair and pulled the black duffle bag onto her lap. Shifting the med kit to the side, Teagan withdrew a silky black mask, holding it up like a trophy.

"You were the executioner," Victoria said. "Oh my god, of course you were."

"Ding, ding, ding. If I can thank Warren for anything, it's for his extensive surveillance skills. For someone who resisted social media so hard, he sure knew his way around a camera setup, and I was able to bypass the Mansion's firewall. Warren wanted to give you a chance to explain. I would've been happy with a private conversation, without the theatrics, but the creepy optics were a fortuitous find in the utilities room. Margaret's got a sick sense of humor when it comes to party games. Too bad her original plan didn't work out. Looked like she'd planned a Purge. *That* would've been a riot."

"You expect me to believe the red room was dumb luck?"

"And a dash of quick thinking," Teagan winked. "It didn't work, by the way. Warren got good and wasted, which put him at Neanderthal levels of susceptibility. But the sneaking around inspired me. X was the perfect solution. The distraction we needed."

"Hacking my email, the camera footage, the graffiti—"

"Okay, but that was a nice touch, right? I thought for sure you caught me coming back inside on your way back from the bathroom, but that's a perk of not having an open floor plan Plenty of blind spots. Warren got one thing right, at least we can agree on that."

"Can we?"

"The follow-up text before I called the police was incredibly effective. Had the message queued up on the other phone. A single tap in my pocket, and you were none the wiser."

"You want a medal? All of that effort to make Meyers look somewhere else ended up making me look guiltier," Victoria concluded.

"I may have gotten a bit carried away."

"You think?" Victoria sputtered.

"A delicate balance, not wanting you to get caught but also creating the right level of doubt to keep people guessing. Had to cover my own ass too."

"Teagan, what about Betty?"

She tucked the mask back into the duffel bag and pushed it to the floor. "What about her? I told you she was blackmailing Warren. I guarantee she was looking for the check when you caught her in his office. People like that can't be reasoned with or talked down. She was going after you next. Convinced herself that Warren had confided in you, and you were holding out for a better deal."

"That's insane."

"Everyone's crazy. She was a gross human being, but even Neon Betty knew you were the one to be reckoned with. Not Warren."

"That's what she said? Betty wanted to make a deal with me?"

"Would that make what I did easier to accept?" Teagan asked, standing. She grabbed the med kit. "Stroking your ego can wait. Meyers is going to wake up. Percolate on your decision for a minute, Hamlet. I'll be right back."

She turned down the hall, ponytail bobbing and syringe raised.

Victoria hustled to the kitchen, settling into her thoughts as she filled a glass at the fridge and drank. The water was cool. Refreshing. She finished it in three gulps and filled it again, chugging quickly and wiping the excess away from her lips.

She couldn't murder Meyers. She couldn't trust Teagan not to do it either, but could she trust Teagan at all after today?

"Thirsty?"

Victoria jumped at the sound of Teagan's voice. "Parched. Long day, you know? Was kind of preoccupied when I got home. Someone tipped off Margaret Connors before the two-hour time limit was up."

"Whoops. In my defense, I didn't think she'd turn the video over so quickly. Barnaby moves at a glacial pace in literally every other circumstance and is the very definition of self-preservation. It was supposed to be insurance in case you audibled. I only have one more dose of propofol left, by the way."

Another countdown.

"The blood was a nice touch," Victoria said. "Love your flair for the dramatic."

"Don't look at me like that," Teagan said as Victoria's face contorted in disgust. "Artist, remember? Just a few hazmat bins waiting to be picked up. No one misses those blobs of fat, trust me. I wish I could've seen you scrubbing it up, but I had this feeling, you know? A tingling in my spine that started when you left the house. Confidence doesn't make me immune to panic. Or moments of doubt. I'm a realist."

"And here I am, homeless."

Teagan joined her at the counter. By all appearances, they were having a leisurely chat. Tired, drawn. Yet the tension was ramping up again, a thrill running like a current beneath the serenity.

"That place was too big for you anyway. Never understood why you moved there, but I suspect Warren was the driving force. His five-year family plan. And Kent Wood Manor isn't nice to its single childless women. After we finish, we'll find you a place that's perfect. A fresh start."

Victoria toed at the tile, alternating between the swirled design and the grout lines. Teagan talked like there would be an after—that this night, their actions, wouldn't be the end. For Teagan, this was a small speedbump. A hurdle, not an insurmountable crisis.

She was missing the finality. Didn't she feel the apocalyptic dread?

"How is this going to end, Teagan?" she asked.

Teagan looped their elbows together. Victoria's breath caught, remembering that the last time they'd clung to each other like this was in the snow outside the Mansion.

"It ends with us. Together."

"I don't see how that's possible," Victoria muttered. "I'm sorry, I don't see how this ends in anything but death."

"There has to be death," she said. "But not for us. Meyers is the enemy, Tor. Not me."

"X could be the enemy," Victoria tried. "We blame it on him. The crime goes unsolved. Almost fifty percent of murders went unsolved last year anyway; it wouldn't even be strange. Warren would be a statistic. A cold case on one of my podcasts five years from now."

"That won't work," Teagan said, shaking her head. "Not with Meyers. This is the only way."

"You said that about sleeping with Warren too. Perspective matters."

Teagan grew grave. "Unless you're willing to cop to a murder, I suggest falling in line behind the one Livingston sister in this room who's not afraid to act. There are no reservations on my end, but I need something from you first."

Victoria met Teagan's eyes. The whites were bloodshot, but her gaze was sharp and alert. "What?"

"Warren's papers. If I'm going to secure the lease for the new building and finish the transfer, I need them."

"I can't do that."

"Come on, Tor. Don't make this difficult. The deal was ninety-eight percent done."

"It was dead in the water; that's what you said. Warren wasn't going to go through with it. Signing over that money would ruin everything I've been working for. Dragging Livingston out of the shit pile that Warren made will take every cent, and whatever you schemed with my deceased husband is not a top priority. There's still plenty of other routes you can take to start your own practice. Loans, drawing from your own savings—"

Teagan slammed a fist onto the counter. "I can't wait that long. Aside from the fact that Glen's driving me to the edge of sanity, I'll lose patients, the location, everything I've already invested personally at this point. And you want me to sign on for a bank loan? Months of kissing ass with associate degrees in finance with jowls hanging over their Brooks Brothers suits. Vampiric interest rates. You're out of your damn mind."

She stomped away. Victoria straightened as Teagan crouched at the bookshelf, throwing open the lid of the box on the bottom shelf. When she stood, Teagan held their father's hunting knife.

"Teagan," Victoria said, raising her hands in defense. "Put that back."

"No," she said, tightening her grip. "Give me the papers, Vic."

"Don't call me that."

Vic. Warren had called her Vic, and she'd hated it, unable to shake the notion that it was short for *victim.*

"I'll ask one more time. Give me the papers, and we'll forget this ever happened. You'll have Livingston. If anyone can save it from annihilation, it's you. Reshape it into your vision; it'll be better than anything Dad or Warren could ever have produced. It's the ultimate comeback story."

"I won't do it. Warren shouldn't have agreed to the deal in the first place. You'll have to do this the old-fashioned way."

Teagan laughed, an unhinged hyena shriek. "Okay," she said, lowering her chin and settling into a wide smile. "If you insist. We can do this the old-fashioned way."

There was no preamble.

Teagan rushed forward, knife aimed at Victoria's heart.

Victoria remembered thinking so many times in the early days of planning that her problems would be solved once Warren was dead, but nothing could have been further from the truth. Staring at the point of the knife, she realized that, despite their best efforts, people can't fight who they are.

Victoria Tate was a rainmaker.

Teagan was the monster.

67

At college orientation, the dorm coordinator had passed out rape whistles to all the incoming freshman girls. Sporting a cheery gap-toothed smile and meaty forearms, she'd placed the whistle in Victoria's hand.

"You never know when you'll need it," she'd said. As if it were a given. As if no matter what choices she made, there would always be danger.

Victoria didn't have the wherewithal to ponder the implications of that memory, but it flashed through her mind all the same as Teagan lunged at her, the tip of the knife just missing her shoulder.

Laughter bubbled inside her chest, so sure she'd been that Teagan would pull away at the last minute. Teagan wouldn't stab her, that little voice in the back of her head insisted. They were sisters—like that word meant something. Another voice, however, a smarter, darker voice, registered the brutality in Teagan's expression and ordered her to *move*.

She sidestepped and cut around the counter. Teagan reared back and swung again. Victoria tucked her arms against her body, the brush of air warm on her face.

"Stop," she shouted.

Teagan didn't speak, the same determined glare on her face as she pursued Victoria. Victoria dodged forward, using the counter as a buffer. It wouldn't last long. Even in childhood games of tag, they'd been evenly matched. The merry-go-round effect would falter, one of them making the first real move.

This was a precursor to the main event, Victoria realized, and Teagan smiled as if she could hear her thoughts.

"Put the knife down," Victoria said.

"Make me."

"Teagan." She whipped the blade again, narrowly missing Victoria's forearm. "Teagan, just—Jesus, just stop."

"No." They rotated again, Teagan blocking the exit. "We've got two options here. One," she said, swiping across the island and chuckling when Victoria grunted avoiding the blow, "you stop being a baby and help get rid of Meyers, give me the papers so I can get the money, and both of us live happily ever after." *Slice.* "Or two, you decline my generous offer and put yourself on the losing team."

Slice.

The blade snagged on Victoria's arm. A tear appeared in the gray cotton fabric of Warren's sweatshirt. She hissed, a reflex more than anything, and watched a thin red line blossom on her skin. The pain came next but was overshadowed when Teagan hacksawed the air, capitalizing on the momentum.

Victoria clamped the wound, backpedaling blindly into the far counter. "You cut me."

"Extremes are kind of my thing," Teagan said.

Victoria had a clear but narrow chance as Teagan went on the offensive, and she took it. She bolted into the living room, searching for a weapon to protect herself. Unless she was planning on papercutting Teagan into submission, the books wouldn't work.

No matter what, she couldn't leave. The front door was right there, but Victoria discounted it immediately. She wouldn't be able to explain Meyers's predicament to anyone before Teagan covered her own tracks. Probably set it up so that Victoria took the fall. She could see it clearly: the rescue squad blasting into the apartment with a power kick and arsenal. Meyers, already dead in a pool of her own blood. Teagan, severely injured but still able to point a bloody finger.

Maybe she could prove herself innocent of Warren's murder, but there would be no way to defend herself against that.

She'd been right all along.

This would only end in death—for one or both of them.

68

In movies, there is inevitably a climactic scene where the hero confronts the villain. They exchange witty remarks. One begs for his life while the other refuses mercy. There is a fight—of course there is a fight—choreographed and predictable, where the hero takes a beating but ultimately ends up on top.

Because he is a hero, and heroes always win.

Victoria was through with heroics, not that she'd ever seen herself as a hero, but she wasn't wholly a villain anymore either. She was somewhere in between, or a combination of both.

She could be both.

To survive this night, though, she had to be more.

"I looked for them, you know," Teagan said, floating into the room with the knife still firmly gripped for attack. They rotated in a tentative circle, fighters waiting to see who would make the first move. "I thought for sure you were going to tell me you'd found them when I realized that you'd packed up Warren's office. Five more minutes in the basement and we wouldn't even be having this conversation. Meyers showing up was a bit of bad luck. Unfortunately, her luck's about to run out, and mine's just getting started."

"Not if you go to jail."

"Who says I'm going to jail?" Teagan asked, inching closer. Victoria retreated at the same pace, dancing a dangerous tango. "The only jumpsuit in my closet is that cute black one I stole from you last year. No one's going to arrest us because we won't get caught. We're a team, and we're going to be okay. As long as you give me the papers, everything is going to be fine."

"We seem to have completely different definitions of 'fine.'"

"I told you before: I don't want to hurt you."

Victoria motioned to the blood seeping through the sweat-shirt. "I know what you said. I also know that you're a skilled liar with a penchant for gaslighting and manipulation."

"You're doing it again," Teagan sing-songed.

"I'm not doing anything."

"Fighting the inevitable is kind of *your* thing," Teagan said. "I'm actually surprised you didn't rebel against Dad when he made it clear he wanted you to join the family business. Completely out of character when you consider your general attitude toward authority figures trying to tell you what to do. We're equals, though, aren't we? And this is happening whether you like it or not."

"Screw you."

Teagan snorted. "Your husband did."

Victoria groaned, rolling her eyes, ready to launch into a rebuttal. Teagan had to push the easy buttons. Low-hanging fruit and cheap shots, because apparently, she had no qualms about winning without dignity. A win was a win.

The comment served to distract her. Victoria was unprepared when Teagan ran full tilt in her direction, tackling her to the ground. The air rushed out of Victoria's lungs with a *whoompf.*

She struggled to reposition herself as Teagan straddled her. Her sister's strength was surprising considering her size, but adrenaline worked in crazy ways, and Victoria was at a disadvantage.

Victoria grabbed Teagan's wrist, blocking a deadly blow of the hunting knife.

"Stop fighting," Teagan said, clawing at Victoria's exposed skin. Teagan's nails grated her cheeks and chin, but she scratched back, dragging red marks onto Teagan's neck and jaw. A scuffle ensued, grunts and huffs of effort and pain. Elbows hit tender spots as the sisters vied for dominance.

Victoria kicked up, her back digging harder into the ground as she tried to knock Teagan off balance. But the angles were wrong and she had no surface to work with. She squeezed Teagan's wrist harder, but she didn't relinquish her hold on the knife.

Then an inadvertent knee kick to the kidney sent Teagan sprawling. In her haste to stop her fall, she tangled with Victoria, stumbling further and losing the knife. It skittered slowly across the floor toward the center of the room.

"Oh, you bitch," Teagan moaned in pain.

Victoria scrambled, hands and knees clutching for purchase as she attempted to find her footing.

And the knife.

With a lunge, Victoria grabbed the knife and scurried forward. She'd spent as much time plotting Teagan's death as any other normal sibling. In an abstract, unrealistic way. The knife's handle, however, was cold and smooth, and as real as the heel that suddenly hit her lower back.

Victoria made an unholy squealing noise and wriggled like a butterfly stuck through with a collector's pin. Teagan hummed and pushed down harder, crushing Victoria's pelvis into the floor and kicking into her torso with the other foot.

Pain exploded in her ribs, but Victoria did not let go of the knife.

"I wanted us to be a team," Teagan said, kicking at Victoria's shoulder and then wrapping her fingers in her hair. She yanked hard, arching Victoria's head back uncomfortably before slamming it forward into the ground.

Victoria yelped, her nose crunching and flooding with warmth. Tears clouded her vision, and a dull roar took up residence in her ears. She remembered the last hunting trip her father had taken. Blood had stained his clothes, his gloves. The folded brim of his ski cap. There'd been none of that in the hospital room after his stroke. Clean and white, any trace of his violence had been wiped away. How easy it had been to pretend that he was worthy of her troubles. That her life would work out because she'd believed in his words, in him.

"We're too much alike," Teagan said, releasing her hold. She stood akimbo over Victoria. "Destined to be alone. As much as we'd like to buy into the fantasy, we know that hell isn't fire and brimstone, it's other people. We work better solo."

She came crashing down, her full weight ushering in the descent as she sat on Victoria's lower back.

"Get *off*." Victoria struggled, flailing backward in futile, wild arcs. She slashed blindly with the knife, but Teagan dodged her easily.

"Last chance," she said. "Give me the papers. Better yet, give me the money." Her face lightened in a moment of epiphany. "Warren had to have left you with a tidy sum."

"No." Victoria growled in frustration.

"No, he didn't, or no, you won't give it to me? Because from where I'm sitting, you don't have grounds to negotiate."

"*No*," she repeated, pushing off the floor.

Teagan recovered quickly, using the upward motion to knock Victoria onto her aching back before plopping down on her stomach.

Victoria couldn't breathe.

"I just had a brilliant thought," Teagan sneered. "No spouse, no kids. Who gets everything when you die?" Her knees squeezed together, keeping Victoria locked in place as she ripped the knife from her hand. She slid the blade along Victoria's collarbone, slowly applying pressure until searing pain sizzled into her brain.

Victoria screamed and bucked. Teagan rode it out, slicing a clean line into the meat of her left cheek until she could jerk away.

"I'll comb through every centimeter of your shit until I find the papers. I'll get Warren's Cayman account and your estate too. This is really working out in my favor. Talk about serendipity, huh? Too good to kill a detective. Leave me the dirty work because you think you're better than me. Let me tell you something, dear sister. Morals mean nothing if you're not alive to use them. And when I line up the scalpel for my first nose job at my solo practice, I'll press that blade in and think of you."

She raised the knife higher and brought it down. The blade sank into Victoria's stomach, to the right of her belly button.

Victoria shouted, the pain excruciating, like nothing she'd ever felt before. Burning and cold. Abrupt and demanding. She closed her eyes.

Whatever bright light they'd told her to expect at the end didn't come. There were no angels or trumpets, no flashback reel of her life's greatest moments. There was only the darkness of her eyelids and the certainty that she'd lost.

That, more than anything, filled her with regret.

She'd tried so hard to be everything that everyone had wanted her to be, but she hadn't done enough to get the one thing she'd wanted for herself.

Too late, her mind whispered. *Too little.*

Teagan's weight shifted, and the knife was yanked from her torso. She pictured herself as a fish on a hook, dangling from the line until some crusty old man in waders ripped out the jagged end. How it could hurt worse on the way out, she had no idea. Heat radiated from the wound. Sticky, wet material clung to her skin.

"Goodbye," Teagan said, lifting the knife again.

A rush of warm air hit Victoria's face, and she imagined the knife swinging through the air in its gleaming, sharpened glory.

She didn't open her eyes.

69

There was regret, yes, and guilt—plenty of guilt—but there was also curiosity. Victoria wondered if the second stab would hurt just as much as the first, or if some biological response would protect her from the worst of it. Would the blood that filled her lungs and throat be thick like syrup, or viscous and thin? Would her last breath rattle, or simply expel into nothingness? She wondered if perhaps she should've given more credence to those Catholic teachings of pearly gates or eternal damnation.

Mostly, she wondered why the end was so loud.

A constant banging like a bass drum echoed through her head. The sound reverberated, a distant tingling she couldn't explain. How long had she been hearing it? Teagan's monologue had taken all her attention—although it could've been the threat of impending doom more than the quality of her speech, Victoria reckoned—but it seemed like the noise had been there the whole time.

I'm still in the red room, she thought. Trapped. *The Gala never ended. I've been here this whole time.* The heart speakers were pounding, and she was kneeling before the executioner, begging for her life.

Was she begging? A whispered word spilled from her lips, repeating over and over as her eyes pinched shut and the booms grew louder.

Please, please, please.

It was only when the banging was joined by a splintering crack of wood and a slurred voice yelling, "Stop!" that she opened her eyes and registered this wasn't the Gala, and they weren't alone.

Teagan didn't stop.

The knife barreled down.

Victoria watched in slow motion. The glint of the steel. The beads of sweat sticking to Teagan's forehead. The garish scrapes and scratches on her face and neck proving Victoria had gotten a few good shots in. Her sister was beautiful; even now, with rage in her eyes and resignation crinkling the lines around her mouth, Teagan was a force of unbridled energy.

They locked eyes, bleary and bloodshot, as a pop ignited the air around them.

Teagan convulsed. Shock filled her face as her right shoulder and arm flew backward in a fizzled burst of red spray. The knife went flying as she fell to the ground.

"Teagan?" Victoria asked. She coughed and pulled her legs toward her chest, immediately regretting that decision as pain crescendoed through her. She flopped to the side instead, rolling toward her sister. "Teagan!"

Meyers was already at Teagan's side, gracelessly slumped to her knees with two fingers digging into the soft flesh under her jaw. She held a phone between her shoulder and ear. Calling for backup. Calling for paramedics.

"You shot her," Victoria said.

Meyers dropped the phone and crawled drunkenly across the floor. She made it a few feet before losing the contents of her stomach. The deep hurling sounds were rough in her throat and made Victoria cringe. Meyers wiped her mouth with the back of her arm and grimaced.

"Are you all right?" she asked. Her breathing was labored. Bits of vomit stuck to her collar. The buttons of her shirt gaped uncomfortably, and she'd lost a shoe at some point. Behind her, what was left of the door lurched into the hallway. Bits of wood and drywall littered the floor.

"Me?" Victoria looked at Teagan, who laid unmoving in a growing pool of blood. "I don't know. My stomach." She looked down, cradling her wound with her arm. The blood looked bright against the gray of Warren's sweatshirt. Dizzy from the view, she fought her lightheadedness and nodded at Meyers. "I'm okay. I'll be okay. You shot my sister."

"She was about to kill you," Meyers deadpanned, a note of irritation coloring her voice. With a groan and a strained expression, she returned to Teagan, pocketing her phone before adjusting her stance over the body. "You're welcome, by the way."

It couldn't be that easy, Victoria thought as she lurched to her feet. On wobbly legs, she shrieked as the skin of her stomach seemed to tug in seven different directions at the same time.

On the floor, Teagan remained still. Blood splattered the side of her face and spread in a dark circle around her.

Will be a bitch to clean, she thought, clamping her teeth down to stop from laughing.

Meyers checked Teagan's pulse again and shook her head, pressing both her hands against the wound. "Need to get the bleeding under control until the ambulance gets here."

343

Victoria winced. Every breath felt like she was being ripped open. Her neck itched as blood dried in the creases. In the distance, sirens wailed. The inky black of the night sky had brightened considerably. The moon was a sliver against an expanse of dusky blue. A few stars peeked through wispy clouds broken only by the blackened branches of winter trees and the city skyline.

Alive.

Victoria's vision clouded with floaters, specks of light jerking in zigzags when she blinked. Braced against the wall, unfazed by the bloody handprint smearing the paint, Victoria noticed the black duffle bag, remembered the executioner's mask tucked inside. Carefully, she bent and scooped it up, biting back a scream, and tucked the silky material into the back of her pants.

The rescue teams would be here soon, police and medics.

She couldn't rest just yet.

There was still work to do.

70

Lying on the starched sheets of the hospital bed, with stiff covers wrapped around her and too-warm socks on her feet, Victoria learned that Teagan was alive.

The shot Meyers had gotten off was a good one, missing most of Teagan's major organs, with a clean entrance and exit wound. The bullet had nicked her lung, though, so she was stabilized and rushed to surgery.

"Will she make it?" Victoria had asked the doctor. He was handsome, with broad shoulders and dexterous hands that held a clipboard. She wondered briefly if he'd still be able to operate if she accidentally broke one of his fingers.

"We'll start her on antibiotics to stave off risk of infection, but barring any unforeseen complications, your sister should make a full recovery."

"Great."

Great.

Victoria hid her dejection just before Meyers appeared in the doorway. She had dark circles under her eyes, and her color was a little paler than her usual ghostly hue, but overall she looked okay. She greeted the doctor, exchanging brief updates in the hallway while Victoria caught broken bits of their conversation.

The doctor nodded or shook her off accordingly, sparing a glance for Victoria through the small window in the door only once before training his entire focus on Meyers. They parted with a promise to reconnect before she left the building, and Victoria had just enough wherewithal to straighten her hospital gown before Meyers returned.

"How are you feeling?" Meyers asked.

"Like I got hit by a bus," Victoria said. "A big bus. With spiked wheels." She motioned to the bandages covering her wounds. Her collarbone had needed stitches. The gash on her cheek would heel but would probably result in unsightly scar.

The ironies didn't cease. The universe apparently had a point to make.

Meyers dragged a chair to the side of the bed and plopped down. It was easy to see the exhaustion in the slow swoop of her arms as she reached for her notepad. "I need to ask you a few questions. Do your best to be thorough, but I might need to come back for a follow-up depending on what your sister has to say when she gets out of surgery."

If, she thought. *If she gets out of surgery.*

"I'm an open book, Detective Meyers. No offense, but are you going to make it?"

Meyers scoffed. "I'm tougher than I look."

"I don't doubt it." Victoria paused to gather her thoughts, choose her words carefully, and then, "How much do you remember?"

"Some," she said. Cryptic. "Too much and not enough if that makes sense. The worst of the grogginess wore off somewhere around my fourth attempt to kick the door down, which is when I realized I could theoretically shoot the lock out."

That explained the wood explosion. "I'm glad you did," Victoria said. Around her, the machines beeped. The sharp smell that was entirely *hospital* enveloped her senses, and Victoria fought the nausea that accompanied her resurfacing memories.

"Mrs. Tate, what happened with your sister tonight?" Meyers asked candidly.

Victoria's mouth opened and closed. Another echo of a fish on a hook. She floundered again, searching for a place to begin. How much should she disclose? Where was the line between truth and justice?

"Teagan confessed to killing Warren," Victoria said. "Apparently, they were having an affair. She was using Warren for money, and when he caught onto her game, she killed him. There are bank statements in my car from offshore accounts he set up before he died, and Judy can confirm some of this story. She was scheduling their lunch meetings. Some of the restaurants probably have footage of them together."

"Romance gone wrong," she said, taking notes. "And the fire?"

"Also Teagan," Victoria said. "She was X. The text threats were from her. Trying to frame me for Warren's murder so she could access the money without setting off alarm bells. She'd been looking for Warren's documents and assumed I was holding out on her. She didn't know what, if anything, I knew, and wanted to keep me close while she searched. I guess Betty Knottier found out about the money somehow; you might want to talk to Dave about that. Teagan . . . Teagan killed her too."

Her throat tightened with emotion. She sipped from a plastic cup of water and crunched an ice chip, studying Meyers's flickering expressions. Her body language spoke of professionalism, her posture straight and closed off. Her eyes, however, softened at the corners.

"We'll interrogate Teagan when she's medically cleared," Meyers said. "Between me and you, though, this seems pretty cut-and-dried. We found the knife in her apartment. I'll have my own testimony." She rubbed the back of her neck and analyzed a very interesting crack in the floor. "We'll get your official statement when you're released, and if you're amenable come trial time, we'll discuss the possibility of you testifying for the prosecution. The DA's going to want to close this down quickly. The people of Kent Wood need closure."

"Of course," Victoria said, slipping into her best HOA complaint voice. "What my sister did . . . it's abhorrent, Detective Meyers. I'm shocked."

"Mm," she said.

That fucking noise, Victoria thought. The burst of anger surprised her, breaking through the façade and slamming her chest with a fiery fist. She swallowed the melting chip, took another long drag of water, then met Meyers's gaze.

Disbelief was written on her face. She was buying the story about Teagan, sure, but she knew that part of it was bullshit.

"Did the doctor say when you should expect to question Teagan?" Victoria asked.

"I'll be back in the morning. She'll be taken into custody for assaulting a police officer, wrongful imprisonment, but I expect there will be additional charges before the week's out."

So much had happened in the twenty-four hours since she'd lost her home and learned the truth. Victoria should've been relieved by the news. Teagan was going to be arrested. There would be a trial.

Victoria didn't feel relieved, however. She was scared. And angry that she was scared.

What would Teagan confess to when she woke up? There were many ways she could spin the story, cast doubt and implicate Victoria.

Was there backup footage of the night of the Gala?

Could any of it be pinned on Victoria?

She hadn't killed Warren, but could Teagan convince a jury that she had? Use circumstantial evidence and theatrics to curry favor?

Yes, her gut screamed. *Yes.*

Everyone loved a spectacle, and Teagan was a star.

Teagan couldn't be trusted. That was the simple, undeniable fact.

As Meyers bid her goodbye and made her way to the door, Victoria knew without a shadow of doubt that Teagan could not leave the hospital alive.

71

It was a cold December night when Victoria Tate decided to murder her sister.

Snow fell gently outside, the puffy flakes descending in the flickering yellow security lights of the hospital. Visiting hours had long passed. Victoria had watched friends and family members ambling to their cars, arms stretched out for balance on the slippery sidewalks. Their footsteps disappeared behind them like ghosts, and she channeled that energy as she swung her legs over the side of her bed.

She'd made friends with the nurse earlier, asking questions about her son and educational experience. The woman hadn't batted an eye when Victoria had taken an interest in the hospital equipment—specifically in how to disable the alarm that would alert the nursing station when a patient got out of bed.

A few clicks of the buttons and Victoria managed to shut the power off. She waited, listening for any signs she'd been heard, but the only sound was her own breathing.

Her feet hit the floor and the tubes in her arms clacked together. With a hiss, she removed the IV and wrapped gauze around her arm, carefully shuffling across the room. The tug in her gut was lessened by the meds, and her path was a little loopy. Opening the closet, she removed the necessary item and inched toward the door.

The nurse's station was empty. She crept down the corridor, cradling her side. Every few steps she'd lean against the wall to catch her breath, but no one stopped her. No one questioned why she wasn't in bed.

Her heart racing, Victoria paused at her sister's door. There was no turning back.

With a final glance to make sure she was alone, Victoria pushed inside. The curtain around the bed was pulled shut, blocking Teagan from her immediate view. Her footsteps were soundless as she approached, heel to toe, scanning the room for obstacles. Her luck continued; Teagan was the only patient in the room.

Victoria wouldn't even have to worry about collateral damage

Teagan looked small beneath the hospital blankets. Dark circles ringed her eyes. Abrasions dotted her cheek and chin, remnants of their fight that already felt like a lifetime ago.

How many lives she'd lived to end up in this place.

Déjà vu rolled over her in waves as she carefully brushed the hair off Teagan's face. She'd done the same thing to her father the night he died, standing over his sleeping form, dedicating his features to memory. Her hair was the same color, the same thick and wavy strands. Teagan's innocent expression mirrored his, vulnerable and serene.

He had made sure that Victoria couldn't have that, so Victoria had taken it from him.

And now, she would take it from Teagan.

With steady hands, Victoria held the mask over Teagan's face. She'd contemplated wearing it herself, an extra touch of pettiness to really drive the point home, but ultimately decided against it. Teagan wouldn't be alive long enough to appreciate the irony, and Victoria was never the executioner.

The black silk was cool against her skin. The eyeholes were prismatic. In their glimmer, her reflection smiled. With the mask in place, Victoria grabbed a pillow from the empty bed, ignoring the twinge in her abdomen and the ache in her bones.

Her father hadn't struggled much. Weak from the stroke and sedated, he'd punched and flopped while she'd held the pillow to his face. Her sister would be no different.

Teagan whimpered in her sleep, a small, tense noise.

How sweet, Victoria thought. *She'll go dreaming.*

Wasn't that the best any of them could ask for? she wondered. To lose themselves in the safety of their minds? Unburdened by crushed hopes and the expectations of others?

Yes, Victoria thought as she held the pillow down, to die dreaming was a merciful ending for a monster.

ACKNOWLEDGMENTS

Thank you to Anne Tibbets, Luisa Smith, Otto Penzler, Charles Perry, Will Luckman, and the entire team at Scarlet and Mysterious Press. From first draft madness to finished product, this book wouldn't have been possible without your hard work and tireless support. You pushed me to be the best writer I could be, and I am incredibly proud of what we accomplished together.

To Sean, Mackenzie, and Jack, always. Never get too old or too cool to ask me animal facts, challenge me to superhero "Who's Better" competitions, break it down for *The Masked Singer*, or demand I taste test the spice levels of your latest creations. You are the best part of every day. I wouldn't be able to do this without you.

To my writing friends-turned-family, from the daily poetry thread to the Twitter writing communities, horror fam to indie loves, I appreciate you beyond words. Publishing is a hell of a journey, but it's the good kind of crazy when you have people you can count on to make you laugh on the hard days, help you work through the blocks, inspire your creativity, and celebrate even the smallest victories. Here's to many more years of whiskey, wine, and words.

To my family, thank you for being my biggest fans and constant readers. I finished a solid chunk of this book on vacation in Wells Beach, Maine, watching everyone in the waves under the blazing sun, and I will forever be grateful for the opportunity to have those moments. I see a celebratory reunion at Scoop Deck in the near future. Love you all so much.

I'd be remiss to not give a shoutout to my Birds, the best hype crew I could ever ask for. Thank you for not only blowing up my notifications with insane gifs, memes, and incredibly classy, not even a little bit crass, jokes, but also for reading my words, recommending my stories, and never hesitating to offer eyes and ears of support. Love you all (the right ones will know).

Extra special thanks to Jaimie Truesdale, Lindsay Smith, Jenn Rebecca Gaylord, Anna Knierim, Alex Andreeva, Dawn Gray, Jenn Beston, Jaime Hendricks, Meghan Crawford, and Melissa Willis. I can't thank you enough for tolerating my spontaneous karaoke sessions, running check-ins, true crime updates, ridiculous FaceTime conversations, con shenanigans, and TikTok hilarity. ILYSM.

And a huge wave of gratitude to the readers, reviewers, bookstagrammers, bloggers, and bookish communities. Thank you for giving my stories a chance.